Double Grudge Donuts

Books by Ginger Bolton

SURVIVAL OF THE FRITTERS

GOODBYE CRULLER WORLD

JEALOUSY FILLED DONUTS

BOSTON SCREAM MURDER

BEYOND A REASONABLE DONUT

DECK THE DONUTS

CINNAMON TWISTED

DOUBLE GRUDGE DONUTS

Published by Kensington Publishing Corp.

Double Grudge Donuts

Ginger Bolton

Kensington Publishing Corp.
www.kensingtonbooks.com

KENSINGTON BOOKS are published by

Kensington Publishing Corp.
900 Third Avenue
New York, NY 10022

Special book excerpts or customized printings can also be created to fit specific needs. For details, write or phone the office of the Kensington Sales Manager: Kensington Publishing Corp., 900 Third Avenue, New York, NY 10022. Attn. Sales Department. Phone: 1-800-221-2647.

The K and Teapot logo is a trademark of Kensington Publishing Corp.

ISBN: 978-1-4967-4022-9 (ebook)

ISBN: 978-1-4967-4021-2

First Kensington Trade Paperback Printing: March 2024

10 9 8 7 6 5 4 3 2 1

Printed in the United States of America

Acknowledgments

I have always loved stories, and to me, books are a sort of magic. When I was seven and learned that people created books, I decided I wanted to write them. Thank you to John Talbot and John Scognamiglio for helping that happen.

And thank you also to the team at Kensington Publishing, including Larissa Ackerman, Carly Sommerstein, Kristine Mills, and all the other people who transform a manuscript to a book, place it in stores and libraries and on websites, and then encourage readers to visit those stores, libraries, and websites.

Special thanks to Mary Ann Lasher. I love the paintings she does for my covers, and so do my readers.

I learn from writing friends, including Catherine Astolfo, Allison Brook, Laurie Cass, Krista Davis, Daryl Wood Gerber, and Kaye George. And others. Thank you!

Sgt. Michael Boothby, Toronto Police Service (retired) keeps me from straying too far from how police officers behave, but I might take a few liberties.

Librarians and booksellers are wonderful to readers and to authors. Thank you.

I appreciate family and friends who understand my wandering off wherever my imagination takes me.

And then there are those of you who hold my books in your hands and join me and my characters in their world. Stories need listeners and readers. Thank you all!

Chapter 1

Summer Peabody-Smith crumpled a business card between her fingers and whispered, "No . . ." Her knuckles were white.

I threw a questioning glance at her, but she merely shook her head and stared with a sort of despair at the lone performer in the ornate Victorian bandstand in the village square.

The tall, slender man in pressed black slacks and a neat white shirt played a third note on his cornet. And a fourth.

With my lack of musical talent, I didn't recognize his tune as quickly as Summer must have. I had never before heard "Reveille" played so slowly. Summer crushed the business card into an untidy ball.

As far as I could tell, the notes the cornetist played were perfect. I could have relaxed and enjoyed the mellow tones, but I was too aware of Summer's anguish.

The cornetist went on, note by painstaking note. People in the rows of folding chairs near us rustled and whispered, and I couldn't help feeling sorry for the young man competing in the Fallingbrook Arts Festival's Musical Monday evening show.

And then it got worse.

Squawk!

I couldn't help turning around on my uncomfortable chair to see what had made the horrendous noise behind us.

A stocky, gray-haired bagpiper in full Highland regalia paraded immediately behind the rear row of seats. His bagpipe let out another discordant squeal. Many of the hundred or more people in the audience laughed.

Frowning, Summer and I focused on the cornetist again. Maintaining his dragging tempo, he continued playing "Reveille."

The bagpipe behind us let out random screeches, and more audience members laughed.

Finally, the cornetist finished "Reveille." He gave a stiff bow and strode out of the bandstand. His face was bright red. The evening was warm, typical for early August in northern Wisconsin, but most of the day's earlier heat and humidity had dissipated to a soft haze.

Brushing past the cornetist in the aisle between seats, the bagpiper marched toward the bandstand. The crisp pleats of his green, black, and white plaid kilt swaying, he climbed up the two shallow steps into the bandstand. He picked up the microphone and announced in a gravelly voice that everyone was welcome to sing along.

I wasn't good at distinguishing one bagpipe melody from another, but I figured out what this one had to be when people around me sang "My Bonnie Lies over the Ocean."

Summer and I didn't sing.

His cornet case in one hand and his face still red, the cornetist sat down in the seat beside Summer. She'd told me she was saving it for a friend, but she hadn't mentioned that the friend was one of that evening's competitors.

The wailing of bagpipe and voices ended. Most of the audience stood and applauded. Summer and the cornetist remained seated, and so did I.

The cornetist leaned toward Summer and me and asked, "Who is that?"

Summer smoothed the card she'd nearly destroyed. "He must be this guy, Kirk MacLean." She held the card where both of us could see it. "Look what his business card says: HE WHO PAYS THE PIPER CALLS THE TUNE."

Although the cornetist's attempt at a smile was tepid, he was stunning—square-jawed with a straight nose and rich brown eyes. "Original." He was probably older than I'd first thought, but still young. I guessed he was in his early twenties. Women his age probably swooned.

I wasn't about to swoon over anyone besides Brent, my fiancé. Summer was interested in another detective, one who didn't live near Fallingbrook.

Summer tore the card in half and thrust the pieces into a pocket of her plaid shorts. "I should introduce you two. Emily, this is Quentin Admiral. I used to babysit him out at Deepwish Lake. He and his parents live in Chicago, but their summer home is down the lake from ours. Quentin, this is Emily Westhill. She's one of the two owners of the Deputy Donut café."

Quentin and I stood. I smiled up at him, shook his hand, and congratulated him on his performance. He muttered, "Sorry I let that rude piper get the better of me."

Summer demanded, "But what happened to you before he made his bagpipe scream in apparent pain, Quentin?"

Audience members stopped clapping and sat down. I eased into my seat.

Quentin sat, too. "Tell you later."

With his bagpipe under one arm, Kirk MacLean strutted out of the bandstand, and a bluegrass group took over. They were followed by a pair of fiddlers, and then, to my surprise, three of Deputy Donut's regular customers. The women wore frilly white aprons over red gingham dresses. Smiling broadly, they wielded their concertinas as fiercely as they wielded their knitting needles weekday mornings in Deputy Donut where they, along with two other women, called themselves The Knitpickers.

People in the crowd seemed to have decided that each performance after Quentin's deserved a standing ovation.

Unlike me, my parents had loads of musical talent. They and the Fallingbrook High School music teacher, Lisa-Ruth Schomoset, were that evening's judges. They conferred, and then Lisa-Ruth went to the bandstand and shortened the microphone stand. With her drab brown curls, oversized glasses, shapeless tan dress, and clunky sandals, she looked tiny in that bandstand.

She tapped the microphone, assured herself that it was working, and announced that third prize went to the concertina ensemble. Hands over their mouths in obvious amazement, the three women stood and hugged one another. Laughing and swishing their full skirts, they hurried to the stage and accepted their ribbons. On the far side of the audience from me, the other two Knitpickers hooted and cackled. I clapped and cheered.

Lisa-Ruth called Quentin to the bandstand for second prize. Red-faced, he collected his ribbon and jumped over the two steps. He landed on his feet without the slightest stagger. He might have been slender, but he was athletic. I guessed from his broad shoulders that he'd spent a lot of time canoeing on Deepwish Lake.

Lisa-Ruth announced that the first prize went to Kirk MacLean. The bagpiper swaggered to the stage.

Quentin strode to us. We congratulated him. He gave us terse thanks. Glaring at Kirk MacLean, he almost seemed to be holding his breath.

Chapter 2

❧

I couldn't help contrasting the pain and vulnerability of people Quentin's age with the enthusiasm of the concertina-playing Knitpickers, who were probably in their seventies. They'd been ecstatic about coming in third, while Quentin seemed upset at winning second place.

I looked up into his face and offered the only consolation I could think of. "Summer and I are going to the Fireplug. Would you like to join us?"

Still frowning toward where Kirk MacLean had disappeared, Quentin seemed to hesitate.

Summer prompted, "Say yes."

He let out a deep breath and grinned at her. "Yes." They were both about six feet tall.

I picked up my tote bag. "Good. You're committed, and now I have to warn you that my parents are coming, too. They're two of the judges who gave you only second place."

Beyond the other side of the rapidly emptying seats, Lisa-Ruth scurried away from the crowd and disappeared among tents displaying arts and crafts.

Quentin flapped his hand in a nonchalant gesture. "Second place is good." I suspected that he had recited that sentence, in that monotone, many times.

Summer ran fingers through her ruby red hair, which for

once fell in waves to her shoulders instead of being pinned on top of her head. "I'll bet that bagpiper has never played with the Chicago Symphony Orchestra. Quentin has."

His face was losing its redness and returning to tan. "The bagpiper played well."

We wended our way south from the bandstand along paths between majestic trees that must have been planted about the time that Fallingbrook's square—it was actually a rectangle—was laid out. Above us, cicadas toned down their chorus.

Summer asked me, "Where's your handsome detective?"

Remembering the days when I had denied that Brent was "my" detective—or my anything—I smiled back at her. "Working, but he should be off tomorrow night for the Troubadour Tuesday show."

Quentin asked me, "Is he a singer?"

"He has a great voice—at least, I think he does—but no, he's not going to compete or perform. He'll sit in the audience with me unless he's sent out on a call."

Summer pushed a low-hanging branch out of her way. "How many more days until your wedding?"

I didn't have to think about it. "Fourteen. Two weeks from today."

Quentin deadpanned, "But who's counting?"

My tall, wiry father and short but equally wiry mother caught up with us and congratulated Quentin. At the south end of the square, we crossed Oak Street together, and then turned south on Wisconsin Street. The sky was almost the color of my pale orange sleeveless dress.

Harold, the balding, fiftyish owner of the Fireplug, was chatting to patrons on his sidewalk patio. He hurried to us. "Welcome! Great to see you all again. I'm afraid we have no tables free out here, but there's probably one big enough for your group inside. Get yourselves settled, and Ed will take your orders."

Inside the cool, wood-paneled pub, all of the booths were full, but a large table in the center of the pub was available. We claimed it.

A big man with a broad forehead emphasized by the way he wore his dark hair pulled back in a ponytail came to our table and greeted Quentin by name. Like Harold and the other staff at the Fireplug, Ed wore a short-sleeved shirt with a fire hydrant embroidered on it. He removed a pencil from behind his ear and took our orders.

A few minutes later, while he was handing us chilled mugs of foamy beer, my mother confessed, "I actually like the sound of bagpipes."

My father gazed toward one of the many framed maps decorating the pub's walls. "I always have."

I stared at a map as if seeing through it all the way to Scotland. "There's something haunting about them, as if they're calling to us from long-ago centuries."

My mother quoted dreamily, " 'The skirl of the pipes, the beat of the drums'."

Quentin repeated, "*Skirl*. Whoever made up that word was probably talking about an enraged squirrel trapped in a metal pipe. Sorry, but bagpipes grate on my ears."

Ed plunked my mug down with so much force that beer nearly sloshed over the rim, and the spider tattooed on his very muscular right forearm appeared to jump out of its web. "I hate bagpipes!" Maybe he realized that his reaction was extreme. He set the remaining mugs down quietly and stalked away.

My mother turned to Quentin. "Your playing was perfect. You hit the right notes and played well. There was just one thing . . ." She closed her mouth tight, like she always did when she was afraid of saying something she might regret.

Quentin supplied the word. "Tempo."

My mother gave him an apologetic grin. "It was like you

wanted to put people to sleep, not wake them up like 'Reveille' is supposed to."

Summer twirled a curl around one finger. "Why did you play so slowly, Quentin? I've heard it out at the lake at horribly early hours, and you always play it at a blistering pace. Perfectly, too."

Quentin set his mug down. "It's this thing I do as an attempt at humor at shows and festivals where audience members might want to have fun. I play 'Reveille' really slowly, then 'Taps' at the same pace, which suits 'Taps.' Then I play them both again, speeding up each time. When I get to the final speedy version of 'Taps,' the audience is usually laughing."

Summer accused, "But tonight, you stopped after one slow rendition of 'Reveille.'"

Quentin reddened again. "The audience wasn't going to laugh as much at me as they were already laughing at that bagpiper. I lost focus and quit."

My mother looked about to cry. "I wish you had done what you planned. You probably would have captured first place. Kirk's the janitor at Fallingbrook High. Lisa-Ruth Schomoset teaches music there, and I got the impression that Lisa-Ruth doesn't like Kirk. Did you notice that, Walt?"

My father winced, almost as if he were in pain. "*Doesn't like* him sounds mild. *Detests* him might be more appropriate." I stared at my father in surprise. He seldom made cutting remarks. He softened it by adding, "But she admitted that his playing was faultless, and that he truly did engage the audience. It was close, though. I'm sorry, Quentin. We were torn about giving him instead of you first prize."

Quentin drew squiggles through the condensation on his mug. "It doesn't matter. And I'm sorry I was less than gracious about accepting my ribbon."

My mother asked, "You were? I didn't notice."

I had noticed, and judging by my father's expression, he had, too.

I noticed something else. Quentin's apology did not quite seem sincere. He studied my face for a second. "I'm angry at myself for quitting my performance before I'd barely begun it. I'm not angry at the bagpiper." He shifted his attention to my parents. "Or at the judges."

I suspected that he actually was angry at Kirk and also at the judges, but his anger had been tempered by the half hour that had passed since the awards were given out—and by being in a social situation with my folks.

Outside the pub's front door, Harold's laugh boomed out. "Come on inside! And next time, be sure to bring your bagpipe. You can play it inside or out!" He ushered Kirk, wearing his Highland outfit, into the pub.

Quentin turned toward me and made a horrified grimace. I had to smile.

Harold pointed at our table. "That gentleman over there in the white shirt has a musical case of some sort. You could play a duet." He waved farewell and went back out to his patio.

Kirk sneered—actually sneered—at Quentin. "A dirge." His voice was loud enough for everyone in the crowded pub to hear. "Only amateurs have to play that slowly."

Quentin looked down at the table and fiddled with his coaster.

My father grinned, leaned forward, and said in a conspiratorial voice, "Imagine the disharmonies of a cornet and a bagpipe playing in different keys at the same time."

Quentin let out a begrudging laugh.

"Golden tones from the cornet, and . . ." My mother seemed to struggle for words.

Summer gave me an apologetic look. "Caterwauling from the other. Not your cat, Emily. Dep would never caterwaul."

I admitted, "She's been known to."

Ed returned to our table. We didn't need anything else, but he stayed and asked me, "Aren't you the one who owns the fifties police car with the huge plastic donut lying flat on top?"

"I'm part owner, along with the father of my late husband. We deliver food and beverages that we prepare in our shop."

"That must be nice. Harold's promising to come up with a fun way of delivering burgers and fries, but for now, we use his van." He looked behind him as if checking to see if Harold were nearby, then mimicked holding handlebars and ringing a bike's bell. He lowered his voice. "I'd go for a bike, myself."

I said, "That would be fun." I thought, *But I prefer our tarted-up 1950 Ford with Deputy Donut on the sides and an enormous fake donut on the roof.*

Kirk hadn't taken a seat. Still standing, he stared at one of the framed maps on the wall near the door.

Ed snarled at him, "Hey, piper, buy something or leave."

Harold must have been right outside the door. He poked his head around the jamb and frowned at Ed.

Kirk reached into his sporran and dumped coins and a small white rectangle on the table below the map. Kilt swaying, he marched out.

Ed lowered his head and apologized quietly to the people at our table. "Sorry, that was rude. I was trying to protect you and everyone else in here."

Quentin focused on Ed, but said nothing.

My father asked, "Protect us from what?"

Ed clenched his fists, causing the spider tattoo to appear to crawl toward our table. "From being robbed."

My mother squeaked, "Robbed?"

Ed quirked a thumb at Quentin. "Hey, Quentin, you know why."

Quentin blinked. "I do?"

"Sure. That's the guy who was hanging around the gym on

Wednesday. He was wearing shorts that time, and he's trimmed his beard and hair since then, but that's him."

Quentin stared toward the doorway where we'd last seen Kirk. "I didn't recognize him, but you might be right."

"Of course I'm right. He robbed both of us. And don't go saying that I was the one who broke into lockers and stole our wallets and my phone. You and I were side by side all morning. That guy's not a member of the gym, but he hung around, not using the equipment, or anything, just sort of . . . watching. It freaked me out. He went toward the locker room, and then he must have left, because I didn't see him in the gym again that morning. Or ever until just now. Did you, Quentin?"

Quentin grasped the handle of his beer mug. His knuckles paled. "I wasn't paying attention. The thief could have been someone else. Anyway, the manager at the gym was probably right that I hadn't locked my locker."

Ed's spider tattoo jumped again. "I locked mine. Someone picked the padlock." He explained to the rest of us, "The locker room has a door to the outside. That bagpiper didn't come back into the gym, so he must have left through the locker room and let the door lock behind him."

I asked Ed, "Do you trust the manager of the gym?"

"Mostly. Nothing like that happened before or since, only Wednesday when that guy was hanging around for no good reason."

My dad asked, "Did you report the theft to the police?"

"Yeah, and I already have some of my replacement cards and ID."

Other customers signaled Ed for more beer. He headed toward their table.

Quentin's face had gone blank, as if he'd stopped listening to Ed. He put bills on our table. "I should go."

My mother pointed at the little pile of bills. "That's too much."

Quentin glanced toward where we'd last seen Ed. "He could use the tips."

Summer asked him, "Do you need a ride back to the lake?"

"I drove." Quentin strode out.

Summer half-stood and watched him go. "I hope he's not planning to search for that bagpiper and confront him about his rude disruptions. Or the theft Ed mentioned."

Startled, I asked, "Would he?"

She put down her empty beer mug. "Probably not. He was a difficult and willful little boy, but he's about twenty-five. He must have outgrown his tantrums. Besides, he's able to make a living with his talent."

My mother opened her eyes wider. "That's impressive! And he's staying out at your lake?"

Summer was still watching the doorway. "His parents are professors, so they usually spend most of the summer out there. I think Quentin has most of August off." She thrust money onto the table. "I should go, too."

My parents and I also left cash and stood. On my way out, I glanced at the map that seemed to have intrigued Kirk. It showed the neighborhood destroyed in the Great Chicago Fire of 1871. The white rectangle Kirk had left on the table below it was one of his business cards.

My father held the pub door open for us.

Thanking him, I glanced back into the pub. Ed paused at the table beneath the map, scooped up Kirk's coins and card in one big hand, and slipped them into a pocket.

On the patio, Harold waylaid us. "Sorry about Ed's outburst to the man in the kilt. Ed's a good employee, but he needs to watch that temper and stay in his own lane."

My father said gently, "No problem, Harold."

My mother added, "It won't stop us from coming back."

My parents, Summer, and I strolled south along Wisconsin Street. Above us, the sky glowed with the final, pinkish remains of the evening's sunset. A breeze brushed my skin like velvet. Neither Kirk nor Quentin was in view. Summer watched traffic as if she were hoping to see Quentin drive past on the way to his parents' summer home. At my street, Maple, my parents and I said goodbye to Summer and turned west.

We passed older, larger Victorian homes and then newer, smaller ones. Built in 1889, my yellow brick two-story cottage still had its charming, ivory-painted gingerbread trim. Alec and I had bought and restored the house before that devastating night when he and Brent were both shot and Brent was the only one to survive.

The porch light and a lamp burning inside the living room welcomed us. In my cozy living room, Dep purred and rubbed against our ankles. My father picked her up and held her like a baby, a small, soft, short-haired tortoiseshell tabby baby with donutlike circles on her sides and an orange-stripy patch on her forehead. She purred louder.

We all went upstairs. My parents were using my guest room, which, when I didn't have guests, was my home office. My mother stopped in the doorway. "We don't have to get up as early as you do, Emily. Go ahead and use the bathroom first."

"You're sure?"

My father called from inside the bedroom. "We're sure. We'll read awhile before we turn out the lights."

When I was ready for bed, I didn't latch the bedroom door. I turned out my light and heard my door open just enough to let a little kitty in, and then her slight weight landed on the duvet covering my shins. She purred. I fell asleep.

And was startled awake by the skirl of the pipes.

Chapter 3

✼

Listening in the darkness, I lifted my head from the pillow. Dep shifted on my legs, and I could feel her tension. No whispers came from my guest room. Were Dep and I the only ones hearing bagpipes?

I didn't recognize the tune, which wasn't surprising, but I was certain it wasn't "My Bonnie Lies over the Ocean." Someone could have been broadcasting recorded music, but to my amateur ears, it sounded live. Slowly, it became quieter, and then I couldn't hear it at all.

Was Kirk celebrating his success in the Musical Monday competition by marching around the community and serenading us, whether we wanted him to or not?

I still heard nothing from my parents. I hoped they'd slept through the music.

I snuggled down underneath the covers. Today was Troubadour Tuesday. Following a schedule, people would sing in front of Fallingbrook businesses during the afternoon, and then they would compete for prizes at the evening show.

Kirk MacLean couldn't be among them. I doubted that a bagpiper could sing more than a few notes at a time while keeping the pipes' bag inflated. Although I liked bagpipes, I didn't want to hear them every day. And I certainly did not want them rousing me out of a deep sleep and calling to me across the centuries.

With a soft grunt, Dep settled down on my shins. I drifted back to sleep.

Dep woke me up by patting my cheek shortly before my alarm was due to sound. I turned it off and quietly showered and dressed in my summer Deputy Donut uniform, black shorts and a white polo shirt embroidered with our Deputy Donut logo—the silhouette of a cat wearing a hat like the ones we wore at work, police hats with fuzzy donuts where the shield would be. The words DEPUTY DONUT were embroidered in a curve above the cat. Dep and I ate breakfast. I snapped her into her harness, attached the leash, and took her out onto the front porch. I didn't know if my parents were sleeping or simply staying out of my way.

Dep walked well on a leash, as long as I let her investigate. That morning, she spent so much time on side excursions that instead of walking along the fronts of shops on Wisconsin Street, I shortened the distance by cutting through parking lots behind the shops.

Two blocks from Deputy Donut, Dep became curious about a camper van next to a fence on the far side of a parking lot from the shops. Someone must have repainted the van by hand. Splotches of deep green peeked through bright orange brushstrokes. Someone inside the van was snoring. I gave Dep's leash a tug. Tail straight up, she walked nicely the final two blocks to Deputy Donut's back door.

My father-in-law, Tom, and I had opened Deputy Donut in an attempt to cope with our grief over Alec's death. Donuts had been some of Alec's favorite desserts. When Alec and I had first brought our tiny tortoiseshell tabby kitten home, Alec had taken one look at the donutlike circles on the little torbie's tricolored sides and had laughingly called her Deputy

Donut. We'd quickly shortened it to Dep. Tom and I had borrowed Dep's full name for our donut shop.

When I was at Deputy Donut, Dep stayed in our office. She had everything she needed plus windows on all four sides so she could watch the parking lot, the driveway leading from Wisconsin Street to the parking lot, our dining area, and the kitchen. Tom and I had designed and built a playground for her in the office. Kitty-sized ramps and stairways led to catwalks and tunnels, painted in shades of coffee, chocolate, vanilla, and butterscotch, near the ceiling.

I shut the back door, confining Dep in our office, and released her from her leash and harness. She nosed through the basket of toys we kept underneath the desk. With a bright red jingly ball in her mouth, she raced up one of her ramps to a platform next to a tunnel.

I opened the door to the dining area. The jingly ball landed on the floor behind me. Laughing but not surprised, I went into our dining area and closed the office door. The walls in our charming dining room were white, tinted with the barest hint of peach, a perfect background for displaying local artists' work that people could purchase through The Craft Croft. All of our tables, whether for two, four, or six people, were round, so of course we had painted donuts on their tops. My mother-in-law, Cindy, who taught art at Fallingbrook High, had helped. No two tables were alike.

I walked behind the half wall into the kitchen and from there into the storeroom. I tied on an apron and put on my Deputy Donut hat with its whimsical faux-fur donut in front. My muscular father-in-law, Tom, came in next and settled his hat on his gray-flecked dark hair. Jocelyn, a former gymnastic star who was home from college for the summer, arrived next. Dressed like we were, she tied her straight black hair into a ponytail and covered it with her hat. Olivia, our other assistant, had the day off.

As usual on weekday mornings, two groups came in about

nine and settled at the large tables near our front windows. The retired men joked with one another and teased the Knit-pickers. That morning, we all, including the retired men, praised the concertina trio. The three women pretended to be shocked that we were surprised about their talent. The two regular groups left as usual before noon.

The afternoon began well. Tom made and decorated donuts in the kitchen. Jocelyn and I decorated donuts and served customers.

Cindy arrived at our patio with her colleague, Lisa-Ruth Schomoset. Cindy made most of her clothes, and I was certain that she had made this outfit—elegantly simple and perfectly seamed linen slacks and top. Their wheat color nearly matched her hair, smoothly tied back in a bun. The tragedy of the death of her only child, my first husband, Alec, had not erased her smile lines or cooled the warmth of her blue eyes.

My parents joined her and Lisa-Ruth in the shade of one of our umbrellas. The pink umbrellas cast a rosy glow over the diners, making Lisa-Ruth and her greenish-brown dress look less sallow. However, maybe Cindy, Tom, and I had gone too far when we'd painted multicolored sprinkles on the umbrellas. The opaque sprinkles cast lozenge-shaped shadows on faces.

My parents asked me if I'd heard bagpipes in the night.

"Yes, but I went back to sleep."

My father nodded. "So did we."

My mother said, "But it was weird."

Lisa-Ruth frowned.

My parents ordered espressos. Lisa-Ruth wanted Colombian coffee with lots of cream and sugar, and Cindy opted for the day's special coffee, a rich and full-bodied dark blend from Ethiopia with grassy undertones. She decided to try one of our new lemon-curd Long Johns. Tom had been experimenting with their recipe at home. My mother wanted one of our wild blueberry donuts topped with lemon glaze. Lisa-

Ruth ordered a fudge donut with fudge frosting topped with swirls of caramel sauce. My father asked for a strawberry shortcake donut with vanilla ice cream and whipped cream.

When I returned to their table, they were talking to two couples at the next table. One of the women made a disgusted face and told me, "We've just been planning what to do about a bagpiper who has been roaming all through town today, deafening everyone with his horrid screeching."

Uh-oh, I thought.

The other woman was as indignant as her friend. "Not only that, but he's also been playing where singers are performing, and no one can hear the singers."

Double uh-oh.

I felt the blood drain from my face. Cindy patted my wrist. "Emily, warn Tom and your assistants. We're conspiring to invade your shop."

Lisa-Ruth corrected her. "Not invade, precisely."

My mother explained, "While you were inside, everyone on this patio agreed that if Kirk MacLean interrupts a performance here this afternoon, we're going inside and turning our backs on him."

I lowered the now-emptied tray and let it dangle from one hand at my side. "Okay . . ."

Lisa-Ruth pointed down Wisconsin Street. "Here come my kids! Not mine, but some of the students I taught last year."

Two boys and two girls, all in their late teens, ran through the hot sunshine to the sidewalk in front of our patio. They wore straw boaters on their heads, red-and-white-striped vests over white shirts, and red shorts. The boys whipped off their hats and held them over their hearts. Harmonizing barbershop-style, the teens launched into "For Me and My Gal."

My mother smiled pointedly at my left ring finger with its solitaire sapphire and mouthed, "Soon!" *Thirteen days now . . .*

Lisa-Ruth sipped her coffee and recorded the teens' performance on the phone she'd set up on a tabletop tripod. It was
no wonder she was proud. As far as I could tell, her former
students sang perfectly. My mother nodded, and my father
tapped his toes on the flagstones.

I wanted to stay and enjoy the performance, but I needed
to make certain that Tom and Jocelyn weren't frantic in the
kitchen and dining room without me.

Of course they weren't. I put the tray away.

And then I heard the bagpipe. I turned around.

In his Highland outfit, Kirk MacLean stood next to the
barbershop quartet. Kirk paid no attention to the teens and
their song. His "My Bonnie Lies over the Ocean" clashed
horribly with their "For Me and My Gal," not that I could
hear much of the teens over Kirk's bagpipe.

Lisa-Ruth stood and shook her finger at Kirk. He ignored her.

The other guests on our patio scraped their chairs back
and clustered in the entryway. They sorted themselves out
and filed inside. Lisa-Ruth followed them but stayed outside
for extra seconds. Holding the door open with one hand and
shoving her other hand into her large tote bag, she yelled at
Kirk. "Stop that!"

The teens ended their song in the middle of a verse and ran
north.

Kirk kept playing.

Cindy pulled Lisa-Ruth inside, and everyone from the
patio turned their backs on Kirk and his rudeness. I didn't
join the lineup of people facing our dining room, kitchen,
and office. I went from table to table inside, explaining to
other patrons why our donut shop had been overrun with
patio guests and their conspiratorial whispers and snickers.

The volume of the pipes dwindled, and a man called,
"He's leaving. We can go back to our tables and our coffee
and donuts."

They trooped outside.

I refilled coffees inside the shop, and then took a pot of fresh coffee out to the patio. Instead of settling in to enjoy their donuts and beverages, most of the patrons on the patio were standing and facing north.

Lisa-Ruth pointed a finger. "He's at the Fireplug. He followed my students, and now he's interrupting their performance up there." She described him in terms that I suspected she would never utter in her classroom.

A man elaborated. "When we came outside again, we could see the kids serenading the people on the patio at the Fireplug, and then that piper went up there and started that awful racket. Now the kids are running toward the square. I hope he doesn't follow them."

Kirk had tossed some of his business cards onto the tables closest to the railing dividing our patio from the sidewalk. My mother removed a card from her plate, scrunched it in her hands, and threw it onto the table. "He's not supposed to be one of the touring performers today. His day was yesterday." It was hard to rile my mother, but Kirk MacLean had succeeded.

I held up the carafe of coffee. "Who wants a refill?"

Lisa-Ruth sat down. "I need one." She lifted the napkin she'd left on the table and stared at the spoon that had been underneath it. "My mug's gone." She said it in a cool and matter-of-fact voice, very different from the angry tones she'd used earlier.

I managed to be every bit as calm. I set the carafe down on the table near my father. "I'll get one."

I turned toward the front door. Cindy thinned her lips but quickly straightened her face.

I wondered if she had also noticed Lisa-Ruth tucking something into her tote bag before she joined the others inside Deputy Donut. The logo embroidered on our aprons and shirts and printed on our dishes was cute, and occasionally, people asked to buy a mug. So far, we had decided not to sell them. Sometimes, though, like at that moment, they simply disappeared.

Behind me, Lisa-Ruth called out, "Never mind."

I went back to their table.

Lisa-Ruth stood and pointed toward the Fireplug. "He's chased the kids from there. Someone needs to stop him."

My parents stood, too. The determination on my mother's face would have scared me when I was a kid and had disappointed her. "Let's go remind him that he was in the spotlight yesterday, and he's not on today's schedule."

Lisa-Ruth asked my parents in a quiet voice, "Can we take back his prize?"

My father looked down at her upturned face. "We didn't put anything like that in the rules."

Lisa-Ruth snapped, "We should have. It needs to go in before next year." Glowering toward the town square, she added, "If we even do this again."

Pain flickered across my mother's face. She'd been hoping that this first Fallingbrook Arts Festival would lead to more. She suggested to Lisa-Ruth, "Bring it up at the next committee meeting."

Without responding, Lisa-Ruth brushed past my parents and Cindy. She left the patio and strode south.

My parents and Cindy watched her wordlessly for a second and then headed north. Kirk stopped playing and marched away from the Fireplug. He headed in the direction the teens had gone, toward the square.

Chapter 4

Three young men with acoustic guitars arrived at our patio and accompanied themselves singing "Greensleeves."

Beyond them, a dark gray compact car crept north along Wisconsin Street. Lisa-Ruth stared through the driver's window toward the trio, glanced at me, and then faced forward and sped away. Cindy and my parents were about halfway to the Fireplug. Lisa-Ruth passed them and continued north. Considering the numbers of people wandering around shopping and enjoying the festival, she was driving dangerously fast.

A man in a rumpled brown suit ignored the musicians in front of our patio, strode between our outdoor tables, and went inside. Jocelyn was serving customers on the patio. I followed the man in the brown suit into the shop. Beyond the window to our office, Dep was in one of her favorite places, perched on the back of the couch where she could watch the diners. She stared grumpily at the man.

He hesitated near the stools pulled up to the serving counter, and then veered to a small table at the corner between the office and the outside wall. He sat down, put his elbows on the table, and plunked his face into his hands like someone who was too tired to hold his head up. Maybe he didn't want anyone to bother him.

Dep flicked at one of her shoulders with her tongue.

I decided that the man needed to talk to someone. He lifted his face as I came near and sighed. "Coffee," he requested, "strong coffee." With a grim attempt at a smile, he added, "Please."

I suggested, "An espresso?"

"Two to start. And an old-fashioned cake donut. Do you make them with nutmeg?" He tugged at the knot of his tie until it loosened. It was tan.

"Lots of it."

The smile became more real. "One to start. No, make it two." He unbuttoned the top button of his shirt. Its yellowish beige was lighter than the tie, which had a pinkish cast. The entire effect was of someone who had tried to put together a matching outfit but had ended up mismatched and drab. Maybe he and Lisa-Ruth both bought their clothes from a store specializing in muddied colors.

Heading to the kitchen, I couldn't help picturing a remake for the man. A suit in a warmer shade of brown, a lighter shirt, and a dark green tie would have made him appear livelier and would also have set off his reddish-brown hair, pale skin, freckles, and hazel eyes.

Filling his order in the kitchen, I figured that the man's mood was affecting his appearance. Something serious was bothering him.

I took two espressos and the donuts to his table. Dep was lying on the back of the couch with her front paws tucked underneath her chest. Her eyes were half open, but I suspected she was again focusing on the man.

He thanked me and explained, "I didn't get much sleep last night."

"I seldom bring people two espressos at once. If you drink both of them, you might not get much sleep tonight, either."

"Tonight doesn't matter. Last night did. I tossed and turned, worrying about this afternoon's job interview, and then when

I finally fell asleep, someone went past my apartment playing a bagpipe. I don't know how many times I fell asleep only to have it happen again."

"Maybe the espressos will wake you up enough for the job interview."

"Too late. I've just come from it. Thanks to that guy and his bagpipe during the night, I did a terrible job at the interview. He should be stopped."

I didn't tell him that Lisa-Ruth had said almost the same thing. I confessed, "A bagpipe woke me in the night, too. I'm not sure if it was being played by the man who has been disrupting this afternoon's performances, but my parents and mother-in-law were here a few minutes ago. They've gone to ask him to stop interrupting other musicians. Maybe they'll also suggest that he shouldn't play his bagpipe when people are sleeping." The man gave me a genuine smile. It made him look younger and less careworn. I figured he was in his early twenties, probably even younger than Quentin. I added, "You probably did better at that interview than you think."

"I could tell by the look on the guy's face that I didn't get the job." I opened my mouth, but the man in the brown suit said it for me. "Yeah, I know I shouldn't be so hard on myself. But sometimes, you can just tell, you know?"

"I suppose. What sort of job are you looking for?"

"About anything. I quit my job at the lumber mill. I was a shift supervisor. I reported unsafe conditions to the company owner. He sided with my boss, the foreman who had changed things and made them unsafe, and then there was an accident that could have been deadly, and I quit. I need a job, so any sort of labor would do, but I hope to find a position where I can work my way up toward management again."

"Public works might be looking for someone."

"That's who just interviewed me. You're not hiring, are you?"

Tom did most of our deep frying, but by this time in the afternoon, he was mostly done for the day. He and Jocelyn were out on the patio with our diners. Everyone seemed to be enjoying the latest entertainers, a pair of sixtyish men wearing tiny top hats and singing while one played a ukulele and the other a banjo. Even though Olivia had the day off, the other three of us had time to spend with customers. I gently answered, "We're fully staffed."

"Who does your cleaning?"

"The Jolly Cops Cleaning Crew."

His shoulders slumped. "Everyone in town says that. Do they hire only retired cops?"

"I think so."

He pulled a business card out of his pocket. "If you hear of anyone hiring, can you let me know?"

His name was Austin Berwin. The card also showed his phone number and his email address, and nothing else. "Sure, Austin."

He smiled and thanked me.

Across the room, a woman held up her mug and pointed at it. I excused myself and headed toward her.

Behind me, a man said loudly to Austin, "I heard what you said about that bagpiper. You're not the only one who didn't sleep last night, thanks to him."

Austin repeated, "He should be stopped."

I didn't turn around. I kept walking. I thought, *Kirk will stop after Cindy and my parents explain the scheduling of the performances.* But I also thought, *Kirk had to know how rude he was.* Maybe he was trying to be obnoxious. That didn't make sense.

Maybe it didn't have to.

Out on the sidewalk, a man in lederhosen and a woman in a dirndl had replaced the previous duet. The new couple played accordions and sang "Edelweiss," and then there were no more acts scheduled in front of Deputy Donut for the day. Our customers left. We prepared dough for the next day, put it into the proofing cabinet to keep it at the perfect temperature and humidity overnight, and tidied for the Jolly Cops. I said goodbye to the others and walked Dep home on her leash. The haphazardly painted orange camper van was still in the parking lot. If someone was snoring inside it, they were doing it quietly.

At home, I heard my parents talking and laughing in the kitchen. I released Dep and followed her through my jewel-toned and white living room and my white, chrome, and glass dining room. Standing at the granite-topped island in the kitchen, my parents were putting the finishing touches on a tomato, cucumber, and leaf lettuce salad. Near them, kabobs of chicken, sweet red peppers, red onions, and zucchini were marinating in a fragrant combination of olive oil, lemon juice, garlic, and lemon zest.

As if she hadn't had food and water available in the office at Deputy Donut, Dep galloped to the chocolate-brown pottery bowls that Cindy, who had been an award-winning ceramicist before she became an art teacher, made for her.

We took the kabobs, salad, and Dep outside. The smooth yellow brick wall surrounding my yard kept Dep safe. She didn't like climbing trees, or at least she'd given up on figuring out how to descend with her dignity intact, and I kept bushes pruned away from the wall. Leaving my father to tend the grill while Dep pounced on bugs in the grass, my mother and I returned to the kitchen for placemats, napkins, dishes, glasses, and cutlery.

Setting the outdoor table, I asked my parents, "Did you convince Kirk to stop disrupting others' performances?"

My mother gazed toward the browning kabobs. "We caught up with him."

My father poked a piece of chicken with a thermometer. "And we talked to him, but not even Cindy, who knows him from working at Fallingbrook High, seemed to get through to him. She told us later that she tries to keep the art room clean, but he always acts like doing his job as janitor is a favor to her."

The kabobs, salad, and the lemonade my father had made were all delicious. Even though each of us had eaten at least one donut that day, I served a new flavor we were trying—raised donuts filled with Door County cherry jam and topped with cherry frosting and toasted coconut. We all agreed that they might be even better if we skipped toasting the coconut.

My parents were already dressed for the evening—my mother in a flowing red paisley top over jeans, and my father in jeans and a casual blue shirt. I put on a lime-green sleeveless dress, and then we left Dep behind and walked to the square for the Troubadour Tuesday evening competition. My parents joined Lisa-Ruth at the judging table. I sat down and saved a seat for Brent.

I didn't have to wait long. A warm, gentle hand landed on my shoulder. I jumped up. Uncaring that people around us might recognize Brent as Fallingbrook's detective, I threw myself into his arms. He gave me one of his bear hugs and then let me go. His gray eyes glinted down at me with affection, and his smile was huge. Because he was off duty, he wore khakis and a white polo shirt. We sat down. Holding his hand, I told him about Kirk MacLean and the way he'd disrupted performances the evening before and during the day. "And I think he was roaming the streets of Fallingbrook during the night, waking everyone up with bagpipe music."

Brent shook his head. "Some people . . ."

We changed to a more interesting subject and quietly discussed our upcoming wedding until the couple in the lederhosen and dirndl began singing and playing their accordions. After their performance, a long-haired woman played a guitar and crooned about thirty verses of a mournful ballad. The teen barbershop quartet clambered to the stage and launched themselves into their cheerful harmonies.

Behind the rows of people in folding chairs, a bagpipe squawked.

Chapter 5

Again in his Highland costume, Kirk was marching behind the audience. He was farther away than he'd been the night before, but not far enough.

Lisa-Ruth leaped out of her seat at the judges' table. With her long batik skirt, in colors of aging mustard, ketchup, and relish, swirling around her legs, she strode toward the back of the audience. She scowled. Her face reddened.

Brent and I followed her.

Behind us, the teens didn't miss a beat.

I caught up to Lisa-Ruth and whispered, "My fiancé will ask Kirk to move. You can go back to judging."

"I'm recusing myself tonight, anyway, unless your parents need me as a tiebreaker. Those kids are former pupils."

"Then go back and enjoy their performance."

She pointed at the bagpiper. "Kirk-the-jerk needs to be told in no uncertain terms to stay away, and your fiancé might be too nice."

"He's nice, but he's also a police officer, and he's good at encouraging people to do what he wants. Maybe you should go back where your former students can see your supportive smiles. They can't be happy that you turned your back on them."

It wasn't a very deft hint, but without meeting my gaze,

Lisa-Ruth turned around and stalked toward the judges' table.

I joined Brent and slipped my hand into his. He calmly, quietly, and politely asked Kirk, "Would you mind practicing farther from the bandstand?"

Kirk thrust his lower jaw out. "Are you trying to harass me, Mr. Policeman?"

Brent remained calm. "I'm only asking you to respect other performers and the audience."

Kirk glowered at me.

I pasted on a smile and murmured, "Congratulations on last night's win."

Kirk studied my face and relented. "Okay, I'll go where I'm welcome. Harold said I could come play at the Fireplug any time." The pleats of his kilt fanning out, he pivoted and marched south.

Brent hugged my shoulders. The barbershop quartet finished their song, and we walked back to our seats. On both sides of the aisle, people stood, cheered, and clapped. They were facing the stage and the obviously exhilarated teens, not us, but I joked to Brent. "I could get used to all this applause."

He grinned down at me. "Do you think we can get our wedding guests to give us a standing ovation after the ceremony as we march up the hill from the lake?" Our ceremony was going to be in a large tent on the shore at Brent's property north of Fallingbrook. Our reception would be higher on the hill, under another tent outside his house.

Picturing how perfect it would all be even without standing ovations, I answered happily, "I'm sure we can."

Brent dropped a kiss on the top of my head, and we edged into our seats as the three singers with acoustic guitars adjusted their microphones. They also received a standing ovation, and so did the rest of the Troubadour Tuesday performers. Kirk and his bagpipe did not return.

Although Lisa-Ruth had recused herself, the other two judges—my parents—awarded first prize to the barbershop quartet.

Walking with my parents to the north end of the square and then across the road, Brent and I told my parents about the praise we'd heard of the teens' performance and the judging.

My mother said, "Those kids are talented."

My father added, "And it wasn't as if some of the others weren't also excellent. The festival is turning out even better than we'd hoped."

We chose a table on Frisky Pomegranate's patio. I sat facing the road and the tree-lined square where people strolled among the easels and tents displaying arts and crafts.

Penny, the sixtyish owner of Frisky Pomegranate, came to take our orders. She and the other servers wore pomegranate-red dresses and aprons trimmed with white piping and embroidered with dancing pomegranates like the one on the sign above the restaurant's front door. Penny asked me, "Did that bagpiper come around your patio, too, Emily, bothering everyone?"

"He interrupted the barbershop quartet at our patio, and then he followed them to the Fireplug and played there while they were still singing."

Penny tapped her pencil on her ordering pad. "So annoying. He kept coming around here yesterday and again today. I'm too old for this aggravation. I don't know how many customers he drove away."

I told her about our customers fleeing the patio, going inside, and turning their backs on the front windows. I added, "He didn't stick around."

She laughed. "I'll get my diners to try that tomorrow. That should teach him. Also, I hear that he paraded around the streets all night making that thing screech and squawk. I'm glad I live outside of town."

My mother told Penny, "We're staying with Emily in town. We woke up to the sound of 'The Skye Boat Song.'"

I toyed with my spoon. "Is that what it was? I could only tell that it wasn't the other song I've heard him play, 'My Bonnie Lies over the Ocean.'" The cutlery at Frisky Pomegranate was darling. Three-dimensional but slightly flattened dancing pomegranates were stamped on the ends of the handles.

Penny quipped, "Wherever Bonnie lies, I wish she'd take a Skye boat and go wherever no one will think of playing bagpipes about it. What can I get you folks?"

Frisky Pomegranate served perfect milkshakes. My mother and I ordered strawberry, Brent ordered chocolate, and my father ordered vanilla. We took a long time drinking and spooning up the satisfyingly thick shakes.

Brent paid for all of us, and then walked us home. The sky glowed, almost turquoise above thunderclouds piling in the west. Brent stayed at my place only long enough to give Dep the cuddle she demanded, and then he kissed me and headed, whistling, back toward the police station where he'd parked his SUV. He should be inside his home above Chicory Lake long before the storms arrived.

With Dep on my lap on the couch, I chatted to my parents until my mother commented, "Again, don't wait for us to go to bed. I'll stay down here and enjoy the cross breezes while I read."

My father assured me, "We'll close the downstairs windows."

I thanked them and went up to bed. Dep stayed downstairs. Later, she nudged the door open, jumped onto my legs, and purred. The light in the upstairs hall was still on. My parents tiptoed upstairs. The hallway darkened, and I dozed off again.

*   *   *

Rain and wind awakened me from a deep sleep. I got up and closed both of my bedroom windows, although one faced north and the other east, and rain seldom came from either direction.

What was buzzing? Three in the morning was a strange time for one of my parents to use an electric toothbrush or razor, but I supposed that if a piece of food between teeth was keeping one of them awake, they might get up and attempt to brush it away. I crawled underneath the covers. The buzzing diminished. Maybe whoever was using the toothbrush had slowly closed the bathroom door.

In a flash of lightning, I saw Dep sitting up, her ears at their pointiest. Thunder rumbled. Dep settled down, snuggled into the crook behind my bent knees, and purred. I dozed off before whoever was in the bathroom padded back down the hall to my guest room.

I woke when the sky outside my eastern window was beginning to lighten. By the time Dep and I were ready to leave for work, it was fully light outside. The rain had stopped, and although clouds were still low and trailing streams of mist, I decided to walk to work. To Dep, a few raindrops were preferable to riding in the car, and besides, my car was in the garage, blocked by my parents' car in the driveway. I shouldered the backpack I used as a purse, harnessed Dep, and let her lead me outside.

Maybe I should have left earlier. The rain seemed to have reinvigorated aromas that my curious cat found fascinating, and she spent extra time investigating. Although Tom and our assistants had keys, I didn't like arriving after any of the others did. I again took the shortcut through the parking lots behind the stores on Deputy Donut's side of the street.

The shortcut wasn't going to save us much time, after all. Dep tried to head toward the camper van, its gaudy orange paint startling in the gray, drifting mist.

Guessing that someone might again be sleeping in the van, I pulled gently at Dep's leash.

She ignored me and strained forward.

Ahead of her, near the fence, a small mound of fabric lay in a mud puddle.

It wasn't just any fabric, either—it was green, black, and white plaid, formed in a shape resembling a crescent. Tubes stuck out from it like skeletal arms and legs.

Why had Kirk MacLean left his bagpipe outside where rain and mud could damage it?

Chapter 6

❈

I stared indecisively at the soaked bagpipe. As if she thought it was a catnip-filled toy, Dep kept straining toward it.

Who would leave his musical instrument in a puddle in a parking lot?

Kirk MacLean had not been acting rational.

A breeze knocked a raindrop out of the trees and onto the back of my neck. I shivered. A drop must have landed on Dep's ear. She sat down, twitched the ear, and rubbed it with a front paw.

An engine sounded to my right. Two blocks north, Tom's SUV pulled into the lot behind Deputy Donut. Gripping Dep's leash with one hand, I beckoned frantically to Tom with the other. The SUV went out of sight, toward where Tom usually parked next to the garage we'd had built for our donut-topped delivery car.

Tom must not have seen me. He briskly crossed the parking lot toward Deputy Donut.

I didn't want to shout and possibly bother people sleeping in the van or in houses on the other side of the fence. My attempt to whistle came out as a wheeze.

Tom climbed the two steps to Deputy Donut's back porch and let himself into the office.

Dep had gone as far as her leash would let her. Stretching her neck, she peered around the far side of the van, puffed up, arched her back, and hissed.

I told myself she was probably only responding to another cat.

But maybe it was a skunk.

Mentally preparing myself to back out of range of any skunks, I ran to Dep, lifted her into my arms, and peered toward where she'd been looking.

I couldn't help gasping.

Dep had not been trying to investigate a cat or a skunk. Either would have been better.

Kirk lay in a crumpled heap near the open driver's door of the van.

No one would intentionally sleep with one arm in a puddle. His grizzled beard, black velvet jacket, and green tartan kilt were wet and muddy.

He didn't look like he was merely sleeping.

I whispered, "Kirk?" He didn't answer.

Hugging my squirmy and puffed-up cat, I whipped out my phone, called emergency, asked for both an ambulance and the police, and gave my name. "A man is lying outside an orange van in the parking lot behind Fallingbrook's bookstore. The man doesn't appear to be alive."

The dispatcher asked, "Is he breathing?"

"I don't think so."

"Bleeding?"

"Not that I can see."

"Can you check for a pulse?"

"Sure." I turned my phone to speaker mode, set it on an almost dry spot on the pavement, and fumbled around Kirk's wrist. I was certain from the temperature of his skin that I would find no pulse, and I didn't. "No discernible pulse," I reported, "and his skin is about the same temperature as the air."

"Stay on the line and remain on the scene. Police and ambulance are on the way."

I picked up my phone and somehow held onto Dep and got to my feet even though the damp and dreary parking lot seemed to whirl around me. Everything became grayer except that repainted van, glaring orange in the mist. Automatically, I reached for the van to steady myself, but I remembered that I shouldn't touch it and possibly smear fingerprints already on it. Still clutching Dep, I backed away from the twisted body on the wet ground.

Had Kirk slipped and fallen on rain-slimed pavement? Maybe he'd been hit by lightning. The hemmed corner of a piece of white fabric stuck out beneath his drier sleeve, the one I'd inadvertently moved when I searched for a pulse. A handkerchief?

His ceremonial dagger was still in the scabbard tucked into his sock and secured with a garter. I stooped for a better look.

All I could see was the handle. It was decorated with an almost three-dimensional sculpture of a dancing pomegranate. The "dagger" must have been a dinner knife from Frisky Pomegranate.

To my inexpert eye, Kirk's death looked like it could have been an accident or the result of a medical crisis.

A piece of off-white crockery lay close to his head. It was curved, a section broken from the top of a mug. There was a slightly thicker rim, and below it, the letters EPU in black.

EPU.

DEPUTY DONUT was printed on our dishes.

Was this part of the mug that had gone missing from our patio the day before? I didn't see the rest of the mug. Maybe it was underneath Kirk or the van.

I couldn't help wondering if Lisa-Ruth had taken the mug and then had done something to Kirk with it.

A marked cruiser rolled through the parking lot toward

me. I told the dispatcher that the police had arrived, disconnected the call, and took quick snapshots of the scene with my phone. The cruiser stopped beside me. Misty, one of my two best friends since junior high, was driving. Her patrol partner Hooligan, the husband of Samantha, my other longtime friend, was in the passenger seat.

They got out and joined me. Tall, slim, and beautiful even when frowning with concern, Misty placed a gentle hand on my arm. "What's going on, Emily?"

With his auburn hair and freckles, Hooligan usually couldn't help looking both boyish and impish. Now he was as serious as Misty.

Dep had calmed down, but she wasn't purring. Hugging her and inwardly quivering from shock, I summarized what I'd found.

Misty wrote down what I said and then put her notebook away. "Go on to work, Emily. Someone will take a more formal statement from you later."

"Okay." Trying to control my uneven breathing, I carried Dep through the parking lots toward Deputy Donut. Breezes blew more raindrops onto me. I couldn't stop shivering.

Ahead, Jocelyn pedaled her bike from the alley beside Deputy Donut. She turned and stared toward me and the cruiser behind me. I waved. Still clutching Dep, I ran to Jocelyn.

She chained her bike to the stand near the back of our building. "What's going on?" Her deep brown eyes were wide with curiosity.

We shut ourselves inside the office, and I briefly explained. Mechanically, I released Dep and put my backpack and her leash and harness away. Dep ran up one of her cute little stairways to the catwalks and tunnels near the ceiling, probably to check on the toys she'd left there or to knock some of them down onto Jocelyn and me.

Dep had been quiet during my quick examination of the

scene of Kirk's death, and hadn't made a noise when Misty and Hooligan showed up, but now she hissed like she had when she'd first seen the body beside the van.

Jocelyn looked up toward the catwalk. "Dep doesn't usually do that, does she?"

"No. She hissed when she caught sight of Kirk on the ground. Maybe she's reliving that." With her fur again puffed up so that she appeared too wide to sit on her catwalks, Dep peered toward the ceiling. Her tail flicked back and forth like it did when she spotted prey. If there was a spider or bug up there, I couldn't see it.

Her pupils huge, she ran down a switchbacking ramp to the floor. She jumped onto our office couch and stared up toward her kitty tunnels and catwalks as if expecting a spider to descend toward us.

I ran my fingers through her soft fur. Although raindrops had landed on her, she wasn't damp. "What is it, Dep? Did you see something terrifying?"

Jocelyn cooed at her, "The sounds of birds splashing in puddles or pecking at things on the roof wouldn't scare you, would they?"

Still puffed up, Dep gave us a baleful look. Then, as if nothing had alarmed her, she vigorously licked a front paw.

Jocelyn and I laughed, although I didn't exactly feel merry. Jocelyn examined my face. Serious again, she asked, "Are you all right, Emily?"

"Just a little shaken." I'd stopped trembling.

"Did the police take your statement?"

"Misty took notes. She and Hooligan were first on the scene. Someone will take an official statement."

Jocelyn gestured at the computer. "You should start it now."

"You sound like Tom."

"I've worked around you two for several years. And this isn't the first time you've come upon a body and needed to write it all down."

Olivia opened the back door. Confining her lustrous, brown, wavy hair into a bun low on the back of her head, she joined us in the office. The tall and serious young woman had walked up Wisconsin Street from her apartment and hadn't noticed the unusual activity in the lots behind the shops. I summarized and then had to dismiss her concerns about me. "Compared to that bagpiper, I'm fine."

Filling Olivia in on Kirk's odd behavior the day before, Jocelyn closed Dep and me into the office. She and Olivia headed toward the kitchen.

The police would want the video files from our security cameras. I turned on our computer and watched the video taken by the camera mounted on the back of our building. I sped through the beginning of the night. Although the video was in color, in the dimly lit parking lot, it might as well have been black and white. The last few cars left the parking lot.

Around one in the morning, three pickup trucks parked behind Deputy Donut. Four retired police officers wearing their black Jolly Cops Cleaning Crew uniforms climbed out of the trucks and headed toward the back door near our loading dock. They were obviously laughing and teasing one another—the "jolly" in their company name was accurate. I fast-forwarded again.

At one fifty-five, something moved. I slowed the video.

In his Highland costume and clutching his bagpipe, Kirk ran south past the back of our building. He glanced over his shoulder and ran faster. Lightning flashed.

I watched a few minutes longer. Nothing.

Kirk must have been running to save his outfit and bagpipe from the impending storm. Maybe he arrived at his van after it started raining, and he opened the door, slipped on wet surfaces, and suffered a fatal fall.

But why had he run faster after looking over his shoulder?

Focusing on the space between two of the Jolly Cops' pickups, I replayed the video slowly from where Kirk appeared.

Someone in dark clothing ran in a crouched position on the far side of the trucks. The hood of the person's jacket was up, hiding the face, and I couldn't make out details or tell if the person was male or female, young or old. He or she was heading south, only seconds behind the bagpiper.

Just over five minutes later, at one minute after two, the Jolly Cops left Deputy Donut, rushed to their trucks, and drove north, out of the camera's view.

Rain sluiced over the otherwise bare pavement.

Chapter 7

In the next few minutes of the video, nothing moved except the rain, and then even it stopped. I fast-forwarded again. About fifteen minutes after that crouching figure followed Kirk through the parking lot, I saw a car. I slowed the video.

A small, dark sedan crept north on the far side of the parking lot. It could have come from Kirk and his van. The camera on the back of Deputy Donut was mounted too high to see who was driving, or even hands on the wheel, and as far as I could tell, no one was in the passenger seat. The car went out of sight. I sped the video again.

I saw no more movement in the lot behind Deputy Donut until Tom drove in to open the shop for the day. I went back and made notes of the times that the video showed Kirk, the person running behind him in a crouch, and the sedan driving away from near where Kirk's life had ended.

I also watched the video from the camera mounted on the front of Deputy Donut. By two in the morning, traffic had died down. No pedestrians were in view. Twenty minutes later, two vehicles drove south in the rain, but one of them remained beyond the pickup truck it was passing, and both vehicles went out of sight. Lightning flashed.

I wrote down the time when the two vehicles passed, and

then I typed my statement, printed it, and slid it out of the printer.

A tap sounded on the back door.

I whirled around as if a murderer—or a bolt of stray lightning—were coming after me.

Brent was outside the glass door. His eyes were bleak.

I opened the door, gave him a quick hug, peeked with one eye past his upper arm, and made an inane comment. "The sun came out."

"A while ago."

I handed him my statement. "I'll get you some coffee and donuts."

He thanked me, and I closed him inside the office with my statement and my cat.

I returned with an eggy cruller dipped in maple glaze and dotted with bacon bits, and also a raised donut filled with key lime custard and topped with meringue. And I brought him a mug of one of my favorite coffees, Kona from Hawaii.

Brent gave me a warm smile. Eating the cruller and the donut, drinking coffee, and commenting on how good they were, he read the rest of my statement.

Customers began filling the dining room. Through windows from the office into the kitchen and dining room, I could see that Tom, Jocelyn, and Olivia were coping without me.

Brent read the last page of my statement and began asking questions. Together, we went to the computer. He stood behind my chair while I filled him in on details and added them to my original document.

Finally, he asked, "What do you think happened?"

I counted on my fingers. "He could have been hit by lightning. He could have slid on wet pavement and hit his head. Maybe he slipped trying to get into that van. Do you know if the van was his?"

"It was."

"Maybe he simply had a fatal heart attack or a stroke. But video from the security camera in the back of our shop shows him running, looking over his shoulder, and speeding up. And it shows someone following him. Do you think he was attacked?"

"The postmortem will show more, but there are signs of a struggle, and I'm calling it suspicious. Show me the video?"

Playing it on the screen, I suggested, "This person following Kirk might have been running in a crouch because he or she knew about the camera on the back of our shop."

"Or guessed."

"But someone drove north past the shop about fifteen minutes later. Maybe they weren't worried about cameras, or they knew or correctly guessed that cameras would be mounted too high to reveal who was in a driver's seat when the car was heading north. Or maybe they were trying to avoid being seen on the street, where there are probably more surveillance cameras. Maybe they figured their sedan was nondescript enough that no one would recognize it. But police can identify makes and models of cars, right?"

"We can usually figure it out." He replayed the video, stopping it when the car was in view. "A dark Honda Civic, one of thousands in the state."

"Too bad it doesn't show the license number."

He joked, "License numbers should be painted in large letters on the sides of cars. It would make my life easier. Send me a copy of the video, please. I'll be checking for security videos from nearby businesses, also. Maybe one will show the plate."

"The video from the front of our shop doesn't show plates, either." I played that video for him, slowing when the car and the pickup truck drove past. "Could the car be the same Honda Civic?"

"I see what you mean. It could be. Footage from businesses across the street might show the entire car."

"Are there security cameras focused on Kirk's van and . . . and on him?"

"A camera on the back of the bookstore might have one that would show the van, but the van itself would be between the camera and Kirk. I'll ask at the bookstore next."

I emailed him the video clips and asked, "Would you like to see the pictures I took this morning before Misty and Hooligan got out of their cruiser?"

"We took some, but yes, please."

Brent had also recognized the knife from Frisky Pomegranate. I reminded him that Penny had complained about Kirk. "However, annoying her customers and perhaps driving them away from her patio is hardly a reason to kill him."

"You never know what might trigger people. Did Kirk and his bagpipe drive customers away from your patio?"

"I think the festival has been a net gain for us." I showed him the next photo. "This piece of crockery must have come from the rim of one of our Deputy Donut mugs. The break looks new."

"I'm sure you're right, and I'm afraid that fatal blow to his head might have been caused by the mug, not from falling, and I don't believe he was stabbed with the dinner knife."

"Could he have been stabbed by his ceremonial dagger, and someone took it and replaced it with a knife from Frisky Pomegranate?"

"I don't think he was stabbed at all, and I have no idea why a dinner knife was in the scabbard in his sock instead of a ceremonial dagger, except these days, kilt-wearers usually carry non-lethal replicas instead of real daggers."

"What was in his sock last night when you encouraged him to practice his bagpipe farther from the show?"

"He wasn't obviously carrying any sort of daggerlike thing. No scabbard and no garter, either. Maybe he added those to his getup to feel safer when he was wandering around at night."

"It's horrible to think that one of our mugs might have been used to kill him." I twisted my fingers together. "I didn't see the rest of the mug. Was it nearby, like maybe underneath him or his van?"

"No. Have any of you thrown a broken mug into the garbage lately?"

"Not that I know of." I told him about Lisa-Ruth's mug going missing the previous afternoon and about her anger at Kirk when he interrupted her former students' barbershop quartet while they were singing at our patio and farther north at the Fireplug.

"Was that the barbershop quartet that won first prize last night?"

"Yes. I stopped Lisa-Ruth from confronting him—by that time, she was in a fury—while you were on the way to ask him to move." I added in admiration, "And while you were automatically checking for weapons, like daggers in socks."

Grinning, he asked, "What do you think happened to her mug?"

"Shortly before I found out it was missing, Cindy and I noticed Lisa-Ruth taking her hand out of her tote bag as if she'd just slipped something into it."

Brent wrote in his notebook. "What other pictures did you take?"

I enlarged the picture of the white fabric sticking out beneath one of Kirk's sleeves. "I wasn't sure what that white thing was, but after zooming in on it, I'm almost sure it's the corner of a cloth handkerchief. It's hemmed with fancy stitches that were probably white once. And there's a monogram." I stared harder. "Some of the thread looks beige, like there could have been blood on the handkerchief, but the rain diluted most of it, except on the thread used to hem the handkerchief and embroider the monogram. The embroidery thread must be denser than the cloth surrounding it. Do you think those beige spots could be bloodstains?"

"I'm almost certain they are. Most of the handkerchief was sheltered from the downpour by Kirk's arm, and the spots on the parts of the handkerchief that didn't get soaked appear to be blood. We'll have it tested."

He bent closer to the computer screen. "Can you tell what letters that monogram might be?"

"It's hard to tell, with all those flourishes and curlicues, but I think there are only two letters, A and O." I looked up into Brent's face. "Who still carries cloth handkerchiefs, especially handkerchiefs with hand-embroidered monograms?"

"Maybe they're part of Highland costuming. We'll check that."

"Or Kirk kept one with him when rain was predicted so he could use it to wipe his bagpipe dry."

"Can you think of anyone with the initials A.O.?"

I remembered Austin Berwin and his anger at Kirk. "Could the initials be A.B.?"

"Possibly. Why?"

I gave Austin Berwin's business card to Brent and explained how I'd gotten it. "You can keep the card. We're not hiring at the moment."

Brent pocketed the card. "Did you touch the deceased?"

"The 911 dispatcher asked me to check his pulse. I touched only his right wrist, the one that's not in the puddle, and I'm afraid I accidentally uncovered some of the handkerchief."

"Did you touch anything else at the scene?"

"Only with my shoes, walking to Kirk, and I grabbed Dep before she touched anything except with her paws on the ground."

Brent probably realized that his question could have been interpreted as insulting—I'd learned enough from Alec, Tom, Brent, Misty, and Hooligan to know not to disturb anything near what might prove to be a suspicious death. Also, I'd had other encounters with similar scenes. Brent said, "I know you wouldn't, but . . ."

I followed his gaze to the screen, and then I saw something that I hadn't noticed in the shock of discovering Kirk's body. I concluded aloud, "His kilt. The pleats are almost as knife-sharp and neat as if he were standing up. It's like someone straightened those pleats after he fell. After he stopped moving. Maybe he did it himself, but . . ."

"Exactly, and I doubt that some uninvolved person came along and straightened only his kilt, left him lying twisted like that, and didn't call for help." Brent pointed at the enlarged photo of the handkerchief. "Why did you say that the monogram was hand embroidered? Why not machine embroidered?"

"I'm not sure. It looked that way. Machine embroidery tends to be more precise and neater." I enlarged the picture of the handkerchief more. "The thread looks heavier than the thread used in machine embroidery, and the knots are bulky and look hand tied. Oh!"

"Oh, what?"

I took my hand off my mouth. "You probably already figured it out. Seeing the knots means we could be looking at the back of the handkerchief, and the initials could be O.A. But it's hard to tell from the back, especially since the letters have all those embellishments."

"Can you think of anyone with the initials O.A.?"

"Not offhand. Can you?"

"No. Maybe the handkerchief is an heirloom or purchased from a secondhand store. How about last names starting with A?"

"There's our former police chief, Agnew, but he couldn't have come back, right?"

"Definitely not."

"And Samantha's maiden name is Anderson, and her parents live in town, but their first names don't start with O."

"I'll ask them if they've lost an antique hankie. Anyone else?"

I thought back. "I met someone recently . . . oh!" Again, I clamped a hand over my mouth.

Chapter 8

Obviously amused, Brent prodded, "Who did you just remember, Em?"

"The letter I thought was an O could be a Q. The name of
the cornetist who came in second on Music Monday is
Quentin Admiral."

"Came in second to . . . ?"

"Kirk. The bagpiper." Although Brent retained his neutral
cop face, I guessed at the conclusion he might reasonably be
drawing, and I defended the young musician. "Quentin's in
his mid-twenties. He's a serious musician, a professional. He
did seem angry when Kirk interrupted his performance—
well, Kirk actually flustered Quentin, and Quentin broke off
his playing before he could really show off his talent."

"How did Kirk fluster Quentin?"

"You've probably guessed. While Quentin was playing,
Kirk marched back and forth behind the audience and let his
bagpipe squawk, but after the awards were handed out,
Quentin calmed down. I don't think that coming in only second bothered him. He's used to not always being first. He
wouldn't risk his future and his career by attacking someone.
Summer Peabody-Smith knows him. She babysat him. His
parents also have a summer place on Deepwish Lake."

"We'll talk to him. And to Summer."

"And there's something else, Brent. One of the servers at the Fireplug, Ed, said that someone stole wallets and phones at the gym where he and Quentin work out. Quentin was with us when Ed made the accusation, and Quentin didn't necessarily agree that the probable thief was Kirk, but he didn't disagree, either. I gather that Kirk, or whoever, might have picked locks and helped himself to Quentin's wallet and Ed's wallet and phone. Ed seemed really angry at Kirk about it, but Quentin seemed neutral and angrier at Kirk for interrupting his cornet solo than for possibly stealing his wallet."

"Do you know if the thefts at the gym were reported to the police?"

"Ed said he reported it, but I don't know about Quentin. The management at their gym knew about it."

"I'll check for incident reports and have a talk with Ed, Quentin, and the management at their gym."

"Are you calling in the DCI?" The Wisconsin Division of Criminal Investigation offered their expertise and resources to help solve major crimes. Their detectives were called agents. Summer really liked Rex, a DCI agent who had visited Fallingbrook recently, and I suspected that the attraction was mutual. If Fallingbrook needed another DCI agent, and it appeared that we might, I hoped that Rex would return. I wanted other people to be as happy as Alec and I had been and as Brent and I were.

Brent stood. "We've already requested their help." He packed my signed statement into his briefcase. "Sorry, Em, but I probably won't be able to attend the Wee Wonders Wednesday show with you tonight, but I'll be in touch. And let me know if any last-minute problems crop up in our wedding plans."

I smiled up at him. "Everything's under control." Knowing that, as usual, he could be called to work at almost any time, the two of us had already done as much as possible. "And our friends and relatives will help if necessary."

Grasping my upper arms, he pulled me close and kissed my forehead. "Stay safe." Anyone in the dining room could have seen the affectionate gesture. What they couldn't see was the warmth in Brent's eyes as he gazed down at me. "I'm sorry you were the one who found him."

"I'm okay."

He opened the door leading to our back porch and the parking lot. "I know. Be careful."

Clutching Dep to keep her from following him, I said, "You, too." Neither of us would ever forget that his and Alec's chosen profession had led to Alec's death. I couldn't bear the thought of possibly losing Brent, too.

He lifted my chin with a gentle finger. "I will." And then he was gone, and I was standing there with my face buried in my cat's soft, warm fur. She purred.

I closed the door, set her down, and headed into work.

Jocelyn and Olivia had told Tom why I'd closeted myself into the office, first by myself and then with Brent. I washed my hands and put on an apron. In the kitchen, Olivia was filling and decorating donuts, Jocelyn was starting another pot of coffee, and Tom was tending the fryers. Seeing them doing their usual jobs like it was any other, more normal day, calmed me, and I was able to coolly describe more of my horrid early morning discovery.

Having been a detective in Fallingbrook and also its police chief, Tom was pragmatic about it all, but to him, I would always be a beloved daughter-in-law. He couldn't help warning me not to interfere with the investigation.

Jocelyn, who was studying to become a kindergarten teacher, would probably never outgrow her youthful enthusiasm. I might have to keep her from throwing herself into amateur sleuthing—and danger.

Olivia was a little older than Jocelyn in years, but ages older in understanding sadness and grief. Her parents had died, orphaning her and her little sister when Olivia was eighteen and her sister was only eight. Olivia had taken the place of their parents in her sister's life. Her sister was now a secure and confident college student, but I was sure that Olivia always lived in fear that the people she loved would be taken from her. She demanded, "You'll be careful, won't you, Emily? What if a killer is after you because you found Kirk, and the killer might be afraid you saw him or learned too much about him?"

I pointed out, "Kirk had been dead for several hours before Dep found him, so I doubt that the killer was still lurking around. The killer could have been anyone. Kirk must have irritated lots of people with the way he was acting."

Olivia argued, "People seemed to accept that he was annoying, like the customers that Tom and Jocelyn were telling me about, the ones who came inside and turned their backs on him."

Jocelyn tilted her head. "That music teacher, though. She was angry at him for disrupting her former students' barbershop quartet." She turned to Tom. "The music teacher is a friend of your wife's, right?"

Tom lifted a basket of donuts out of the deep fryer and hooked it on the side. "I'm not sure *friend* is the right word. They're colleagues. I'm not sure Lisa-Ruth Schomoset has many friends."

I did not mention that I'd seen a piece of a Deputy Donut mug near Kirk, and I didn't tell Tom, Olivia, and Jocelyn about Lisa-Ruth's mug disappearing around the time she left her table and came inside or about her anger during the Troubadour Tuesday show when Kirk had again interrupted her former students' singing.

Although the tour of Wee Wonders Wednesday performers wasn't scheduled to start until afternoon, our patio was filling up. I went outside to take orders.

The first woman I approached asked me, "What's going on with the police tape a couple of blocks away?"

I didn't want to lie, but I also wasn't about to give out information that the police weren't ready to share. I settled on, "I'm not sure."

Lisa-Ruth strolled north on our side of Wisconsin Street. She didn't look toward the patio or acknowledge my smile and wave. She focused on the other side of the street as if she were wondering if anyone in those buildings could have seen what went on in the parking lot behind the shops on our side of the street. I didn't think that anyone could have without a long-necked periscope, and maybe not even then. Maybe Lisa-Ruth was merely shy, and not about to look toward our patio unless someone she knew, like Cindy, was on it.

It seemed that more than the usual number of pedestrians wandered into the alleyway between Deputy Donut and Frills and Thrills, the bridal shop on the other side of the alley. However, police tape blocked the far end of the alley, and everyone who ventured up it had to return to Wisconsin Street.

On our patio, people were making conjectures about what might have happened during the night. I didn't want to talk about it, hear about it, or even think about it. It was a relief when a brawny man headed straight toward our front door instead of joining the gossiping people on our patio.

It took me a second to recognize the man with the long dark ponytail. As far as I knew, Ed, the server from the Fireplug, had never before come into Deputy Donut, but I usually had Wednesdays off. That week, I was working every day, partly because we expected the performances in front of our patio to keep us extra busy. Also, I wanted to see the acts. And most importantly, in twelve days, I was taking two weeks off for Brent's and my wedding and our honeymoon in the Rockies.

Smiling at the thought of spending all that time alone with Brent, I followed Ed inside. He sat at one of the smaller tables. "My turn to wait on you, Ed," I told him. "What can I get you?"

"Um, what do you have?"

"Coffee, tea, donuts, hot chocolate, whatever you'd like."

"Just coffee. You know, I have to wake myself up and get to work. We open the Fireplug at eleven."

"The special coffee today is Kona, from Hawaii."

He was wearing a white dress shirt and black jeans. He reached for his right sleeve as if to roll it up and then moved his hand away from his wrist. Maybe he'd noticed me staring at the spider tattoo on his forearm on Monday evening and thought it had frightened me, when in reality, I'd been fascinated by the way it had seemed to move independently. He asked, "Don't you have just plain, regular coffee?"

"Yes, a medium roast from Colombia."

As if he didn't quite know what to do with his hands, he rubbed them together. "I'll have that."

"And a donut?"

His ruddy face reddened more. "Nah. I always eat lunch at work."

I brought him the coffee. As if he couldn't help being a server, he took the mug from me, set it down on the table, and turned the handle to his right. "I have to apologize for when you and your friends were in the Fireplug. My boss said I was rude when I told that guy in a kilt to go away."

Ed didn't seem to have heard that Kirk was dead, and I wasn't about to tell him—or anyone else—before the police released the information. Instead, I said, "It didn't bother us, and you explained why you did it."

He dumped cream into his coffee. "I didn't tell you the worst of what that thief did to me. I didn't want Quentin spreading it around to the guys at the gym. My charge cards were gone, and I had to postpone buying an engagement ring for my girlfriend. I'd invited friends and family to the public beach up at Little Lake to watch me propose. My girlfriend didn't know what I planned, and everyone else thought I had a ring. I got down on one knee in the sand, and all I had to offer was an envelope with a picture of a diamond ring I'd cut out of a magazine. I didn't handle it well. I was nervous, so I laughed. She got all insulted, said I wasn't serious, and turned me down in front of my friends and family. It was the worst day of my life." He tore open a packet and poured sugar into his coffee.

"I can see why. Maybe you could take her out to a nice dinner, just the two of you, and explain what happened, and then offer her the actual ring." Feeling like the sapphire on my ring finger was suddenly too showy, I thrust my left hand into my apron pocket.

Ed emptied another packet of sugar into his coffee. "I called her a few minutes ago. She didn't answer."

"Maybe she needs more time."

He brushed at invisible crumbs on the tabletop. "I don't think anything is going to fix it." Glumly, he stared out through the front window toward the street.

I followed his glance. Quentin was standing with his back to the patio, looking up toward the false front at the top of a one-story building across the street.

Ed pointed at Quentin. "I should warn you about that friend of yours. He might dress in a white shirt and black pants like he also works in a restaurant, but he's really a snooty rich kid. I heard he was angry Monday night because he came in only second in the contest, and that guy in the kilt won, with a bagpipe, of all things. All I can say is that everyone else must've been really bad if that screeching won first prize. I'm guessing that Quentin was already furious at that bagpiper for stealing his wallet. Losing the contest to him must've just piled fuel on his fire and broken the camel's back, you know?"

Not sure what to say, I merely nodded.

The nod was all Ed needed. He went on, "I came to warn you. Quentin's arrogant and often angry. Flies off the handle if he thinks he's entitled to gym equipment someone else is using."

My smile was probably not very genuine. Could the willful, difficult little boy that Summer babysat years ago have become a murderer? I thanked Ed. "I'll consider myself warned. Do you think that Quentin could have been the one who stole your wallet and phone? And maybe only claimed that his wallet was stolen?"

"Nah. Quentin worked out beside me. That bagpiper was sneaking around there that day and had no reason to be inside."

Quentin walked on past without coming in.

Ed glanced at his phone. "Oops. I'd better get to work. I'm supposed to open the Fireplug before Harold gets there."

Ed paid me and left. He'd only sipped at his coffee, which wasn't surprising. He'd dumped so much sugar and cream into it that he probably hadn't been able to taste the coffee.

Chapter 9

Because of the Wee Wonders acts that would take place in front of Deputy Donut that afternoon, we expected a larger than usual crowd for lunch. We battered and fried zucchini spears, mozzarella sticks, and poblano peppers stuffed with garlic-and-herb cheese. Tom, Jocelyn, and Olivia must have sensed that I was still unnerved by having come across Kirk's body. They told me to take my lunch break first. Needing to be in familiar surroundings, I ate in our office.

Dep watched me from a carpeted tunnel near the ceiling. I gazed through the windows to the alleyway beside our building and to the nearly empty parking lot. In addition to taping off the end of the alley, the police had strung their yellow tape across the steps to our back porch. Kirk had run past our building, and someone might have been chasing him, so the lot behind Deputy Donut and the lots between it and where I'd found Kirk had to be considered part of the crime scene. The police wouldn't allow the public into those lots until all the possible evidence had been collected.

I mopped up the last of the cheese from my poblano pepper. I still shuddered from a combination of shock and horror, but the delicious lunch helped me feel more normal. Like that morning's curiosity seekers, I wanted to know what was going on. And maybe I hoped for a glimpse of Brent. I opened the back door and stepped out onto the porch. Noon-day heat, humid after the early morning thunderstorm, sur-rounded me.

I leaned over the police tape attached to our porch railings and peered south. Two blocks away, investigators in head-to-toe white outfits milled around Kirk's van. One of the taller ones might have been Brent. Despite the heat, I hugged my-self and whispered nearly silently, "I miss you."

Voices and footsteps warned me that more gawkers were coming up the alley to the parking lot. To the left of the porch and several feet back, Ed's boss Harold stopped beside the police tape blocking the alley. He was with Penny and Tiffany, one of Penny's waitstaff at Frisky Pomegranate. The trio craned their necks as if hoping to see as much of the parking lots as possible. Although they looked south, the cor-ner of Thrills and Frills blocked their view of Kirk's van and the investigators near it.

Harold looked up at me on our porch and pointed at the tangle of wildflowers and grasses at the base of the fence across the parking lot. "What's going on, Emily?"

I didn't have to answer. Penny chimed in. "I usually park a couple of blocks south of here." She gestured toward Tiffany. "We park down there because we like to keep the spaces near Frisky Pomegranate available for our customers, and besides, we can always use the walk. But today we had to park far-ther away."

Harold explained, "The lot two blocks south of here is just buzzing with people wearing protective gear. And police vehicles. It looks like a police investigation to me."

The police tape was a dead giveaway, but I was not going to say that aloud.

Harold asked, "Why is it taped off all the way up here?"

I peered north, but our loading dock obscured the view in that direction. Still not wanting to say anything about the in-vestigation before the police made it public, I gave another of my not-the-whole-truth answers. "The police must have a reason."

Harold shrugged. "I guess I'll have to stop cutting through these lots on my way to and from work, at least for now. Will we see you at the Fireplug after tonight's show, Emily?"

Penny jostled him with an elbow. "Maybe she'd prefer to visit us at Frisky Pomegranate. What's the show tonight, Emily?"

"Wee Wonders Wednesday." Expecting to need to make up evasive responses to comments about Kirk perhaps disrupting performances that afternoon, I held my breath.

None of them mentioned Kirk. Tiffany clapped her hands. "The kids' talent show! I hope to see some of them at our patio when they tour around town."

Harold and Penny agreed, and then all three of them turned and headed toward Wisconsin Street.

I went back inside and worked at the deep fryers while Tom ate in the office. He barely took any time.

Olivia and Jocelyn often went for walks together during their lunch break, but our patio was packed. They took turns eating in the office.

After all four of us had returned to work, Cindy came in. She was wearing another of her creations, a neatly sewn slate blue dress. "I couldn't find a place to park anywhere nearby, with so many people coming downtown to see the kids' performances. Plus the lots behind the stores in your block and the two blocks south of here are taped off for a police investigation. What's going on?"

From the counter between the dining room and the kitchen, Tom beckoned. Cindy and I edged onto stools at the counter. No one else was nearby. Tom murmured to me, "Cindy's discreet. I think we can tell her what happened, don't you, Emily?"

I lightly grasped Cindy's wrist. "Yes, and I'm sorry to tell you, Cindy, but your school janitor is dead."

"Kirk?" She was obviously startled.

"Yes." I briefly described Dep's and my discovery that morning and added, "Brent said it appeared that Kirk might have been attacked."

Cindy took a deep breath. "In a way, I'm not surprised. I hate to say it, but I don't know if anyone is going to miss him. He moved here in September, and I don't think he had close family or friends. Not here, and maybe not anywhere."

Tom might have retired from being a detective, but he still asked pertinent questions. "Where did he live before?"

Cindy gazed toward the proofing cabinet and refrigerators lining the rear wall of the kitchen. "I asked him that question when he started working at Fallingbrook High. All he said was, 'out east,' but he pointed south, so I don't know." Cindy turned toward the dining room. Very few people were in it, but the patio was crowded. "I see you're busy outside. Can I lend a hand?"

We thanked her. I pointed out that Jocelyn and Olivia were now sitting at different tables on the patio and chatting with customers. "We have everything under control. Besides, you came to watch the kids' acts, didn't you?"

"Yes, but I probably wouldn't miss much by pouring coffee and delivering plates of donuts. And all of your patio tables are taken."

I grinned at her. "Then, feel free to help serve people. But since our customers seem content to linger over what we've already given them, let's get coffee and donuts and sit at one of the big tables next to the front window."

The smile crinkles beside Tom's eyes deepened. "Go sit down. Give me a few minutes, and I'll bring you a surprise."

Cindy and I raised our eyebrows at each other, exclaimed "Oooh!" at the same time, and then burst out laughing.

We went to the table that the Knitpickers occupied weekday mornings, turned the two chairs nearest the window to face the patio, and sat down. Cindy smoothed her dress over her lap. "This is perfect. We'll see the children perform, but we'll be in air-conditioned comfort."

A woman pushed a bright red and blue stroller resembling a stagecoach to the sidewalk in front of the patio. The "stagecoach" contained four children who looked about three years old. The woman lifted the children out of the stroller. She arranged, and then rearranged, them into an uneven row facing the patio. Complete with darling if uncoordinated gestures, they sang, "I'm a Little Teapot."

The audience, including Cindy and me, applauded, and so did the charming toddlers, vigorously. The woman settled all four of them into the stroller and buckled them in.

Cindy watched them head off toward the next stop on the schedule, the Fireplug. "That woman's back must be strong. I'm glad I decided to teach high school rather than run a daycare."

Although the other diners in Deputy Donut had gone out to the patio, and no one was inside except Tom, puttering in the kitchen, I leaned closer to Cindy. "Speaking of high school teachers, do you have any idea what happened to Lisa-Ruth's mug yesterday? She was the last one to come inside, and when she was standing in the doorway scolding Kirk, I thought she might have slipped something into her tote bag. I'm not sure. All I saw was her empty hand coming out of her bag."

Cindy thinned her lips like she had the day before when Lisa-Ruth asked for a new mug. "I noticed that, too. I had to wonder, because of something that happened after the spring concert. She was in charge of the ticket money, and twenty dollars went missing."

Not knowing what to say, I muttered a quiet "Oh."

Cindy added, "Only temporarily, but it was strange. Lisa-Ruth said she counted the money, locked the cash box, and wrote down the amount. Then she heard a student scream, and Kirk was the only staff member near Lisa-Ruth. In her panic to find the screaming girl, Lisa-Ruth asked Kirk to watch the cash box." Cindy made a semi-exasperated face, but a smile pulled at her lips. "The girl was fine. A boy had thrown a rubber snake at her. Lisa-Ruth calmed the situation, confiscated the toy, and returned to the cash box. It was where she'd left it, still padlocked, but Kirk was gone. The concert was a Friday night. Lisa-Ruth took the cash box home for the weekend. The following Monday, she unlocked it and announced that twenty dollars had disappeared, and that someone must have picked the padlock and opened the box."

I groaned. "Ed, a server at the Fireplug, is certain that Kirk picked locks in the locker room of the gym where Ed works out."

"I wouldn't put it past Kirk. At school that Monday, Lisa-Ruth didn't accuse Kirk, exactly, but he claimed that he had also needed to leave the locked cash box for a few minutes, and someone else must have, as he put it, 'broken into' it. He didn't accuse Lisa-Ruth. He came up with another theory, that no one had broken into the cash box, and Lisa-Ruth could have counted incorrectly."

I winced. "Ouch."

"Lisa-Ruth turned bright red and swore that she knew how to count. She also said that the students who collected the money had kept track on paper. She gave the principal their names and told the principal to ask them for their records."

"Did the principal do that?"

"I don't know, but the next morning, while Lisa-Ruth was teaching a class, Kirk brought the principal to the music room. From the art room across the hall, I saw them barge into the room without knocking. I thought that Lisa-Ruth could use support, so I told my students to keep working, and I followed Kirk and our principal into the music room. Kirk loudly announced that he'd found the money the night before while he was cleaning. He told the principal to look behind the trash can. The principal pulled out a ten and two fives."

"What did Lisa-Ruth do?"

"Clamped her mouth shut, but I could almost see her curls frizzing in the steam coming off her scalp. Her students fidgeted and murmured. They love Lisa-Ruth. I didn't think the principal handled it well, but I guessed that Kirk had convinced her to go to the music room with him right away, even while class was in session, before the money disappeared again. I kind of bullied both the principal and Kirk out of the music room. Lisa-Ruth pounded on piano keys, her students began singing, and I returned to a class full of contented sophomores up to their elbows in wet clay."

"What do you think really happened with the money?"

"I suspect that Kirk took the twenty dollars, and then when he heard that a paper trail existed—as far as I know, the principal never did ask those students for the records— Kirk hid the money in the music room in the hope that people might believe that Lisa-Ruth stashed the money there to take home later."

"What did other people who know Lisa-Ruth think?"

"Most of the other teachers and I believed that Lisa-Ruth was innocent, but none of us had proof. And the principal smoothed things over by saying that no money was missing. Nothing more was done, and the school year ended. But suspicion can be insidious. Yesterday when Lisa-Ruth asked for a new mug, I briefly wondered if she might occasionally take things that didn't belong to her. However, I want to believe that Lisa-Ruth is honest. I do believe it." Cindy looked out at our happy customers in the shade of the pink umbrellas. "Besides, when the barbershop quartet was singing, Lisa-Ruth was recording their performance with her phone. What do you bet she slipped her phone and its little stand, not a mug, into her tote bag?"

"That's probably what she did." I hoped I sounded convinced. I was thinking that Lisa-Ruth might have had a legitimate grudge against Kirk for the way he'd cast suspicion on her. Would that, along with anger over Kirk's interruptions of her students' performances, have caused her to take drastic revenge?

Chapter 10

❧

Tom brought a tray to our table. "Try this and see if you think we should add it to our menu." He handed us each a spoon and a small glass bowl containing something that looked like a hot fudge sundae except that the topping was liquid and smelled like delicious coffee. "*Affogato*," he explained. "It's an Italian dessert—espresso poured over a scoop of vanilla ice cream."

He picked up the third bowl of *affogato* and a spoon and sat on the other side of Cindy from me.

The melting ice cream swirled slowly into the coffee. I slipped a spoonful of softened ice cream, hot espresso, and still-frozen ice cream into my mouth. Closing my eyes, I rolled the hot, sweet, cold, and heady combination on my tongue. I couldn't help a groan of pleasure.

I opened my eyes. Leaning forward, Tom peered around Cindy and grinned at me. "What do you think, Emily?"

"Where has this been all my life?"

Cindy said firmly, "Add it to your menu."

I tasted the ice cream by itself. "This is vanilla bean ice cream from Freeze, right?" Using machinery from the 1940s, recipes from the same era, and no artificial flavors, our local ice cream shop made the most delicious ice cream I'd ever tasted.

Tom's grin widened. "Only the best goes with our espresso."

Four girls trooped to the patio. Cindy tapped Tom's arm. "Here they are!" She turned to me. "The biggest one is fourteen and looks after the other three during the day, all summer. She and the smallest girl live next door to us. The other two live across the street."

The three youngest girls wore frilly pastel bathrobes. Although they scrunched their faces into exaggeratedly mean expressions, they couldn't help looking sweet. The tallest girl was in a patched brown bathrobe and knuckled her eyes as if crying. She held up a sign that said CINDERELLA.

With great enthusiasm, the three smaller girls stomped their feet and pointed at the sidewalk. Cinderella flopped down onto her hands and knees and pretended to scrub. The tiny evil stepmother and her tinier evil daughters turned their backs on the audience as if they'd gone somewhere. The evil stepmother placed a tiara on her own head, faced the audience again, and pulled a magic wand out of one floppy sleeve. Now obviously Cinderella's fairy godmother, she waved the wand, and Cinderella shrugged off the patched brown bathrobe to reveal a princess dress. She traded her sneakers for silvery sequined slippers. The fairy godmother placed the tiara she'd been wearing on Cinderella's head, and Cinderella skipped behind the other two girls, who still had their backs to the audience. Cinderella came back into view. Now she was wearing only one slipper. Turning away from the audience, the fairy godmother shoved the other slipper into a bathrobe pocket.

Cindy told us, "The girls wanted Cinderellas and her little sister's dachshund to play the part of Prince Charming, but their parents talked them out of it, so let's see what they devised."

The evil stepmother who had transformed herself into the fairy godmother turned to face us. Now she wore a crooked mustache that made us laugh and a golden paper crown. She was carrying Cinderella's lost slipper.

Even from the sides of Tom's and Cindy's faces, I recognized their expressions of longing. The untimely death of Alec, their only son, had eliminated the possibility of grandchildren, and they both loved children.

When Alec had first introduced his friend and partner Brent to them, they had opened their home and their hearts to Brent. He and I, and my parents when they were in town, already spent most family holidays with Tom and Cindy. If Brent and I were lucky enough to have children, Tom and Cindy would be another set of grandparents.

Out on the sidewalk, the two evil stepsisters unsuccessfully tried stuffing their feet into the silvery slipper that Prince Charming, still in a pastel frilly bathrobe, offered them. Sadly, the evil stepsisters shook their heads.

The slipper fit Cinderella. Prince Charming went down on one knee. Cinderella jumped up and down and clapped her hands, and then all four girls curtsied to the audience.

Naturally, we applauded. Cindy and Tom went outside to congratulate them on their performance, and I cleared our dishes.

Although I was smiling about Tom and Cindy's neighbors and their clever miming of Cinderella's story, I was again thinking about what Cindy had told me about Lisa-Ruth. Was it possible that she had taken that mug the day before and used it to kill Kirk?

I went out to the patio, stood beside Tom and Cindy, and watched two brothers play small violins.

The boys headed toward the Fireplug, and three little girls in shiny red, gold, and royal blue costumes tap-danced to recorded music. They made quite a clatter, and I couldn't be sure if anyone was tapping with the beat, but they were adorable and received enthusiastic applause.

A boy played an accordion that was almost as big as he was.

Another one stacked and restacked cups.

Finally, a girl in braids, cutoff jeans, and a yellow T-shirt caused everyone's eyes to mist over with her clear-voiced and, as far as I could tell, perfect rendition of "The Star-Spangled Banner." Cindy whispered to me, "She's eleven. I hope she sings tonight at the show. Lisa-Ruth will start counting the days until that little diva arrives at high school!"

Far from looking like a diva, the girl plucked at the side seams of her cutoffs in a nervous curtsy, and then, with her beaming father following, scampered north toward the Fire-plug.

It was nearly our closing time, and no more acts were scheduled for the day. Our clients headed off. Many planned to attend the show that evening.

Cindy offered to help us close, but Jocelyn firmly told her that Tom had spent a long day at work and deserved a home-cooked meal that night. Cindy laughed. "Guess who does the grilling at our house. But okay, I'll go marinate the chicken and make a salad." She kissed Tom and headed toward her car.

The rest of us cleaned and tidied. Tom unfastened the police tape so he could drive out of the parking lot. I refastened it. My phone rang.

Brent.

His tone was surprisingly formal. "A DCI agent would like to talk to you."

"I'm at Deputy Donut. Want to bring him here?" I was picturing Rex, my favorite of the DCI agents I'd met, the one Summer liked.

"We'll be right there."

I told Jocelyn and Olivia to go on without me, refastened the police tape after they left, and called my father. He, my

mother, and Lisa-Ruth were judging the Wee Wonders show
that night. I told my father, "Go ahead and eat. I discovered
Kirk MacLean's body this morning, a couple of blocks from
Deputy Donut, and his death looks suspicious. Brent and a
DCI agent are about to come talk to me."

My father's response was short. "Kirk MacLean. I'm not
sure I'm surprised." We disconnected.

To prevent Dep, who was batting toys all over the floor,
from running outside when Brent arrived, I put her into her
harness and attached her leash. Holding the leash, I looked
out through our glass back door.

Brent and another man—not, I was sorry to see, Rex—
strode north through the parking lot toward Deputy Donut.
They both wore gray suits and white shirts. The DCI agent
was a slighter build, more like Alec's size, but unlike Alec,
this man had slicked-down dark hair, dark eyes, and a thin
face with a pointy nose that reminded me of a bird of prey.
Although taller and more obviously muscular than the DCI
agent, Brent walked with his usual loose-limbed grace. The
DCI agent's shoulders and his gait were stiff. Needing to interview another detective's fiancée had to be nerve-racking.

The two men ducked underneath the police tape and came
up onto our back porch. I picked up Dep, let the men in, and
shut the door.

The DCI agent was Victor Throppen. "Call me Vic," he
said. The twitch of his thin lips barely registered as a smile.

Still clutching Dep, I smiled and shook his hand. His grip
was strong, but not overbearing. His skin was dry.

I felt clammy. And like I might fidget.

Vic studied me with those piercing, nearly black eyes.
"Brent tells me you were first on the scene. Can you tell me
about it?"

I gestured to the couch. "Sure. Have a seat." Still holding
Dep, I turned the desk chair to face the couch and the coffee

table and sat down. Brent led the way to the couch. The two men sat at opposite ends of it. Brent looked relaxed and comfortable. Vic sat up straight, a notebook in one hand and a pen in the other.

Without mentioning that I'd already given Brent a statement, I described the scene. I told Vic that the embroidered monogram on the handkerchief appeared to match the initials of the musician who had placed second on Monday night. I mentioned the knife from Frisky Pomegranate. "Kirk had annoyed Penny, the owner of Frisky Pomegranate, by driving customers away from her patio." I glanced at Brent and added, "Since I talked to you this morning, Brent, Penny told me that she and her assistant, Tiffany, usually park south of here instead of near Frisky Pomegranate, and they walk to work from there."

Vic demanded, "And that's important because?"

I was certain that Brent understood, but I explained to Vic, "Frisky Pomegranate closes around one in the morning. If they parked where she said they usually park, they could have been near that orange van in the early hours of this morning. Maybe they heard or saw something."

Vic wrote in his notebook. "I see. Anything else?"

"One of our mugs disappeared from the patio Tuesday afternoon, and Cindy Westhill, who is the mother of my late husband, and I had seen Lisa-Ruth Schomoset pull her hand out of her tote bag as if she'd just tucked something into the bag. At the time, Lisa-Ruth was yelling at Kirk MacLean for disrupting the singing of a quartet of her former students." I stated the obvious. "She was angry." I glanced at Brent. "And this afternoon, I learned more about Lisa-Ruth. Cindy can tell you the whole story."

Vic put down his pen. "We'll talk to her, but in the meantime, can you give us your version?"

I did, and then Vic asked if I minded showing him the

videos from our surveillance cameras. "You emailed copies to Brent, but I'd like to see them now, before we go out and look around some more."

It took a long time to scroll through the videos and slow the important parts.

Vic peered toward our back windows and door. "Who owns the garage on the far side of your parking lot?"

"Tom Westhill and I do. Tom's my father-in-law. The two of us own Deputy Donut."

Vic continued staring toward the back. "And do you have a camera mounted on that garage, Emily?"

"Unfortunately, no, but I guess it would make sense."

Brent's slow nod was accompanied by an empathetic smile. He turned to Vic. "I've collected videos from this side of the street, but I have not yet talked to the businesses across the street."

Vic said, "We can go there next."

Brent said, "And maybe pick up some dinner at the Fireplug. Emily tells me that one of the servers there had a grudge against the deceased."

I explained and told them what Ed had said since I last saw Brent. "He said that having his proposal turned down in public was the worst day of his life."

Despite Vic's presence, Brent reached across the coffee table and squeezed my left hand. "Poor guy," he said softly. He let go of my hand.

Vic wrote in his notebook and then looked at me. "One more thing, Emily. Was anyone with you early this morning, say from about two thirty until you found the body?"

I couldn't help blushing. "No. I mean, my parents are staying with me, but they were probably sleeping and wouldn't be able to say if I left home during the night."

"Do you know if either of them went out between the times I mentioned?"

"I don't know, but I think I would have heard them going down the stairs."

Vic pinned me with a glare. "Above the sounds of the storm?"

I succeeded in giving an almost calm answer. "Maybe not, but also, they wouldn't have gone out when lightning threatened."

Vic checked something in his notebook and returned his gaze to me. "You said they're 'staying with' you. Do they not live there?"

"They live in their RV in Florida during the winters. They bring the RV up here for the summer and park it in a site they've leased in the Fallingbrook Falls Campground since before I was born."

Vic asked Brent, "How far away is that?" From the tone of his voice, I had a feeling he knew the answer.

Brent might have thought so, too, but he answered, "About a half hour away by the quickest route."

Vic returned his attention to me. "If they're camping that close, why are they staying with you?"

"They often stay overnight at my place if something in town goes on late, and Fallingbrook is having a festival all week with talent shows every evening. My parents are judges for the musical and mostly musical competitions. Also, they're helping with Brent's and my wedding preparations." Becoming more defensive than I knew I should be, I added, "My parents and I enjoy one another's company. I sometimes stay with them at the campground, just for fun." Although I'd been holding the loop at the end of Dep's leash, she had crept underneath the coffee table to the couch and was curled, apparently asleep, on Brent's lap. I let go of the leash.

Vic put his notebook and pen into the inner chest pocket of his suit jacket and gave me another twitch of a smile. "I'm sure they're good people. Do you understand that I'm asking nearly everyone similar questions?"

"Yes. That's okay."

He stood. "Thank you for your help, Emily. We'll be back if we have more questions."

Brent gathered Dep's leash and handed it and her to me. "Were you about to leave when I called?"

"Yes, but I don't mind."

He gestured toward the door leading to the back porch. "You usually take Dep in and out through the back door, don't you?"

"Yes, but the cleaners will be here later. I can carry her through the dining room."

"I'll help you duck under the tape so you can take her down the driveway."

Vic lifted one shoulder slightly. I guessed he was agreeing.

We all went out. Brent untied the tape blocking the porch steps. Hugging Dep, I went down to the parking lot. Vic followed and then hurried past me. He lifted the tape that crossed the parking lot end of the alleyway so high that I barely needed to bend. I thanked him and set Dep down. We started toward Wisconsin Street.

Brent called, "Talk to you later, Em."

I turned around, smiled, and gave him a thumbs-up. Vic was striding south through the parking lots toward the crime scene.

At the sidewalk, I looked back. Brent was at the other end of the alley beside the police tape. We waved to each other, and then Dep and I turned south on Wisconsin Street.

Breezes had dried most of the day's earlier humidity, but the evening was warm. I didn't turn west into our neighborhood until we reached Maple Street, several blocks south of the spot where I'd found Kirk that dreary morning. Even though I might have caught another glimpse of Brent, I had no desire to go anywhere near that site.

Chapter 11

❧

At home, I found a note propped against a saltshaker on the kitchen island. My parents had left for the evening show. Potato salad and cold fried chicken were in the fridge. They'd added, "Frisky Pomegranate for dessert after tonight's show, if you can make it."

I ate and then changed from my work uniform into a sleeveless dress, navy sprinkled with tiny white flowers. I strapped on sandals and put my wallet and keys into a small white shoulder bag.

Downstairs, Dep was dozing on the couch. She opened one eye. "We might be home late," I told her. "Enjoy your nap." She closed the eye, and I started toward the square.

I'd barely turned the corner from Maple Street when a woman behind me called, "Emily!" Summer jogged to me. "Are you going to the Wee Wonders talent show?"

"Yes. I was hoping to find you there so we could sit together."

"Great!" She walked beside me, matching her long-legged strides to my shorter ones. "Rumors are going around that the bagpiper died and the police are investigating. That bagpiper! He must have really upset someone. I hope that won't keep Brent from tonight's show."

"I'm afraid it might."

"Fallingbrook's lucky to have him. He works too hard, but he likes what he does, right?"

"Definitely."

"Quentin would probably have enjoyed talking to him. Quentin will probably join us."

I suspected that when Quentin talked to Brent, neither man would enjoy the discussion, but I only said, "Nice!"

Summer sent me a skeptical glance. "Don't you like him? He's a good kid, really. Well, he's not a kid anymore, but he's a good guy."

"I like him fine. It's just that . . ." I didn't have Brent's permission to tell anyone about the handkerchief with Quentin's initials on it. "Everyone saw how angry he was when Kirk won first prize."

"Emily! You don't think Quentin would actually hurt anyone, do you?"

"I don't, but a DCI agent is here."

She looked down at me. Her eyes glowed. "Rex?"

"No. Someone named Vic, and he's not nearly as charming as Rex."

"How disappointing! But do you want to know why I'm sure Quentin wouldn't hurt anyone? His hands. He's a musician. He can get angry quickly, but he's careful not to injure his hands."

I wondered how she could be sure that in the heat of uncontrolled anger, a musician might forget to protect his hands. Brent had said there had been signs of a struggle, but that didn't necessarily mean that the killer's hands had been in danger.

Standing next to seats that we'd found four rows back from the bandstand, Summer and I spotted Quentin coming from the part of the park where the arts and crafts were displayed. Quentin was again carrying his cornet case and wearing black slacks and a white long-sleeved shirt.

Summer waved both arms above her head, and Quentin

turned toward us. When he was close enough to hear, Summer gestured toward the chairs. "We saved you a seat."

"Thanks! Hi, Emily, nice to see you again." He shifted his cornet case to his left hand and offered his right hand. His right sleeve rode up. Shaking his hand, I tried not to stare at the bandage just above his wrist.

He must have noticed. He let go of my hand and pulled his sleeve down until it again covered the bandage. "I was gathering firewood, reached underneath a tree, and didn't notice the jagged end of a broken branch sticking out. It wasn't much of a branch, but it gave me quite a scratch."

I couldn't help wondering what had become of Kirk's ceremonial dagger and whether Quentin's "scratch" had actually been made by either the dagger or the Frisky Pomegranate knife. I hid my thoughts by reciting a warning I'd learned during first-aid training. "Maybe you should let air get to it."

"The bandage is loose. That's why it catches on my sleeve. But yes, I'll leave it uncovered after I'm sure it won't bleed over my shirt. Or anything else. Did you hear what happened to that bagpiper?" His tone was casual and chatty, and I was sure that Brent and Vic hadn't questioned him. Or Summer, either.

She and I acknowledged having heard about Kirk. Luckily, we didn't have time to discuss it. The daycare toddlers wobbled up the shallow steps to the bandstand with the help of several adults. Summer, Quentin, and I sat down. The audience rustled to near silence.

The children again sang "I'm a Little Teapot." I couldn't hear all of the words, but I recognized the actions. One little boy tipped himself right onto the floorboards. The audience gasped. He struggled to his feet, took a bow, and then clasped his hands above his head in a gesture of victory. People laughed and clapped, and the boy clowned his way off the stage behind his fellow troupers.

Tom and Cindy's neighbor girls rushed through their Cinderella skit but were even more charming than they'd been earlier in the day.

The last performer was the eleven-year-old singer. She wore a plain, long white dress, and flowers were braided into her hair. Fearing that the large audience would make her nervous, I held my breath, but she again sang "The Star-Spangled Banner" perfectly and without accompaniment. All of the performers had received standing ovations. Hers went on for a few minutes after she left the bandstand.

At the end of the show, my mother smiled broadly and announced that every performer that evening was receiving a gold ribbon.

I invited Quentin and Summer to join my parents and me at Frisky Pomegranate for dessert. The three of us headed north through the crowd.

Clutching her gold ribbon and smiling shyly, the eleven-year-old who had sung the national anthem was listening to Lisa-Ruth. I couldn't hear what Lisa-Ruth was saying, but the girl's eyes shined.

Quentin joked, "That's what they should have done for us on Monday night—given us all gold ribbons. That girl deserved first prize if anyone ever did. She's more impressive than a middle-aged bagpiper." He took a deep breath. "Okay, I know we're not supposed to speak ill of the dead, so I'll just say that there was nothing wrong with his actual playing. I was only angry at myself for letting him distract me. And anyway, I know why I didn't come in first, and it has nothing to do with his or my playing." He grinned down at me. "I lost my good-luck handkerchief."

I looked away from him and kept walking without, to my surprise, toppling over or gasping. I didn't say a thing.

Summer, who couldn't have known about the possibly blood-spattered handkerchief I'd photographed near Kirk's body, asked with a laugh in her voice, "Your what?"

"My good-luck handkerchief. I carry it when I'm going to audition or perform. I must have lost it before I went onto the stage Monday evening."

Summer teased, "I didn't know that men, especially young men, carry handkerchiefs."

Quentin patted his chest. "We do if we can fold them neatly enough to let them peek fashionably out of the pocket of our suit jackets if the occasion demands it. But I wasn't wearing a jacket Monday evening, so I shoved it into my pants pocket. That handkerchief was special. My great-grandmother embroidered my initials on it when I was born, and she said it should always bring me good luck."

Summer pointed out, "You came in second, so maybe you did have it with you."

"I didn't. I noticed it was gone almost as soon as I left the bandstand."

I finally found my voice and asked a question that would probably sound more innocuous than it was. "When did you last see it, Quentin?"

"I remember putting it into my pocket on the way out of my bedroom in my parents' cabin that evening. After I left the Fireplug, I retraced my steps but didn't find it. However, that bagpiper had tucked one of his cards underneath my windshield wiper. I don't know when he did that, probably before the performance, not after. My car was northeast of the square." He pointed. "In that neighborhood over there. I don't think he had time to go all the way to my car and back between winning the competition and showing up at the Fireplug, and then when he left the Fireplug Monday evening, he turned south."

I contributed, "I think Kirk might have been staying in a van in a parking lot south of the Fireplug, a couple of blocks south of Deputy Donut."

Quentin spread his hands apart in a gesture of losing all hope of finding lost objects. "The most likely thing is that I dropped the handkerchief when I got out of my car. Maybe that bagpiper picked it up, and the good luck it brought him turned into the worst possible luck." Quentin let out an unmirthful laugh. "Not that I really believe the handkerchief was responsible for my success. Or his, or his death. I don't remember my great-grandmother, but she was supposedly very sure of her suspicions and predictions."

"She sounds like quite a character." Summer's voice was warm. "I'd have liked to have met her."

I agreed. "Me, too." I wasn't about to tell Quentin that I'd seen a similar—probably the same—handkerchief near Kirk's body, several blocks southwest of the square and one and a half days after Quentin thought he'd lost the handkerchief.

I couldn't help wondering if Quentin knew that he had accidentally left the handkerchief near Kirk after fighting with him. And if, after the fact, Quentin made up detailed stories about how and when he lost his handkerchief and how and where he got the "scratch" he was hiding underneath a bandage . . .

Chapter 12

❧

Summer, Quentin, and I snagged a table on the patio at Frisky Pomegranate. My parents joined us a few minutes later.

Penny took our orders and told me in a conspiratorial tone, "Customers told me what that police tape was all about this morning—a man was found dead in the parking lot near where Tiffany and I usually park."

The other four people at our table were talking together, and probably hadn't heard what Penny said, and they also probably didn't notice that I merely nodded my head.

Not that I would have had a chance to say much. Penny lowered her voice and informed me, "And I hear it was that bagpiper." She straightened and tapped her notebook. "Well, it's always sad when someone dies, and it's a shock, but at least that man is no longer disrupting the performances of other people and driving our customers away, right?"

"I don't think he drove Deputy Donut customers away."

"Well, maybe he didn't exactly drive mine away, either, but he annoyed them. It was hard for them to make themselves heard over all that screeching."

Quentin had apparently stopped listening to the other conversation and was watching us. Penny said to him, "You didn't drive anyone away or interrupt other acts. The piece you played on the bugle when you came to the patio was nice and short."

Quentin's smile was genuine, but I thought he was trying not to laugh. "Thank you."

I pictured Monday afternoon at work. "I'm sorry I missed your playing at Deputy Donut. I must have been in the kitchen."

My mother asked Quentin, "What did you play while you were touring around town?"

Quentin blushed. "It was only a short piece that I composed, something meant to be cheerful."

Penny smiled. "It was. Everyone liked it. And now"—she made a hand into a loose fist and held it in front of her mouth like she was blowing into a bugle or a cornet—"Ta da! I have an announcement!"

My mother folded her hands on the table and put on a brightly interested face. I realized I was making the same gestures.

Penny raised one palm like a game show host displaying a prize on a pedestal. "For some time, I've been thinking of retiring and going to live near my adult children, and yesterday I received an offer for Frisky Pomegranate." Waggling both hands above her shoulders, she did an impromptu dance. "I accepted it!"

My mother asked, "Where will you go?"

The steps of Penny's dance ended, and the corners of her mouth went down. "I can't decide. My kids are each trying to convince me to move near them. At my age, I should probably move closer to the doctor in Duluth. But the veterinarian in Milwaukee has kids. My youngest is a teacher. He doesn't want kids, but he's down near Madison, a city I really like. So, I have lots of choices!"

Summer asked, "Will the new owner continue this as a restaurant?"

"She's buying the business, so yes, I think she will, and it will still be Frisky Pomegranate." Penny pointed at the cutlery still wrapped in my napkin. "She adores the cutlery."

Quentin unfolded his napkin and studied the pomegranate on the handle of the spoon. "Did you have it specially made?"

I thought Penny was about to dance again, but she only snapped the fingers of one hand. "No. When I was planning the restaurant and trying to come up with a name for it, I found this cutlery at an auction. It was from a restaurant that went out of business in Chicago. I bought it all and came up with the name. Unfortunately, no more of it is available. As Emily can probably tell you, one of the problems with owning any sort of eatery is that things seem to walk away, and my knives, forks, and spoons have a habit of disappearing. Emily's dishes are cute, too, with that silhouette of a cat on them, so they probably go missing all the time, too, right, Emily?"

I shook my head. "Not all the time. It's not easy to hide a mug or a plate." I thought, *But it's not hard to tuck a mug into a large tote bag . . .*

Penny put her notebook and pen into her apron pocket. "I think Tiffany and I told you that we like to park down beyond your shop every day. Tiffany and I are neighbors, so she rides to and from work with me. We finish here around one every morning, and then we enjoy our brisk walk back to my car. But sometimes, whoever steals our cutlery just drops it. We've been lucky enough to find a couple of pieces, one in the square, and another behind a shop north of Deputy Donut."

I hadn't told Quentin about the handkerchief with his initials, and I wasn't about to mention the knife I'd seen at the murder scene, either. I'd leave that to the police.

I tried not to show my dismay. Both Quentin and Penny had come up with believable stories that could have explained how their belongings had landed in someone else's hands. Was either of them lying to cover for losing something near the body of the man they had attacked?

Luckily, Penny didn't seem to notice my attempts not to squirm. She left us and returned several minutes later with our sundaes. She placed mine—Frisky Pomegranate–made thick, rich hot fudge—in front of me. "Emily, don't worry that I often take up one of the parking spaces down near Deputy Donut."

I hadn't tasted the sundae. I put down my spoon. "It's no problem. Fallingbrook has lots of parking."

Penny seemed determined to explain. "I don't always park down there, like when bad weather is predicted. We were expecting rain early Wednesday morning around the time to go home, so on Tuesday I parked close to our pub." She pointed east, toward where Quentin had said he'd parked Monday evening. "Good thing I did. It was pouring when Tiffany and I left. It was later than usual, and I drove straight home and let Tiffany out at her front door. Well, I'll stop gabbing and let you folks eat your sundaes. Enjoy!"

As always, the sundaes were perfect.

Summer licked her lips. "I hope the new owner will make the sundaes the same way."

I spooned up the sweet creamy sauce from the bottom of my sundae dish. "You'll all have to stop in at Deputy Donut for Tom's *affogato*. He tried it out on Cindy and me after lunch." I described the treat.

My mother pretended shock. "You had ice cream for dessert for both lunch and dinner?"

I defended myself. "Obviously, I need to change. I'll have to start having ice cream for breakfast, too. It goes well with donuts."

After we finished, the five of us headed to the square together. It was dark already in the park, now lit by fixtures resembling old-fashioned gas lanterns.

Quentin asked Summer, "Do you need a ride?"

She thanked him. "I drove this morning."

He shifted his cornet case to his left hand and reached his right hand out to shake all of ours. The bandage peeked out again. "Then I'll say good night." He pulled his sleeve down and headed toward the bandstand.

My parents walked ahead.

When they were out of earshot, I asked Summer, "Do you know what kind of car Quentin drives?"

"Something used, probably. His parents come up here in an SUV with all-wheel drive most summers, and he usually drives something old but reliable."

"An SUV, too?"

"Probably not. Their driveway isn't as treacherous as ours. He usually drives something that doesn't guzzle gas and can get him from concert to concert." She was quiet for a second, and then she said in earnest but possibly annoyed tones, "I believe his story about scraping his arm. He is cautious about possibly harming his hands, but he works around his parents' place. When he was a little boy, he was in charge of gathering kindling, so it's not surprising that he would be collecting and cutting firewood."

Wondering if, before Kirk's murder, Quentin had told anyone about losing the handkerchief, I tried to hide my skepticism. "I like him."

"He's not perfect, but he's not a killer."

We walked together, not saying anything, and I wished we hadn't lagged so far behind my parents. Summer and I had always gotten along. I worried that by not quite concealing my concerns about her young neighbor, I might have strained our friendship.

From the bandstand behind us came the haunting notes of a cornet playing "Taps."

Chapter 13

Ahead of us, my parents stopped and turned around. My mother placed a hand over her heart and mouthed, "Wow!" My father put his arm around her shoulders and pulled her close to his side. They stared toward the bandstand.

Summer and I turned toward the bandstand, too, but trees and the fountain in the middle of the square hid it from us.

The last notes died away, and all we could hear was water splashing in the fountain and nighttime insects singing and chirping.

Wordlessly, Summer and I caught up with my parents.

"He's good, isn't he?" My mother spoke quietly.

My father, Summer, and I agreed. Summer added, "He sometimes plays 'Taps' at dusk at the lake. It gives me chills every time."

My mother tilted her head as if listening for echoes of the music. "If he'd simply played 'Taps' like that on Monday night, he would have won."

My father frowned. "Sorry, Summer, but I have to confess that Annie and I voted for Kirk instead of your talented friend."

Summer's laugh was almost as musical as the cornet we'd just heard. "Quentin's a professional. He knows he can't always come in first. He participated in the festival to support it and Fallingbrook. He's spent almost all of his summers at Deepwish Lake, and he loves this area. He might have been surprised that someone else won, but he wasn't angry at anyone except himself for his failure to ignore that bagpiper." Walking with us through the square, she told my parents about Quentin's having been an indulged but talented child. "He and I have a lot in common, mostly our love of Deepwish Lake."

By the time we said goodbye to Summer and headed into my neighborhood, I wondered if I had mentally exaggerated a constraint between Summer and me. I hoped I could mend the damage I might have done. I also hoped to find out, beyond a doubt, that Quentin was innocent of harming Kirk.

At my house, my parents and I paid homage to Dep until she decided she'd had enough, stalked to the kitchen, and crunched on kibble.

I offered my parents snacks and drinks.

My mother stretched. "I couldn't eat another thing!"

My father's eyes twinkled. "If I get hungry in the night, I know where the cookie jar is."

My mother gave his arm a love tap. "But you'll stay in bed so you won't disturb Emily. You must be tired, Emily. You get up so early, and you must not have gotten as much sleep as usual last night. Did you have something caught in your teeth that bothered you so much that you got up at three in the morning to brush your teeth?"

I'd been starting up the stairs, but I stopped with one foot on the bottom step. "I heard that, too. It wasn't me. I thought it was an electric toothbrush or shaver. Dad, were you shaving at three?"

He rubbed his chin. "Not me, and I wasn't brushing my teeth, either."

Playfully, I slapped my hands against my cheeks. "Someone broke in and brushed their teeth! And don't look at me like that, you two. Brent has a key, but he wasn't here."

My mother shrugged. "Maybe he should have been."

My father gazed toward the front window. "That buzzing must have come from outside. Did either of you hear bagpipes last night?"

We hadn't.

I asked, "Can bagpipes make a noise like that?"

My father answered, "They have those low-pitched whines underlying the tune, but this sounded different."

"But if they could imitate electric shavers," my mother suggested, "that Kirk guy would have known how to do it. Maybe he'd been told off for playing his pipes the night before, so he found a slightly quieter way to wake us up."

Climbing up another step, I laughed. "Maybe he had a battery-powered toothbrush or shaver, and he was wandering through the streets brushing his teeth and shaving." If he had been, he was still alive at three, which was about an hour after he'd run past Deputy Donut with someone apparently chasing him. Maybe he hadn't been killed when I'd guessed he was. Maybe he had run on past his van around two and had come down our street making buzzing noises. Maybe buzzing was the only "music" he could make with a bagpipe after it had been soaked in a storm.

The person I'd seen following him could have gotten into a Honda Civic and driven around until he or she found Kirk near his van.

My parents murmured to each other, and then my father called up the stairs, "We saw flashing lights, too, around the time we heard the buzzing. Could first responders have been heading to the murder scene around three, and the buzzing was something else, not a bagpipe?"

I leaned over the banister. "If it was first responders, they weren't attending the murder scene. I was the one who reported the death, and that was a little before six thirty. I didn't see flashing lights at three, but maybe they weren't visible from the back of the house, especially when my eyes might not have been open."

My mother started up the stairs behind me. "We weren't wide awake, either, so who knows what we heard and saw?"

Dep meowed at me from the top of the stairs. I told my folks, "Go ahead and use the bathroom. I have a call to make."

I went into my bedroom. My mother sang out, "Say hi to Brent!"

I closed Dep in with me and sat on the edge of the bed.

Brent's phone went straight to message. I suspected that he and Vic were busy. "Hi, Brent," I said into the phone. "You missed a fun show this evening, and we missed you." I took a deep breath. "This message might be long. I learned a couple of things this evening. Quentin Admiral has a bandage on his right wrist. He said he scratched himself while collecting firewood. Also, I didn't tell him about the handkerchief I saw with his initials, but out of the blue, he told us that early Monday evening, he'd lost his good-luck handkerchief. His great-grandmother embroidered his initials on it when he was born."

Dep climbed onto my lap. Stroking her comforting fur, I summarized the rest of the gossip I'd picked up. "After the show, we went to Frisky Pomegranate. I didn't say anything to Penny about having seen one of her knives at the crime scene, but she conveniently told us that people like to steal her cutlery. The timing of her mentioning it was interesting. And speaking of interesting timing, she said she'd made the decision yesterday to sell Frisky Pomegranate and move away. Also, she made a point of saying that on Tuesday, she didn't park where she usually does, south of Deputy Donut. Because of rain in the forecast, she parked closer to Frisky

Pomegranate. And my parents said hi, and I say I love you and good night." I disconnected and sat staring at my phone.

The Jolly Cops worked all night and slept during the day. Figuring that they were probably awake and getting ready to go clean their clients' premises, I phoned them.

As always, the one who answered knew who was calling. "Hi, Emily, what's up?"

"The parking lot behind Deputy Donut is part of a crime scene, so you'll need to come and go through our front door tonight. You have a key, don't you?"

"Yes."

"Also, the murder might have occurred while you were at Deputy Donut. The victim ran south through the lots, and I think someone chased him, but that person was running in a kind of crouched position on the far side of your trucks, so he or she doesn't show up clearly. I wanted to tell you that if any of you were outside shortly before two and saw anyone, call the police station, ask for Brent Fyne, and tell him what you saw."

"I heard about that bagpiper's death, but I don't personally know anything about it. I stayed inside your place the entire time, and I can vouch that the other three did, too. But I'll check in case anyone saw anything outside a window."

"It started pouring during that time."

"Did it ever! Even if we were in the habit of taking outdoor breaks, we wouldn't have done it then. Oh, by the way, before that storm, Tuesday night around midnight, we were cleaning a dental office north of Deputy Donut, and we heard a bagpipe in the distance, like that bagpiper was wandering playing the pipes then. After I heard about the death, I reported that the bagpiper, unless there was more than one of them, was alive around midnight."

"I heard bagpipes outside my house the night before. On

the video from early this morning, I saw you get into your trucks while it was still raining. Did you go straight home?"

"We work all night."

I knew that, but the conversation wasn't going the direction I'd hoped it would, so I needed to be less subtle. "Do you still go to Frisky Pomegranate after you leave Deputy Donut?" He was a retired cop, so I wasn't surprised that he didn't answer. I gave him only a second and then quickly added, "Penny told us she was selling it and moving away."

"She told us that, too." I heard him take a breath. "I'll answer the questions you didn't ask. She and Tiffany were both in their restaurant when we arrived. They often are. None of Penny's other staff were there. And Penny and Tiffany didn't appear to have been out in the rain before we arrived. They were dry. They left almost right away. That would have been about five after two. That's normal. They never stay long after we get there. Does that answer all of your questions, Emily?"

"I, um, did Penny say if the new owner would continue to use your services?"

"No." I could hear a laugh in the back of his voice.

"I hope they do."

"So do we. Listen, Emily, you're safe asking us questions, but don't go nosing around the wrong people. Stay out of trouble." Tom and his friends always said things like that.

"I will."

"You'd better! Talk to you later, Emily." He disconnected.

I set my phone down on my summer comforter and traced the forget-me-nots embroidered on the soft white cotton. Penny and Tiffany had worked late at Frisky Pomegranate and had not appeared wet when the Jolly Cops arrived. The Jolly Cops had left Deputy Donut only minutes after the crouching person had appeared to be chasing Kirk.

That meant that neither Penny nor Tiffany could have been Kirk's pursuer.

But had the person following Kirk actually killed him, or had someone else come along later?

Penny and Tiffany, for instance. They might have parked close to Frisky Pomegranate, but where had they gone after they got into Penny's car?

Chapter 14

✣

Walking Dep to work the next morning, I wished I knew what kind of car Penny drove. Frisky Pomegranate didn't open until lunchtime, so it was unlikely that she would have parked before six thirty in the morning, but I couldn't help hoping I might spot a vehicle decorated with pomegranates or something else that I could link to Penny.

In front of Deputy Donut, I realized I should have left Dep at home with my parents for the day. Tape still blocked off the parking lot. If I carried Dep or let her walk through the dining room, I would break health rules. It was too late to take her home, though, so I risked getting into trouble with the police, led her up the alley, and ducked underneath the tape. I could have temporarily untied the tape across our porch railing. Instead, I crouched and crept up the two steps to the porch. Dep's pupils widened, and she swished her tail back and forth. I stood, and Dep must have realized we weren't in the middle of a new game. She walked more or less sedately into the office and let me remove her leash and harness. I shut her into the office with food, water, and a litter tray, and headed into the dining area.

Jocelyn was already placing creamers and sugar bowls on our cute tables. "I turned on the fryers," she told me. "I left my bike at home and came in through the front. Are you going to admit to Brent that you traipsed through the crime scene?"

"He let me out that way last night, but yeah, I guess I should."

Tom must have found somewhere to park. He walked in through the front. Olivia arrived several minutes later, and the four of us eased into our comfy rhythm of frying and decorating donuts, starting coffee, and, beginning at seven, greeting customers.

Around nine, the Knitpickers came in and sat at their table across from the retired men's table. In addition to trading their usual jibes and jokes, they gossiped about the murder.

Other customers discussed the murder, too. Many people hadn't heard of Kirk until he won the Musical Monday competition. Some had been awakened by his bagpipe at strange hours of the night, while others had been disgusted when he interrupted the Troubadour Tuesday touring performances. A few people had not heard of him until his death.

After lunch, Austin, the man who'd been afraid his job interview on Tuesday hadn't gone well, came in. This time, instead of a rumpled, mud-colored suit, he wore jeans and a dark blue sweatshirt. He looked happier. He wanted to try our special coffee of the day, a crisp yet fruity single-origin coffee from El Salvador. He also asked for a fudge donut frosted with fudge and topped with chunks of peanut brittle.

I set his mug and plate in front of him. "How are you doing, Austin?"

"I didn't get the job." He shoved a piece of peanut brittle into his mouth.

"I'm sorry to hear that. Do you have other prospects?"

"In a way." He gave me a smile. "And this peanut brittle is cheering me up. Did you folks make it yourselves?"

"Yes." I loved how it had turned out, translucent like amber and studded with peanuts and sparkling bubbles. I asked him, "What do you mean, 'in a way'?"

He added cream to his coffee. "I decided to broaden my search. That night, I just drove around and around, trying to come up with ideas, and I realized something about myself. I like driving. I commuted a half hour each way to and from my last job, but I wouldn't mind commuting an hour or maybe even more each way. I'm going to look farther away for jobs."

I barely heard the last part of what he said. I'd started holding my breath after he said he'd driven around and around that night, which also happened to be the night—actually in the early morning—that Kirk was killed. I exhaled as non-dramatically as possible. "Did the espressos you drank here on Tuesday keep you awake?"

He took a sip of his less-fierce coffee and gave me a rueful grin. "I should have heeded your warning. I didn't fall asleep until it was almost light. Which meant I didn't start my job search very early on Wednesday. But that's okay. I needed time to get my head on straight. So, the espressos really helped. And the driving around."

That gave me an opening for the question I wanted to ask. "Where did you go?"

"Just around town. Back and forth. It's quiet and peaceful at night."

"No bagpipes?"

"Once, early on, maybe around midnight, I thought I heard some, so I closed my windows and turned in the opposite direction. I didn't hear them again, and I wasn't even sure I'd heard them the first time."

"The thunderstorm that morning was anything but quiet and peaceful. It woke me up. Did you get home before it started?"

"No. The rain was so heavy that I couldn't see, even though I kept driving slower and slower. I pulled over and just felt safe in my car, like it was a cocoon. I watched the rain pour down over my windshield, watched what I could of the lightning show, and felt the car shake with each clap of thunder. It was kind of surreal. I've always liked storms. They're exciting."

"I agree, as long as I'm in a safe place. Where did you stop?" My question was too pointed, so I added, "Were you able to get far enough off the road so that no one else could come along and hit you?"

"I was south of town, and there was no other traffic that I could see. Later, after the rain let up, I passed a pickup truck going even slower than I was."

"Around here?" Now he would know for certain that I was trying to get information out of him.

"I don't remember."

Of course he didn't.

I finally had to give up. I wanted to ask direct questions, but I had promised Tom, Brent, and the Jolly Cop that I wouldn't place myself in danger, not that I wanted to. I let Austin finish his donut and coffee.

After he got up and waved goodbye to me, I cleared his table. He'd left me a larger tip than an unemployed person should have. I sighed. The next time he came in, I would try to give him the biggest donut or the one with the most peanut brittle on top.

I glanced outside in time to see him pull out of a parking spot across the street.

He was driving a small, dark burgundy car.

It could have been the car that crept past the back of Deputy Donut about fifteen minutes after Kirk had dashed past, looked over his shoulder, and started running faster.

Austin had denied driving near Deputy Donut around the time of the storm, but he'd seemed evasive. He had to know by now that Kirk had died and had possibly been murdered, that police investigators had taped off parking lots behind the stores on our side of the street, and that the main investigation was two blocks south of Deputy Donut. He hadn't brought any of that up, and he'd claimed he hadn't been driving near our shop.

Maybe I was too ready to suspect everyone.

I liked Penny and Quentin. I didn't want either of them to be arrested for a murder they didn't commit, but objects belonging to each of them had been near Kirk's body.

Carrying dishes into the kitchen, I muttered to myself, "But so was a piece of a mug belonging to us."

Olivia and Jocelyn were joking with the retired men and the Knitpickers near the front windows, so they couldn't have heard me. Tom was frying donuts. I didn't think he could have heard my voice over the sizzling dough, but he lifted his head. "What did you say, Emily?"

"Just talking to myself."

Tom stared wordlessly at me.

I kept going, into the storage room. I loaded and started the dishwasher.

My delay didn't distract Tom. I emerged, and he asked me, "Who was the customer who ordered the double fudge peanut brittle donut? Wasn't he wearing a suit the last time he was here?"

"Yes. He'd come from a job interview last time. He didn't get the job. I was commiserating with him. And don't worry, the last time he came in, I did tell him that we were fully staffed."

"I wasn't worried," Tom said. "Not about that."

I understood the hint. Tom was again warning me not to ask dangerous questions. I grinned at him. "I'll call Brent. He'd probably like to hear my description of the car the man drives."

Chapter 15

I left Brent a quick message and apologized for not knowing the make and model of Austin's car.

The organizers of the Fallingbrook Arts Festival were calling the day Theatrical Thursday. Cindy again came to Deputy Donut to enjoy the afternoon's performances. This time, she found a place at a table outside, and I sent Tom out to join her while I looked after the frying.

A half hour later, Cindy rushed inside and told me, "Emily, my neighbor kids are on their way with today's skit." She hurried outside again.

All of our current customers were on the patio. I lifted the last basket of donuts from the oil and hooked it on the side of the fryer. Wiping my hands on my apron, I joined the others on the patio.

The four girls, now wearing witch costumes varying from almost scary to just plain cute, set a cardboard carton on the sidewalk. On the three sides of the carton that I could see, they'd painted a cauldron on a blazing fire. Each of the cauldrons and the fires were different. Three of the girls thrust large wooden spoons into the box and made stirring motions. The tallest girl stood to one side and recited, "Double, double, toilet . . ." Clapping her hand over her mouth, she bent over and giggled. The three smaller girls waved their spoons in the air, stomped their feet, and hooted and shrieked before also subsiding into giggles. The tall witch finally got control of her thespian talents. Red-faced, she corrected herself in a loud and dramatic voice. "Double, double, toil and trouble!" She finished the rest of the monologue faultlessly, as far as I could tell. The diners on our patio stood and applauded, and the four girls dragged their carton toward the Fireplug.

I told Tom to watch the rest of the show with Cindy and to come inside only if masses of customers suddenly arrived. I expected to see all of the acts that night at the bandstand.

Mixing yeast dough for the next day, I glanced out at the sidewalk in front of our patio from time to time. Most of the rest of the traveling Theatrical Thursday performers seemed to be adults delivering monologues. A group of six teens juggled with energetic frenzy. Their mouths were moving, but I couldn't hear what they were saying. The audience on our patio clapped and cheered. Next, a man hauled a rolling cart to the sidewalk and opened the doors of an intricate stage. Hiding behind the built-up front and sides of the stage, he worked two marionettes.

Tom came inside after the final performance of the afternoon. "You'll enjoy tonight's show, Emily." We put the dough I'd made into the proofing cabinet.

We closed, tidied, and cleaned, and then I took Dep home. My parents weren't judging that evening. We ate together on my patio and then left Dep behind and strolled to the square through streets still warmed by evening sunshine. We arrived early enough to tour the arts and crafts displays. My father talked to friends while my mother and I admired handmade jewelry, handwoven linens, pottery, wood carvings, and all sorts of sewn, knitted, and crocheted clothing. My father joined us, and the three of us strolled among paintings and photos on easels. I was still looking for the perfect artwork for my guest room but didn't find anything that was exactly right. My parents' RV had no room for anything else to hang on walls, but we all appreciated the artists' talent.

We left the display tents and easels in time to find seats with a good view of the bandstand. I sent a text to Brent telling him where we were. He responded, thanking me for my message about Austin's car and adding that he wished he could join us.

While I waited for the show to begin, I looked around for Summer and Quentin. I didn't see either of them or hear Summer's laugh. Samantha joined us with her adoring husband, Hooligan. Samantha was an emergency medical technician. She wore a dark red dress that matched streaks she'd added to her brown curls, while Hooligan was more boyish than ever in jeans and T-shirt. I asked him, "How's the investigation going?"

He ran fingers through his hair, causing some of the wavy ends to stick out. "No good leads yet, as far as I know. We've been helping Brent and the DCI detective review videos from security cameras in the area, but so far, nothing has shown up besides the people and vehicles that cameras on the front and back of Deputy Donut picked up. Brent said that you were the eagle-eyed person who caught most of that."

"He was hoping cameras at the bookstore might have been aimed at Kirk's van."

"They have only one camera. Its video shows the passenger side of the van but only the back half of it. Kirk ran along the side, looked over his shoulder, dashed around the van's rear, and disappeared. His attacker must have come at him from the van's driver side. He or she never shows up in the video."

I guessed, "Could the killer have fled by climbing a fence and running through the yard of one of the houses behind the parking lots?"

"Possibly, or he went back the way he came, but not past the front or rear cameras on Deputy Donut, and not past a camera across the street from Deputy Donut. We're not sure how he left the scene."

"Did the camera on the bookstore capture an image of the dark Honda Civic that crept north past the back of Deputy Donut, and then might have gone south on Wisconsin Street?"

"That car didn't pass the back of the bookstore. However, a video from the east side of Wisconsin Street, almost directly across from Deputy Donut, shows that the car that quickly passed the pickup truck was a dark Honda Civic. Apparently, once the driver got onto Wisconsin Street, he felt he needed to overtake the truck, although the truck was going relatively fast, considering how hard it was raining."

I asked, "Could you make out the driver's face?"

"It isn't visible. I'm guessing the hands are a man's, but I can't be sure."

"Could you tell who was driving the pickup truck?"

"No, but again from the hands, we're guessing it was a man. We didn't get a license number for it, either."

"Could it have been one of the Jolly Cops?" Maybe one of them had left Frisky Pomegranate early.

"Could have been."

A stiff-shouldered man in a dark suit that looked too hot for the evening went into the bandstand. The audience around us quieted, and Hooligan and I stopped talking. The man in the bandstand spoke more loudly than necessary into the microphone. "I'm Mr. Wordsworth, Fallingbrook High's English teacher, and yes, Wordsworth is my real name. Maybe that's why I chose my profession." His smile wasn't terribly genuine. He'd probably made the joke—if it was one—so many times that it bored him. He introduced the first act and then stayed in the bandshell, standing beside a railing instead of watching the show with his colleagues at the judges' table.

I was sure that the man reciting Hamlet's "Alas, poor

Yorick" soliloquy did it well, but I was not in the mood to watch anyone talk to a realistic skull.

He was followed by a Lady Macbeth with "bloody" hands. I could have done without that one, too, though her gold and silver brocade gown, trimmed in lace, was amazing.

And then it was time for the three young witches with their cauldron and their tall witch narrator. This time the tall witch enunciated "toil and trouble" perfectly. All of the performers had been receiving standing ovations, but I was sure that the applause for the four girls was louder and more prolonged.

Members of Fallingbrook's amateur theater group enacted a snippet from the play they were rehearsing. The opening was still a month away, and I suspected that this hilarious preview was going to sell tickets.

Last, the six teens I'd watched from inside Deputy Donut lined up across the bandstand. The boy on the left juggled three small balls while delivering his lines, then tossed the balls to the girl beside him, who faultlessly carried on the story and the juggling. The six of them passed the balls and the conversation to one another while moving around the stage and acting out a tale of teenage love triangles that eventually resolved into three happy couples. They ran off the stage to enthusiastic applause.

The judges had a tough decision. In the end, they gave the amateur theater actors third prize, Lady Macbeth second prize, the teen jugglers first prize, and then they awarded an unexpected prize, "audience favorite," to the girls in the witch costumes. Those little witches quickly went from sad eyes to happy smiles.

Like the rest of the audience, we stood and gathered our belongings. My parents and I looked at each other. "The Fireplug," I suggested, "since we went to Frisky Pomegranate after last night's performance?"

"It's on our way," my father said, "and we might need sustenance to walk the rest of the distance."

My mother batted at his elbow. "Speak for yourself." She turned to Hooligan and Samantha. "Can you two join us?"

Hooligan and Samantha traded one of the looks that always nearly melted everyone else around them. "Sure!" Samantha said.

The five of us joined the people ambling through the square's shady pathways.

Across the street from the south end of the square, Misty's husband, Scott, was in front of the fire station with some of his firefighters, washing fire trucks. We waved and continued.

Again, the Fireplug's patio was crowded. Harold and one of his servers were handing around mugs of beer. Instead of their usual polo shirts embroidered with a fire hydrant, they wore white long-sleeved dress shirts, mostly untucked over their black jeans.

Ed greeted us inside and pointed to a booth along the far wall. We squeezed into it, and he took our orders. My parents and I ordered beer. Samantha and Hooligan asked for tonic water. My first-responder friends often avoided alcohol before a shift or whenever they thought they might be needed later. I again texted Brent to tell him where we were, and he again said he wished he could join us, but he expected to be working long into the night.

Harold brought us our drinks. My father pointed behind me to the wall near the door. "Harold, you have a bare spot down there. You should go to the north end of the square for new artwork."

Harold boomed out his laugh. "I should. I have quite a few bare spots, and not only on top of my head. My staff complained that my fire-related artwork depresses them, so I'm going to hang more upbeat pieces. I'll check out the square when I get a break. If I don't make it while the festival's going on, I can always go down to The Craft Croft." He gave us a big bowl of freshly roasted and salted nuts and then went off to welcome other people.

After we finished, my father and Hooligan went to the cash register, where they would probably argue over who would pay. My mother, Samantha, and I headed to the ladies' room.

I was the last of the three of us to come out of a stall. My mother had already gone back into the pub, and Samantha was drying her hands at a hot-air dryer that was smaller than the previous one. Around its edges, the wall was a darker yellow except where paler yellow paint had dripped down behind the older dryer. Waiting for my turn, I glanced at the wastebasket. The dryer must have been brand new. An instruction book peeking out of the trash seemed to be in several languages, none of which I could read. Installing the dryer must have been more complicated than I'd have guessed. I could see part of a diagram labeled with letters that must have corresponded with the text.

Samantha stepped away from the dryer. "See you outside, Emily!"

I placed my hands in the stream of warm air. "Okay. Are you working tonight?"

"I hope not!" She left the ladies' room.

I checked the mirror and fluffed my curls. Walking toward the front door through the pub, I noticed that the bare spot on the wall that my father had mentioned was where I'd seen the map of the Great Chicago Fire of 1871. I wasn't sure that the map had been more depressing than some of the other maps and pictures still hanging on the walls.

Outside, my parents and I walked with Samantha and Hooligan to their car. Hooligan gently ushered Samantha into the passenger seat. My parents and I said goodbye to them and then continued south until we turned onto Maple Street.

As always, Maple was a delight of tall trees, blooming hedges, and flower borders. The layouts of the front yards might not have changed much since Victorian days. After several blocks of breathing in scents of alyssum, bee balm, and late-blooming roses, we climbed up to my porch. Dep was waiting for us inside on the living room windowsill. Waving through the window at her, I glanced down at my glass-topped wicker table. I had arranged the zinnias and daisies, picked from my own garden, in one of my vases and had centered it on the table.

But there was something else on that table, almost hidden by the vase of flowers.

A Deputy Donut mug.

It was not just any Deputy Donut mug. A large piece was missing from near its rim, the piece where the letters EPU should have been.

Chapter 16

❧

I pointed at the chipped mug. "Where did that come from?" My voice was too shrill. I tried to tone it down. "Did someone bring it while we were out?"

My mother spoke in calm tones, undoubtedly to prevent me from panicking. "I put it there." She reached toward it.

I became even more panicked. "Don't touch it!" I unlocked the front door and hustled my parents into the living room, where a welcoming light was burning and a demanding cat purred around our ankles. I closed the door and, out of habit, locked it. "I . . . I believe the police are looking for that mug. I'll call Brent."

I slid my backpack off my shoulders, let it fall to the gleaming pine floor, and took out my phone.

Brent answered right away. "Hi, Em. Sorry I couldn't join you this evening."

"It's okay. My mother found a Deputy Donut mug—"

My mother interrupted and said loudly enough for Brent to hear, "Actually, Walt found it."

I corrected myself. "My father found the mug. A large chip is missing. The letters that would be on the broken-off piece are EPU."

"Where are you?"

"At home."

"Are both of your parents there, too?"

"Yes."

"I'll be right there to talk to all of you. Okay?"

"Sure. See you soon." We disconnected, and I told my parents, probably unnecessarily, "He's on his way. He wants to talk to all of us."

I took my backpack up to my bedroom. When I came downstairs, my parents were in the kitchen. My mother was heating water for tea, and my father was taking some of my homemade sugar cookies out of the cookie jar and putting them on a plate. I explained why I thought the mug might be important in the investigation.

The doorbell rang.

I picked up Dep and answered. I wasn't surprised that Brent had brought the DCI agent, but I was disappointed. I preferred Brent's warmth and understanding to Vic's chilly implied suspicion. I stepped out onto the porch with the two men and pointed at the broken mug behind the vase of flowers. "There it is."

Although my porch light was on, both Brent and Vic shined their phones' lights on the mug, and I noticed something I hadn't seen before—black marks on the handle. I made a tentative guess. "It looks like someone already fingerprinted it."

Vic retorted, "That's something that was rubbed onto the surface, not brushed-on powder." He put on gloves, slipped the mug into an evidence bag, and sealed it. "I'll put this in the cruiser, then I'll come talk to you and your folks, Emily."

Still cuddling Dep, I led Brent inside and left the door ajar for Vic.

In the living room, my parents stood together with my father's arm around my mother's shoulders. They had placed a teapot, a tray of mugs, and the plate of cookies on the coffee table.

Vic ran up onto the porch and came inside. I made the introductions. Vic and my parents quickly reached first-name basis. My mother poured us each a mug of tea. "It's chamomile. It won't keep anyone awake."

My father passed the cookies. "Emily made them."

My parents and I sat on the couch, Vic sat in the matching red velvet armchair, and Brent took the dark blue wing chair where he often sat. Dep slithered out of my arms, padded across my mother's lap, and settled on one of my father's thighs.

Brent and Vic took out notebooks. Vic asked, politely enough, "Who found that mug?"

My father raised one hand from Dep's back. "I did, last evening around six thirty. Annie and I were leaving for the show in the square. We'd already gone outside and locked Emily's front door. I went to our car for a sweater for Annie, and there was the mug, upright, between our car and Emily's garage. I hadn't noticed it before. Our car hid it until I got close. I poured about an inch of water out of the mug onto the grass and then brought the emptied mug up onto the porch. Sorry for putting fingerprints on it. We had no idea that we shouldn't."

My mother echoed my father's apology and added, "Walt showed me the mug. We guessed that Emily had been using it to water plants, or something, and had forgotten it in the driveway."

Brent's eyes held their usual affection. "Had you, Emily?"

I lifted both hands off my knees and turned them palms upward. "No. I've never brought broken dishes home from work."

My father contributed, "I'm sure that mug wasn't there when we parked the car in the driveway on Sunday. We would have noticed it."

Vic repeated, "Sunday? Didn't you move your car between Sunday and last evening?"

My father stroked Dep. "We've walked everywhere."

Vic prodded, "Are you sure?"

My mother answered. "Yes." She seldom spoke in such clipped tones.

Vic turned to my father. "What made you pick up the mug?"

My father stretched his legs and bumped the coffee table. The teapot jiggled. My mother leaped out of her seat, but the teapot settled without tipping over. She sat down. My father patted her arm. "I didn't think a mug belonged on the driveway or that Emily had meant to leave it there. Annie put it on the table on the porch. Then we walked to the village square, and I didn't give it another thought until Emily spotted it."

Both Brent and Vic were taking notes.

My mother smoothed her long skirt over her lap. "Our fingerprints will be on that mug." Maybe I was the only one besides my father who recognized from her voice and her unusual twitchiness that she was trying to hide her nervousness.

Brent asked my parents, "Do we have your fingerprints on file anywhere?"

My parents looked at each other and shook their heads. "No."

Brent smiled at them. "If we decide that mug is part of our investigation, and maybe it's not, we'll fingerprint you."

My parents said in unison, "Okay." Tension radiated from them.

Vic looked up at them for a moment from underneath his dark and heavy eyebrows, and then he again studied his notebook. He paged back through it. "Walt and Annie, did you at any time leave the patio of Deputy Donut to chase after the man playing the bagpipes and make him stop?"

My father set down his mug of tea. "We did, on Tuesday afternoon. I wouldn't say we were chasing after him, but we went in the direction he'd gone. We gently reminded him that the performers were supposed to follow a schedule and that his day to serenade various businesses had been the day before, Monday. I don't think we changed his behavior at all."

My mother cradled her mug between her hands as if trying to calm herself with its warmth. "We'd already heard bagpipes around three that morning. Three in the morning!"

Vince asked, "To clarify, you heard bagpipes around three in the morning on Tuesday?"

My mother lifted the mug higher, as if to let the tea's fragrant steam caress her face. "Yes, Monday night, sort of, except it was already Tuesday, if you can follow my reasoning."

Vic gave her a brief smile. "Got it. Did the bagpipes at three on Tuesday morning wake you up?"

My parents and I all said that they had.

Vic posed his pen over his notebook. "Did that make you angry?"

My mother set her mug on the coffee table. I could tell that she was regaining some of her usual composure and confidence. "I was more amused than anything. You too, Walt?"

My father pulled his feet closer to the couch. "I thought it was funny. Odd, but funny."

Vic and Brent both looked at me. "Emily?" Vic asked.

"I mostly thought it was peculiar, but it didn't make me angry. I was able to go back to sleep. The sound of bagpipes did keep one man awake that night, and he was still angry about it the next day. I told you about him, Brent. Austin Berwin. He said twice that Kirk needed 'to be stopped.' "

Vic stated, "We've talked to Mr. Berwin."

Aha, I thought, *I told Austin that my parents and Cindy had gone to try to end Kirk's playing his bagpipes during other performances. Maybe Austin reported that my folks and Cindy left the Deputy Donut patio to "chase after" Kirk. Had Austin claimed that they had done it angrily and forcefully?*

Vic stood and tucked a notebook into his pocket. "We'll have a look around your yard and driveway, and I'm afraid we'll have to tape some of it off until investigators go over it in daylight. In the meantime, will any of you be needing the car that's in the driveway or access to the garage?"

My father answered, "Annie and I won't need our car. How about you, Emily?"

"I won't, but if I need to go into the garage for any other reason, is it okay if I go in through the rear door?"

Brent nodded. "Sure. And if you need a car in an emergency, undo the tape and put it up again."

Vic didn't look thrilled about the suggestion, but my parents and I agreed to it.

Vic and Brent went out and shined flashlights around my front yard and driveway.

I wasn't happy about the way the conversation had gone. When I'd told Austin that my parents and mother-in-law were going to stop Kirk, I should have been more specific and said that they were going to politely remind him not to disrupt others' performances.

Was Austin innocently trying to help the investigation?

Or was he a murderer trying to divert suspicion from himself to my parents and Cindy?

Chapter 17

✣

I woke up the next morning with an uneasy sense that something was wrong and about to become worse.

Then I remembered.

Vic could possibly suspect my parents, and maybe Cindy, also, of murder. And Brent was a detective, too. He couldn't eliminate suspects simply because he liked them. Or was engaged to one, for that matter.

I sat up, put my feet on the floor, and shoved my curls away from my eyes. Dep stepped across the comforter onto my lap and looked up into my face. The end of her tongue was sticking out. "It's okay," I murmured. "I must have let my mind exaggerate my worries while I slept."

But had I?

The mug my father found in my driveway must have been the mug that had disappeared from the murder scene. My parents' fingerprints could be the only ones on the mug. When I'd talked to Vic earlier, I hadn't been able to say for certain that my parents had been inside my house the entire night that Kirk was murdered.

However, it would not have made sense for one or both of my parents to go out in the middle of the night for any reason, much less to clobber Kirk with a Deputy Donut mug and then bring the mug back to my place and leave it sitting in the driveway where anyone could have seen it before my father "noticed" it.

Maybe the murderer knew where I lived. It was easy to find out. My name and address were in the Fallingbrook community directory. Maybe the murderer had brought the mug to my place to frame me.

How could the person who set the mug in my driveway have known that I wouldn't simply throw it out? Were they planning to send an anonymous hint to the police to search my property, including my trash?

Possibly, the killer tossed the mug somewhere, and someone who knew where I lived thought I would want it back even though it was broken. And they brought it to my house instead of to our shop because they'd found the mug close to my house.

I would probably never know. Besides, the mug in my driveway might have had nothing to do with the piece of pottery I'd seen near Kirk's body.

I showered and tiptoed downstairs. While I fed Dep and made my own breakfast, I closed my mind to the idea of my parents possibly being suspected of murder. Instead, I thought about my friends and how much I'd enjoyed being around Samantha and Hooligan. I loved the way Samantha glowed around Hooligan and the way he treated her like a precious and fragile flower when she was really a tough emergency medical technician.

Then I remembered that Samantha hadn't ordered a beer the night before. I had asked her if she expected to work later, and she'd said that she hoped not. If there was any doubt, I shouldn't have been surprised that she didn't drink while we were at the Fireplug. But then she had almost run out of the ladies' room as if she didn't want to answer more questions, as if she had a secret that she didn't want to divulge. . . .

She'd been more radiant than usual.

My thoughts warmed me and made me smile. Could Samantha and Hooligan be expecting a baby?

Happily imagining myself as a sort of aunt, I put bacon and eggs on a plate and took it out to the patio. Dep came with me and batted at beetles in the dewy grass. When I scraped up the last bite, the sun was beginning to peek over my yard's eastern wall. I took Dep and my plate inside, locked the back door, and tidied the kitchen.

As far as I could tell, my parents weren't up. I leashed Dep and took her outside.

Walking along with my dawdling cat, I wanted to call Samantha and ask if she was pregnant, but I knew that she and Hooligan would tell us when they were ready. Still, I couldn't help humming a joyful lullaby, or what might have passed for one if my humming hadn't been terrible. I again avoided the site where Kirk had died and stayed on Maple all the way to Wisconsin Street.

Tom had the day off, and I arrived at Deputy Donut before Olivia and Jocelyn did. In the office, I let Dep loose to play on her catwalks and in her tunnels or snooze on the couch. I went into the kitchen and turned on the fryers.

Olivia and Jocelyn came in, and the three of us began filling our display cabinet with colorful and appetizing fresh donuts. Shortly before our seven o'clock opening, we started the day's first pots of coffee.

Halfway through the morning, Penny opened the door slowly, as if she wasn't sure she wanted to come inside. I was surprised to see her without Tiffany. They occasionally came in for coffee before they started the day's preparations at Frisky Pomegranate. I waved from the kitchen. Beckoning in what seemed an urgent way, Penny took a seat.

Olivia was spreading fudge frosting on an assortment of different flavors of donuts. I asked her, "Can you take over the fryers for a few minutes, Olivia? Penny from Frisky Pomegranate seems to want to talk to me, and I suspect she's in a hurry to open her own restaurant for the day."

"Sure. I've scraped all of the fudge out of this bowl."

I thanked her. Perching on the edge of her chair, Penny gripped the sides of the glass-topped table with both hands. I asked her, "What can I get you? You serve delicious chocolate delicacies, so would you like to try our double fudge donuts? Or triple fudge. We cover the fudge topping with mini chocolate chips."

"Two kinds of fudge sound chocolatey enough for me, so I'll pass on the chocolate chips. What's your special coffee today?"

"A mild coffee from Tanzania that has a natural sweetness to it." I winked. "It goes well with fudge."

"I'd love to try it."

I went back to the kitchen, poured her coffee, and plated her donut.

I took them to her. She pulled the mug closer. "Do you have a minute, Emily?"

I looked around. Jocelyn was teasing the Knitpickers and retired men, and no one was demanding, or even asking politely, for service. "Sure, unless crowds descend on us." I pulled out the other chair at her table and sat down.

Staring at her mug, Penny turned it so that the logo was no longer facing her. "Emily, you have a reputation."

I couldn't help making a face of pretend shock. "I do?"

She glanced up at me, her eyes wary. They were gray, flecked with gold. "Not a bad one. Your reputation is for being sweet and helpful." She waved her hand as if taking in the entire shop with its peach-tinted white walls and the artworks hanging on them. "And for having a wonderful place where people feel welcome and cozy. Frisky Pomegranate never quite achieved that." She gave a self-conscious laugh. "Maybe because I'm not welcoming and cozy."

"But you are." Feeling like she had strayed from her original purpose, I waited quietly for her to say more.

She looked pointedly at my left hand, resting on the table. Without meaning to, I'd gotten into an unconscious habit of placing my sapphire ring where I could see it. Penny asked me, "You're engaged, right?"

I couldn't help a big smile. "Yes."

"To that tall detective?"

"Brent Fyne, yes."

She thinned her lips and glanced at me in a sort of sidewise way. "Are you happy?"

"Very."

Her answering smile seemed wan. "That's wonderful." I wasn't sure she meant it, but I continued smiling. I was afraid that she was leading toward asking for a favor that I could never grant, like telling Brent he shouldn't investigate her. Even if I were willing to do such a thing, Brent wouldn't listen.

Penny broke off a chunk of donut and tasted it. "Delicious. In addition to having a reputation of creating all of this wonderful food and atmosphere, you've figured out who committed murders before, haven't you?"

I put both hands in my lap. "Not really. I might have helped, but I don't deserve any credit."

Her smile seemed more genuine. "That's not how I heard it."

I merely shook my head.

"Here's the thing." She leaned closer and spoke more softly. *Uh-oh*, I thought, clenching my hands together. And sure enough, Penny started telling me about the police and their questions. "I've never hurt anyone. Those detectives—your fiancé and that weasel-faced guy—asked me if that bagpiper upset me or my patrons, and to be honest, no, they didn't." She gave me another sidewise, assessing glance. "Not much, anyway. The annoyance, if any, was slight and didn't last. I might have told some people, you know, for the sake of drama, that the horrid screeching drove customers away, but no one stayed away. Our customers are loyal."

I relaxed my hands slightly. "We are."

That got me another uncertain smile. "In addition to my having exaggerated about how much that bagpiper bothered us, apparently a Frisky Pomegranate knife was found with his body."

Not knowing what to say, I finally murmured, "Horrible." I wasn't about to tell her that I'd seen both Kirk and the knife, and that, since the knife was still tucked inside the scabbard in his sock, the knife might not have played a part in the murder. *But maybe a Deputy Donut mug did . . .* I said nothing more and hoped that Penny would go on talking.

She did. "I certainly did not put a knife near the bagpiper's body. I didn't even know he was dead."

What does that mean? Did she see him lying on the ground?

I must have maintained a neutral expression. She went on talking. "I think I told you that cutlery often goes missing from Frisky Pomegranate. Maybe Kirk took a knife, and that's why it was with his body."

"Did he eat at Frisky Pomegranate?"

"Not when I was around, but he could have grabbed a knife off a patio table when no one was looking. Or one of the other people who stole knives over the years could have kept it until he found a disgusting use for it, like killing someone and leaving that recognizable knife with the body so I'd be blamed." She gulped at her coffee, and then added, "But I'm totally innocent."

"Who has eaten at your place recently?"

She looked pleased that I was asking questions that might help solve the murder—and exonerate her. "Who hasn't?

You have, and your fiancé, and your parents have, and just about everyone else who lives anywhere near or visits Fallingbrook."

I wanted to ask about specific people, but knew I shouldn't go around naming possible suspects. All of them could be innocent. Or all but one of them . . .

Penny folded her napkin into smaller and smaller triangles. "The high school music teacher, that mousy little woman, has eaten there, and that guy with the bugle was with you and the tall woman who manages The Craft Croft." Penny let go of the napkin. It started unfolding itself. She plunked a fist on it, holding the remaining folds in place. "I told the police that sometimes the people who steal our things just drop them, and Tiffany and I find them on our walks to the car late at night. The police seemed to know that I often park near where they've taped off the scene instead of close to Frisky Pomegranate, so they asked who we usually saw around there after we close the restaurant. Then they tried to trick me into saying we were in that area around the time the bagpiper was killed. They asked me who I saw there that night. But Tiffany and I didn't go down there that night. We knew that rain was forecast for Wednesday morning around the time we'd be closing, so when I drove Tiffany to work Tuesday morning, I parked near Frisky Pomegranate. Not that I can prove it."

"You might not have to. Lots of people have security cameras that could show where your car was and that it wasn't near the scene."

She took a deep breath, and I thought that the tentative smile she gave me looked relieved, but it quickly disappeared, and she frowned again. "Another thing that made them wonder is that Tiffany and I worked later than usual that morning. We'd been excited to start planning and organizing things for the new owner. Then it was pouring when we left, so we just put up our umbrellas and ran."

I tried to reassure her. "I'm sure the police will be able to confirm what you're telling me."

She broke off another piece of donut. "They can, and I'm not asking you to confirm it. You weren't there, so you can't know. The people who clean Frisky Pomegranate must have told the police approximately what time Tiffany and I left work, and that's why the police are trying to place us at the scene of the crime when it happened. But there's someone else who can tell them exactly when we arrived home. Her testimony will prove that we didn't have time to go a quarter mile south, commit a murder, and then fly home at three hundred miles per hour."

I put my hands on the table again. "That's great! Get her to talk to the police."

"Easier said than done. She hates Tiffany and me, and she'd probably lie in order to put us in jail."

I couldn't help opening my eyes wider in surprise. "That sounds extreme."

"You don't know Deborah."

"You said she can tell them exactly when you reached home. How can you be sure?"

"She lives across the street from our houses, and she spies on us. She has ever since we refused to pull our milkweed up."

This was becoming confusing. "Milkweed?"

"Yep. It showed up in our yards by itself, and we found out that monarch butterflies lay their eggs on it, and it's the only food that monarch caterpillars will eat. There are lots of varieties of milkweed. Tiffany and I have the most common type. We want to help prevent monarchs from going extinct, but Deborah says milkweed is poison to farm animals."

I succeeded in not scratching my head, but my mouth twisted. "Does Deborah have farm animals?"

"No, but if it wasn't milkweed, it would be something else. She has to have something to do, and what she wants to do is spy on people, and she rationalizes that arguing with them is a good reason to spy on them. On us. I think she's hoping to catch us breaking a law, and she can put us in jail or get us to move away. Well, as I told you, I have decided to move, but poor Tiffany doesn't have that option and will have to put up with Deborah's spying." Penny took another long drink of coffee. "Tiffany and I see Deborah twitching her curtain aside, just barely, and peeking out."

"She can't spy on you all of the time. Doesn't she have anything else to do?"

"She has cameras that help her, but I swear she barely moves from her position by the front window. She must eat and sleep there, if she eats or sleeps at all. Sometimes, I wonder if she's even human." Penny ate the rest of her donut.

"Is she retired?"

"I don't think she's old enough. I'd guess she's only in her fifties, but as far as I can tell, she never goes anywhere."

I suggested, "How about calling the police and telling them that she probably knows when you arrived home Wednesday morning? They can go ask her."

"That might work, but if they somehow dropped the information that she could get us out of trouble by being honest about when we arrived home, she'd probably lie and say we got home an hour or so later." She finished her coffee.

"The police will be discreet. They have experience separating truth from lies." I gave her Brent's phone number.

Penny thanked me and entered the number into her phone. "I hope you're right." She paid me, said goodbye, and left. She looked and sounded totally discouraged.

She'd asserted her innocence, possibly too dramatically to be compelling. I wondered if she'd told me the truth.

Chapter 18

✺

After lunch, Austin Berwin came to Deputy Donut in crisp, dark green pants and a matching, long-sleeved shirt. He edged onto one of the high stools at our serving counter and told me, "I'm on my way to work. Afternoon shift, to start."

"Congratulations. Does that mean you need a strong coffee?"

"Yes, one to take out, and two dozen donuts for my new staff."

"New staff," I repeated. "It sounds like a good job."

His smile was genuine and a little smug. "Better than my old one and better than the public works one that I didn't get. So that bagpiper did me a big favor, not that his playing during the night really bothered me. I didn't have a grudge against the poor guy. May he rest in peace." He said that last sentence quickly and without, I thought, sincerity. "I can't imagine how anyone can kill another human being except if they really have to. I couldn't hurt anyone." He looked down at his hands, folded on the counter.

"Me, neither." I started toward the display case. "Come tell me which donuts you'd like."

He eased off the stool, ambled to the display case, and gazed down through its curved glass top. "Two of those with pink icing and sprinkles, two of those chocolate ones with the fudge icing. What do you call them?"

"Double fudge donuts."

"Great. Two of those. Four of the raised donuts with vanilla icing, because everyone likes those, right?"

"It seems so."

He licked his lips like he was anticipating trying each of the donuts. "What others are, like, general favorites?"

"Old-fashioned cake donuts like you had before, flavored with nutmeg."

"Excellent. Four of those, two with powdered sugar and two without. So, that's the first dozen, right?"

"Right. Another favorite is maple bacon."

"Okay, two of those, and—let's see. What are those with the round things on them?"

"Raised donuts decorated with slices of mini pecan rolls."

"I love pecan rolls. I'll have four." He stepped back and forth, staring down into the display case.

I suggested, "How about apple fritters? And we have zucchini fritters made with sugar and cinnamon. They taste like apple fritters."

"Just apple fritters. Two of those, and then, you know what?" He didn't wait for a response. "Everyone loves chocolate. The rest of them can be your double fudge donuts."

"Good choices." I finished filling the boxes and closed them. "What coffee would you like?"

"Can you put an espresso in my travel mug? It'll be sort of lost in the mug, but I hate to use disposable things if I can help it. And I have a bag I can put the two boxes in to make them easier to carry."

"I can, and you get a discount for using your own cup and bag." I made his espresso. He paid me, picked up his purchases, and went out the front door.

I watched him go. He drove away in the small burgundy

sedan I'd seen him in before. This time, I could read the make and model.

It was a Honda Civic.

I went into the kitchen and told Olivia, "I need to call Brent. I'll be right back."

She gave me one of the genuinely patient smiles that she must have learned at the age of eighteen when her parents' deaths threw her into being both mother and father to her eight-year-old sister. "We'll be fine. Take your time."

Again, Brent's phone went directly to message. I quickly rattled off that Austin Berwin had come in to tell me that he hadn't really minded Kirk's wee-hours bagpipe playing. I added, "You've probably already discovered that the burgundy car Austin drives is a Honda Civic."

None of us at Deputy Donut knew quite what to expect from the Funny Friday traveling performers in the afternoon. Our patio filled up again, keeping Jocelyn, Olivia, and me busy, but since our clients were all out on the patio, we saw many of the acts.

An improv group asked three members of the audience to give them a word. Flustered audience members came up with "dish," "fish," and "sky." Within seconds, the actors had us all laughing with a skit involving bald eagles flying over a group of picnickers and dropping, among other things, fish into their dishes.

I was inside making fresh coffee when a stand-up comic delivered his jokes. From what I could tell, the laughter was strained.

I went out to the patio in time to watch a clown deliberately recite nursery rhymes incorrectly while riding a unicycle in tight circles. "And the dish ran away with the knife," he said. A coincidence, or did he know something about Kirk's murder?

A pair of teens delivered a fast-paced recital of Abbott and

Costello's "Who's on First?" Diners were laughing so hard they couldn't eat their donuts or drink their coffee.

The last act of the afternoon was done with no props. A woman and a man stood facing the audience but angled away from each other. The woman pretended to peer through a window and report the neighbors' shenanigans to her husband. The more outrageous the neighbors became, the more intent the husband was on narrating a surprisingly violent golf game on a TV which, like the window, was invisible to the audience. The woman became shrill, the man blustered, and neither of them paid attention to anything the other said. Both of them seemed to be responding to the other one, although they were actually reacting, quite loudly, to different dramas. The characters ended up apparently satisfied that they'd communicated with each other. They bowed. We clapped, and they wandered, arm-in-arm, toward the Fireplug.

Our guests finished their drinks and sweet treats, paid us, and left. Jocelyn, Olivia, and I closed the gate to the patio, cleared the tables, folded the umbrellas, and leaned the chairs against the tables. Inside, we locked the front door and made dough for the next day. Hardly anyone had eaten in our dining area during the afternoon, and we quickly readied it for the Jolly Cops Cleaning Crew.

The three of us went into the office. During the day, police officers had removed their tape from our porch railings. The tape was also gone from the end of the alleyway, and the parking lots were again available except for the one where I'd found Kirk's body. I blinked to be certain—the police tape was still around that lot, but Kirk's bright orange van was gone.

I told Olivia and Jocelyn, "You two go ahead. I need to do some work on the computer."

Jocelyn narrowed her eyes and studied my face. Knowing that Tom and I often stayed to go over accounts, I attempted to appear innocent.

It must have worked. Jocelyn and Olivia said goodbye and left, Olivia on foot, and Jocelyn wheeling her bike beside her.

I sat down at the computer. Dep jumped onto the desk and helpfully patted the keyboard with her front paws. I picked her up, put her on my lap, and deleted the string of symbols she'd typed.

The Fallingbrook community directory nicely gave me Penny's home address. She lived northeast of Frisky Pomegranate. It would take less than ten minutes to drive there, but was too far to walk and return in time for dinner with my parents and the evening show. "Okay, Dep," I said. "Let's go home."

Maybe she was eager to see my parents. Or she understood my mood. Maybe she was hungry for the fishy cat food I gave her every evening. She pranced along nicely with very few stops.

The police tape was gone from my yard and driveway. I took Dep into the house. My parents were at my dining table, not eating, but apparently writing. I let Dep out of her harness, hung it and her leash up, and put on a jacket, even though it was still warm out. I called toward the dining room, "I have to go somewhere for about a half hour or maybe a little longer. Eat without me. I'll grab something when I get back."

My mother put down her pen. "One of the larger lasagnas that you made and froze is heating in the oven. It won't be out for a half hour, and then it needs to sit, and we're not judging this evening's show. We'll wait for you."

My father pulled a set of keys out of his pocket. "Are you driving?"

I nodded.

He started toward the front door. "I'll move our car out of the way. Or you can take ours."

I didn't want to interrupt whatever he was doing, and I'd be back sooner if we didn't jockey cars around. I accepted his keys. "Thanks. I'll take yours. See you soon."

Their car was a small one that they towed behind their RV to and from Florida. My father had obviously been the most recent driver. I had to pull the seat forward. Backing out of the driveway, I couldn't help checking for stray dishes. There were none.

I drove east to Wisconsin Street, turned north, passed the square, and then turned east again. About a quarter mile beyond Tom and Cindy's neighborhood, a sign marked Penny's road. It was paved in little more than gravel and wound through trees to a large clearing. Two houses were on the left, and a third one was on the right, facing the side yards separating the other two houses. All three houses were small like mine, but newer, maybe built in the 1950s. Penny's address was on the mailbox in front of the first house on the left. Avoiding glancing toward the house on the right, the one that had to be Deborah's, I pulled into Penny's driveway and stopped near the road in the shade of a graceful maple tree. At the other end of the driveway, a single-car garage stood by itself, tethered to the house by a long clothesline.

My first impression of Penny's house was that it had been maintained, but possibly not loved. It lacked personal touches, as if Penny had never planned to live there long. Perhaps she'd spent her time and energy on raising flowers. The wild growth in the gardens in front of her house and the next one, which must have been Tiffany's, would not have appealed to people who preferred tidy flowerbeds. Milkweed pods formed on leggy, big-leaved plants. Goldenrod showed hints of yellow, while the buds of wild asters were still tightly furled. I walked up a curving pathway between pink, purple, and white cosmos that were attracting bees and butterflies. The front of the house was squarely symmetrical, with a door in the center between two windows. On the second floor, three windows lined up with the windows and door below them. The siding was mint green, and the trim was white.

I climbed up the single step to a roofed porch that was barely wider than the door. I rang the bell, heard it jangle inside the house, and waited. I was almost certain that Penny was at work and that no one would answer. Hoping I was right and determined to be patient, I glanced to my right, toward Tiffany's house. It was almost identical to Penny's, except the siding was white and the trim was dove gray. No vehicles were in the driveway, and from where I stood, I couldn't see a garage, if there was one.

I rang the bell again and listened, not for sounds within the house, but for sounds across the road. With any luck, Penny's nosy neighbor was at home and would become curious enough to come out and ask why I was there.

Hoping to be heard across the street, I knocked on the screen door's wooden frame. The frame rattled hollowly and satisfactorily loudly.

I adjusted my position slightly to see, beyond the screen's grid, my ghostly reflection in the window in the top half of the front door. My jacket did not completely cover the Deputy Donut logo on my shirt. Although the late afternoon was still too warm for a jacket, I zipped it to hide the logo. Grateful for the shade of the porch roof, I waited.

Maybe this wasn't going to work. I could give up, go home, and have dinner with my folks. I could tell Brent what Penny had said, and he could drive up here and question Deborah.

Hoping that Penny hadn't already talked to Brent and that he wouldn't suddenly appear across the street, I moved over

until, in the door's window, I could make out a distorted reflection of Deborah's house.

Did a curtain move in the front window?

And then I heard it—the *snick* of a deadbolt being drawn
back.

A voice, rusty from disuse, called out, "She's not there!"

Chapter 19

I didn't want to pivot quickly toward her and make it obvious that I had been hoping for a response from across the street, but I also didn't want to take my time and let the woman retreat inside before I could talk to her.

I hoped I turned in a natural way, though I felt as jerky as Theatrical Thursday's marionettes.

It had to be Deborah. From what Penny had said, I wasn't surprised that Deborah looked eccentric, but I hadn't expected her to appear to have stepped out of a time machine. Her brown slim skirt and its matching fitted jacket appeared brand new, as if she were wearing a costume for a play or a film set in 1949. I couldn't help wondering if her stockings had seams up the back.

Her hair, a shade lighter than her suit, was pulled back and sparkled in the sunshine. Hairspray, I guessed, not glitter. She was tall with large hands and wrist bones that stuck out beyond the jacket's cuffs, as if the jacket had been tailored for someone with shorter arms. She strode down the arrow-straight concrete path from her house. Not wanting to force her to cross the dusty road and perhaps mar her shiny brown, chunky-heeled pumps, I met her at the foot of her path.

Despite the day's heat and the sunshine still beating down

on her house and on her immaculately shorn and weedless green lawn, her suit was heavy, probably wool. I no longer felt conspicuous in my light cotton jacket.

Deborah was younger than her outfit implied. Penny had said that Deborah was probably in her fifties, and that seemed right, though the eyeliner, powder, rouge, and bright red lipstick made it hard to be sure. Faint odors of onions and mothballs drifted from her. She repeated, "She's not home."

"Do you know when she'll be back?" I tried to speak with a nicely interested but impersonal tone that might prevent Deborah from becoming too curious about my reason for visiting Penny's house.

Deborah pursed her reddened lips in obvious disapproval. "That husband-killer? She stays out until all hours. She runs some sort of a nightclub and doesn't get home until one or two. And sometimes not until nearly three. Probably out killing more people."

Preventing my mouth from hanging open, I squeaked, "Husband-killer?" Could Kirk have left a widow behind, and had this woman in the pristine vintage suit been his wife? I had trouble imagining this personification of a 1950s stenographer being married to a somewhat scruffy bagpipe player. To do him justice, although his hair and beard had been mostly untamed, his Highland outfit had been impeccable except for the dinner knife he carried instead of a ceremonial dagger.

Deborah folded her arms. "She'll say she didn't kill her husband, but I know she did."

"When was this?"

"Ten years and five days ago."

Schooling myself not to look amazed at the precision of Deborah's answer, I pointed with a thumb over my shoulder. "In that house?"

"No, they lived in Turquoise, a suburb north of Chicago. She skedaddled from Illinois and came here loaded down with her husband's money." Deborah glanced toward Penny's house. "Enough to buy that place, which she can't bother to look after, plus that nightclub down in Fallingbrook." She said it like Fallingbrook was hundreds of miles away instead of less than ten. And I didn't think that anyone else would call Frisky Pomegranate a nightclub. She folded her arms across the front of that intricately tailored jacket and, in a coy gesture that also could have come from the 1950s, gracefully tapped one elbow with the fingers of her other hand. Her nails were the same shade as her lips. "It's terrible how some people can just get away with murder."

"Yes, it is. How do you know it was murder?"

She gave me a sharp look from those dark-rimmed eyes. "Are you familiar with the case?"

I was able to say honestly, "This is the first I've heard of it."

I was afraid she wouldn't answer my question, but she did. "I know it was murder because I researched it."

I tilted my head, still portraying the interested listener. "Did you work in law enforcement in Illinois?"

"Oh, no. I've lived here all my life. So did my mother. This was my grandparents' house. But I am in law enforcement."

Again, I had to prevent myself from gaping. I thought I knew most of the people in law enforcement in Fallingbrook or recognized them unless they were new. Could this woman be DCI or FBI?

She explained, "I'm a pre-licensed private investigator. I've studied all of the texts, and more. I just need to write the exams and do whatever else is necessary for certification."

"In the meantime, you researched Penny's husband's death?"

"Yes, I did. I needed to know more about her because of her behavior after she moved here. O'Lander isn't a common name. I have a computer and an internet connection, and I looked up her name, and there it was. Her husband's death was a mystery. They said he died of natural causes, but they were wrong. Knowing what Penny was like, I drove down to Turquoise."

I pictured Deborah driving something like a majestic, chrome-blinged Cadillac or Mercury and staying well under the speed limit even on superhighways. "That's a long drive."

"It's farther than I like to go, but even though I don't yet have my PI license, driving there was my civilian duty. Turquoise is a small town, and the people there told me what really happened. Penny returned from the nightclub where she waited tables and found her husband dead in his bed. The neighbors swore that Penny smothered her husband with a pillow before she went to work that day. And even if she didn't outright kill him, they said, she knew he was in a medical crisis before she went to work, but instead of calling for help, she dashed off to collect big tips in the nightclub. It was greed, pure and simple, that caused her to leave her husband that day, even though he was in dire straits. If it wasn't outright murder, it was neglect leading to death."

Deborah's nostrils widened as if she'd caught her own scents of onions and mothballs. "One of the first things we PIs learn is to follow the money. Who benefited from his death? She did, with a hefty life insurance settlement. But she didn't stick around to let the authorities investigate. She came up here, opened a nightclub, and started letting weeds overwhelm her garden and send their seeds over here."

I restrained myself from stepping back, away from the negativity and, I thought, outright hatred that seemed to flow from Deborah. I should have told Brent what Penny had said about Deborah and let him and Vic talk to her. "I see," I said. What I saw was a lonely, vindictive woman who disapproved of wildflowers and whose research into crime detection hadn't been thorough enough to tell her that criminals could be extradited from Wisconsin and taken back to Illinois.

Deborah lowered her voice, as if the milkweed pods across the road held hidden microphones. "And there's more. A man was killed near Penny's nightclub Tuesday night or Wednesday morning, and that was one of those nights that she 'worked' late. She usually arrives home around one thirty, but on Wednesday morning, she didn't pull into her driveway until twelve minutes after two. I know it was her car, because she drives a newer model black Honda Civic, and she got out of it, and so did her neighbor. The O'Lander woman keeps junk in her garage, so she never parks in it, which makes it easy to tell when she's home. Her neighbor cadges rides from the O'Lander woman."

If Deborah was right about the timing, and I suspected that she was as specific about that as she was about the number of years and days since Penny's husband died, and if the Jolly Cop I had talked to was right that Penny and Tiffany had left Frisky Pomegranate that morning at five after two, Penny and Tiffany could not have murdered Kirk after the Jolly Cops saw the two women go out into the stormy night.

Penny or Tiffany could have left Frisky Pomegranate, killed Kirk, and returned before the Jolly Cops arrived at Frisky Pomegranate, but the Jolly Cop had said that neither woman was wet. In the video taken from the back of Deputy Donut, Kirk had still been alive minutes before the rain started that night.

Penny had guessed that Deborah could exonerate her, and it appeared that she could, but I wasn't about to let Deborah know that. I put admiration into my voice. "You keep close track."

She nodded, causing glints from her lacquerlike hairspray to dance in the early evening sunshine. "I have a spreadsheet."

I came up with an honest response. "Impressive!"

"It's all part of being a PI."

"I don't think that anyone has been arrested for the murder early Wednesday morning." I raised a forefinger in the air as if I'd just had a brilliant idea. "What if you told the police what you saw? They must know things about the case that they could put together with what you discovered."

Deborah hesitated, and I was afraid I'd have to send Brent to her after all, but finally she said, as if thinking aloud, "I probably should. I could solve the case on my own, but they can do it faster, and get that murdering woman off the streets." Her padded shoulders shook in a patently fake shudder. "It's gotten so that honest people can't sleep in their beds at night without fear."

I could have given Brent's number to Deborah, but I didn't want to make it obvious that I was close to members of Fallingbrook law enforcement. And maybe a pre-licensed private investigator wouldn't have trouble finding the number of Fallingbrook's police department.

I gestured toward Penny's house. "Are you sure she's not there?"

"I'm positive. And to tell you the truth, I hope she gets arrested and never comes back." Deborah turned around and headed toward her porch. Those chunky heels thudded on her concrete pathway.

In the slanting sunlight, her hair, neatly tucked into a French roll, sparkled. Her sheer stockings glimmered like silk.

The stockings had seams up the back.

Chapter 20

I returned to my parents' car and texted them that I'd be home in about sixteen minutes. Deborah's precision must have been contagious.

Pulling out onto the road, I risked a glance toward Deborah's house and yard. A garage like Penny's was near the back of the property. Maybe it was just as well that I couldn't peek into the garage's windows. I would have been disappointed if Deborah's car had been built after 1960.

Not wanting to spew gravel, I started slowly down the road, and then the irony of the situation struck me. There I was, borrowing my parents' car, and I might have strengthened Vic's suspicion of them by possibly helping Penny prove her innocence. "Great," I muttered to the steering wheel.

I was still wearing my jacket, and the car had heated in the sun. I cranked up the air-conditioning. By the time I parked in my driveway, I was almost cold.

I went inside. Dep didn't come into the living room to greet me, the little traitor. She must have been in the kitchen with my parents.

My mother called out, "Perfect timing! The lasagna's ready to be cut."

I hung up the jacket and headed toward the kitchen. Seeing what was spread out on the table in the dining room, I halted. When I'd left to visit Penny's home when I knew she wouldn't be there, my parents had been writing, but I'd been too preoccupied to notice what they'd been doing. My parents had taken courses in calligraphy in Florida during the winter, and now the table's glass top was covered with stylish and artistically written place cards for Brent's and my wedding reception.

Feeling guilty about my lack of attention to these two wonderful people who gave love and asked nothing in return, I called into the kitchen, "These are beautiful! Thank you!"

Drying her hands on a towel, my mother came to the doorway between the kitchen and the dining room. "Our pleasure."

From the kitchen, my father added, "It was fun. And you knew we were going to do it." I heard the squeaks of a cork being pulled out of a wine bottle.

I followed my mother into the kitchen and gave her a quick hug. "They look totally professional."

Pouring ruby red wine into glasses for us, my father asked, "What did you expect?"

I laughed and hugged him, too.

My parents had made garlic bread and a salad to go with the lasagna. Because the Funny Friday show was starting soon, we didn't want to spend time carrying things to and from the patio outside the sunroom. We ate in the kitchen.

My mother pointed at the fridge. "We went out this morning while you were at work and bought a watermelon. It's cooling. How about if we have dessert here after the show?"

"Sounds great."

I didn't change out of my Deputy Donut uniform. I grabbed the jacket I'd worn earlier, my mother picked up her sweater, and we walked quickly to the village square.

We were almost at the bandstand when the show began. We found seats near the back. The audience seemed to be in a party mood, and nearly everyone laughed all through the show. The pair who had written and acted the skit of the mis-communicating married couple won first prize, and the teens who did the "Who's on First?" act came in second.

After the judges handed out the awards, my parents and I saw Quentin at the back of the audience with other people who had arrived too late to find seats. We threaded our way to him.

The admiration in my mother's smile was authentic. "The way you played 'Taps' Wednesday evening after we were at Frisky Pomegranate was lovely, Quentin. If you'd played like that on Monday evening, you'd have won." My father agreed.

Quentin made a dismissive shrug. "It doesn't matter. And as things turned out, it's a good thing that the bagpiper won. I'm glad I didn't deprive him of that pleasure."

The evening was cooling. I slipped into my jacket. "Summer said you sometimes play 'Taps' at the lake."

Quentin frowned. "I hope it doesn't bother anyone."

My mother demanded, "Are you kidding? They must love it."

I asked, "Is Summer here?" Realizing that my question could be misunderstood, I corrected it to "Is Summer Peabody-Smith here?"

"Yes to your first question. No to your second." Quentin said it humorously, but I thought I could see remnants of the little boy he had been—maybe slightly bratty, but also admirably confident and competent.

We started south. My mother asked him, "Did you enjoy the Funny Friday show?"

Quentin walked beside us. "It was entertaining."

Knowing he might be under suspicion for Kirk's death and could be worried about it, I asked, "How are you doing?"

"Mostly okay, Emily, thanks. Want to hear the good news first, or the bad?"

"Um . . ." I managed.

My mother had no doubt. She tipped her head up and looked into Quentin's face. "The good news."

Quentin winked at her. "My good-luck handkerchief was found."

I clenched my fists so tightly that my fingers hurt. Quentin was here, not in a jail cell. That had to be good news, at least for him. I asked in a small voice, "And the bad news?"

Quentin's Adam's apple raised and lowered. Finally, his voice came out in a sad rasp. "It was with the body of the bagpiper."

My mother rested her hand briefly on his forearm. "Does that mean you'll get it back, Quentin? Eventually, after the police no longer need it? Or would you prefer to never see it again?"

He looked over her head toward the sun slipping down behind trees beyond Wisconsin Street. "I . . . I'm not sure. Apparently, there's blood on it."

My mother flapped one hand as if to dismiss his concern. "That can be removed with cold water and a little bleach. But don't soak it too long if the handkerchief is old and delicate. The fabric could disintegrate. Did your great-grandmother make only one of those for you?"

"Yes, and I know it doesn't actually bring me good luck, but I hate to lose it. I don't remember her, but she made it with love before I was born and finished it with a monogram after she learned my name."

My father slung his arm around my mother. "Women's love is hard and true."

My mother smiled toward his chin. "Men's, too."

He kissed the top of her head.

I glanced around. No one else seemed to be within earshot, so I asked Quentin, "Do you know if the police tested the handkerchief for the blood type? They probably haven't had time to work out the DNA."

Quentin raised both thumbs. "There's good news, bad news, and then there's more good news, at least for me. I'm a regular blood donor because my type is rare. I showed my blood type card to that DCI agent before he told me about the blood on the handkerchief. That handkerchief probably carries some of my DNA, because I've owned it for so long and handled it frequently, but the blood on the handkerchief could not have been mine."

It was my turn to raise both thumbs. "The blood must be Kirk's, then."

Quentin widened those gorgeous dark eyes. "It's not. The DCI agent was so surprised that my blood wasn't on the handkerchief that he let slip that the blood wasn't the victim's, either."

"So . . ." my mother began.

My father finished for her. "It must be the murderer's."

"Might be," I said. "Who knows how many people touched that handkerchief between the time that Quentin lost it and it ended up with Kirk's body?"

Quentin glanced back toward the northeast corner of the square. "I'm guessing that Kirk was the one who put his business card on my windshield. He probably picked up my handkerchief while he was near my car."

I thought, but didn't say, *And, just like he might have attempted to steal twenty dollars, and could have stolen Ed's phone and wallet and Quentin's wallet, Kirk might have taken a knife from Frisky Pomegranate and a mug from Deputy Donut's patio. If Kirk stole those objects, the murderer probably didn't bring them along when he or she committed the crime. We can't say that Penny wielded the knife or that Quentin dropped his handkerchief at the scene. Or that someone from Deputy Donut clobbered Kirk with one of our mugs . . .*

I must have let out a loud sigh as we walked along. My mother turned and stared at me, but she didn't say anything.

At the south end of the square, Quentin waved toward the east. "I parked over there, beyond the police station." He headed in that direction.

Wishing Brent could be with me, I couldn't help a longing glance at the building housing the police station and town offices.

Chapter 21

✣

My parents and I rounded the corner onto Wisconsin Street.
I muttered, "Blood type isn't necessarily conclusive."

My father said, "Neither are fingerprints."

My mother added, "Lots of the stuff you see on TV about
crime-solving is simplified. But let's forget all that. I'm sure
that our watermelon is nicely chilled and will be sweet and
delicious."

We'd barely arrived home and given Dep the greetings she
demanded—and deserved—when Brent called me. "Are your
folks still up? Vic and I would like to talk to them, but if it's
too late, we can see them tomorrow. I thought they might
prefer to get this over now instead of coming to the station
tomorrow."

I was still wearing my jacket, but I broke out in goose-
bumps. "Get what over, Brent?"

"We'd like their fingerprints."

I tried not to sound as uneasy as I felt. "I'll tell them. We
were just about to dig into some watermelon. Should we cut
you some, too?" He hesitated, so I answered for him, making
it into a question. "You're not coming alone, so you don't
know?"

He exhaled audibly. "You got it. But don't let us delay you."

We disconnected, and I relayed the conversation to my folks.

My mother decided, "Let's wait until they're done with us, or all they'll get is sticky fingerprints."

We went into the kitchen and set out a businesslike knife and five plates and spoons.

While I gave Dep fresh kibble and water, my father wandered off toward the living room. The doorbell didn't ring, but I heard the front door open and my father say, "Come in."

"Thanks for seeing us, Walt."

Dep's ears perked up at the sound of Brent's voice. She galumphed toward the living room. My mother and I followed at a more dignified pace.

Brent held up a small black case. "Sorry, Walt, and Annie, but we'll need your fingerprints." Beside him, Vic nodded.

My father offered his hand. "No problem."

Brent showed him where to place his fingers on the inkless scanner. Within seconds, it seemed, both of my parents had given Wisconsin their fingerprints.

Dep rubbed against my ankles and meowed loudly. I picked her up. "Have a seat, everyone." I thought that Vic and Brent might take it as their cue to leave, but Vic sat in the armchair, Brent sprawled in the wing chair, and my parents and I, with my mother between my father and me, perched on the sofa facing the police officers. I hugged Dep. "Does your wanting my parents' fingerprints mean that the mug my father found in my driveway was the murder weapon?"

Brent sent me an apologetic glance and repeated what he'd said to me earlier. "It was involved."

Dep had become almost boneless. I lowered her to my lap and stroked her. "That means that the murderer might have placed the mug in my driveway." I couldn't help shuddering. "I'm glad we keep the doors locked."

Vic's glower was ferocious. "As if that would stop anyone who was determined to get in." He paged back through his notebook. "Now, what can you three tell me about the black marks on the handle of the mug?" He pierced my father with a slatey look. "Walt?"

My father apologized. "I didn't notice them."

My mother didn't wait to be singled out. "I didn't, either."

Brent asked gently, "Emily, do some of Deputy Donut's dishes have black marks on them, maybe from rubbing against something in the dishwasher?"

With my hands around Dep's warm, furry body to keep her from sliding off my lap, I recrossed my legs. "I've never noticed marks like that on our dishes. Could someone with greasy hands have handled the mug? Maybe a car mechanic had a grudge against Kirk."

Vic frowned. "It wasn't grease."

"What was it?" I thought my question was reasonable, but Vic only grunted, so I forged ahead with a slightly different subject. "I didn't notice blood on the mug." I turned toward my parents. "Did either of you?"

They said they hadn't. My father reminded me, "The blood could have been washed away in Wednesday morning's storm."

I stared straight at Vic. "But if there was blood, couldn't the rain have washed it deeper into the break in the mug? Wouldn't that ragged edge of earthenware be porous?"

I thought a flicker of acknowledgment might have crossed Vic's face, but he didn't answer.

Brent did. "The mug and the piece broken from it are at a state-of-the-art lab. They'll find whatever's there."

I thought, *Blood on the mug would more likely be Kirk's than the murderer's.* My mother might have been thinking the same thing. She was staring down at her hands, clenched together in her lap. She looked as sad as I felt. Maybe Kirk hadn't been a wonderful person, but he hadn't deserved what happened to him.

The room became silent except for a fly buzzing at the

front window and Dep's contented purrs. I cleared my throat. "As I said in a phone message to Brent, Austin Berwin came into Deputy Donut this afternoon. He seemed to want to make a point of telling me that, although he'd seemed angry at Kirk for disturbing his sleep, Austin had not really been angry, and now he was giving Kirk credit for inadvertently helping Austin receive an offer for a job that was better than the one where he hadn't done well at the interview."

Vic repeated slowly, "Austin Berwin." He asked Brent, "Is he the O-positive with the lumber mill accident?" It took me a second to recognize what Vic meant by "O-positive." It was the most common blood type. Quentin had told us that the blood on the handkerchief was not the rarest type. Could it have been the most common type, O-positive? *The same as mine. And my parents'.*

Brent gave a terse nod. "That's the man."

I decided not to mention my parents' and my blood type. Instead, I said, "As I told Brent in my phone message, Austin was driving a burgundy Honda Civic this afternoon."

Vic's wordless stare at me made me nervous. I feared that he believed my parents might have killed Kirk. I stammered through an explanation. "As far as I could tell, it looked like the car that crept past the back of Deputy Donut shortly after Kirk ran past in the rain."

Vic informed me coldly, "We know what car Berwin drives."

Brent must have wanted to make the conversation more congenial. "Berwin admitted that his car was in the videos that night."

The back of my neck heated. "I specifically asked him if he'd driven around near Deputy Donut that night. He said he hadn't."

Brent's mouth twitched. "He 'forgot.' A look at some of the videos from the street jogged his memory."

My mother said more or less what I was thinking. "Uh-oh."

I guessed that Brent and Vic did not have adequate evidence against Austin. Yet. Maybe they truly had come to my place only to rule out my parents as suspects.

I asked a question that I didn't expect either Brent or Vic to answer. "Is it possible that Kirk was murdered because he stole something from someone?" Brent and Vic gazed at me without saying anything, so I went on. "Originally, I thought that Lisa-Ruth Schomoset had taken one of our Deputy Donut mugs, but Kirk could have reached over our patio railing and grabbed it after everyone went inside and turned their backs on him."

Vic asked, "Was there a break in his playing during that time?"

I thought back. "I didn't notice one."

My parents said that they hadn't, either.

The hint of sarcasm in Vic's voice became more than a hint. "Seems to me that playing a bagpipe requires both hands."

Brent came to my rescue. "He could have taken the mug if he stopped playing before he headed north from Deputy Donut. Remember, Vic, in the video from Booked, Fallingbrook's bookstore, early Wednesday morning, Mr. MacLean was clutching his bagpipe in one hand and a mug in the other. It did not appear to be broken."

Vic pointed out, "We still don't know how or where he obtained that mug."

I scratched Dep's chin. "He could have taken it from Lisa-Ruth. Those two didn't get along. I told Brent the story my mother-in-law, Cindy Westhill, told me, about suspicions of a theft at the high—"

Vic interrupted me. "I know all about that. We interviewed your mother-in-law and the principal."

I continued to defend my theory. "I suspect that Kirk picked up other things that didn't belong to him. A knife from Frisky Pomegranate, for instance." I waited, almost holding my breath, for Vic or Brent to say they'd interviewed

Penny's neighbor and knew about my visit to her. Their expressions remained neutral. I added, "And Quentin thinks that Kirk found Quentin's handkerchief and took it." I waved my hand in the general direction of Fallingbrook's business section. "Ed, who's a server at the Fireplug, believes that Kirk stole Ed's wallet and phone and Quentin's wallet."

Brent quickly informed me, "The wallets were in Kirk's van. They contained the two men's charge cards and ID, but no cash. We have not yet found Ed's phone. However, Quentin's parents' cabin is a small one, and they are positive that Quentin was inside it all night. The three of them got up and closed windows together during the storm."

Brent might have mostly ruled out Quentin, but I was sure that Vic was thinking that parents might lie to protect their son.

Vic reminded Brent, "We don't know who put those wallets in the deceased's van, or when. It could have been after the murder."

I guessed aloud, "If you fingerprinted the wallets, you might get the original owners' fingerprints, but if Kirk's prints were on the wallets, then it's a pretty good guess that Kirk did steal them from the locker room in the gym."

Vic's phone buzzed briefly, as if he had received a text message. He examined the phone's screen, and then raised his head and looked at my father. "You held the mug by its handle." He transferred his attention to my mother. "And you cupped the mug in the palm of your left hand with your fingers touching the sides of the mug, and you also grasped it by the handle with your right hand."

My father glanced toward the ceiling. "That's exactly how I remember it. She was holding the mug by its handle when she put it on the table."

My mother raised her pointed little chin. "And that's basically what we told you we did. I didn't remember exactly how I held it, but I'm right-handed, and what you said makes sense. There. Now that we've established that we touched the mug we told you we handled, can we offer you two some watermelon?"

Maybe Vic was afraid of being poisoned by more than my mother's suddenly acid tongue. "No, thanks. Brent and I have work to do tonight."

Brent gave me a rueful smile. "Sorry, I guess we'd better not."

He let Vic precede him outside, and then he rubbed a comforting hand through my curls. "See you soon, I hope."

Chapter 22

Standing in the open doorway and pressing my cat to my heart, I watched the two men head toward the unmarked cruiser in front of my house. I felt guilty for not having confessed that I'd lured Deborah out of her house to talk to me instead of simply telling Brent what Penny had said. But would the police by themselves have achieved as much as I had?

Then again, maybe I hadn't succeeded. Deborah might never contact them, and I would have to send the detectives to talk to her.

If she called them, would she tell them about the short woman with the dark curly hair and blue eyes who had asked questions about Penny?

I hoped she wouldn't. She saw herself as a private investigator. Maybe she would resist providing information that might give me or anyone else credit for discovering evidence. With luck, she'd never know that I had tricked her into proving Penny's innocence.

As if he were a chauffeur, Brent opened the unmarked cruiser's passenger door for the DCI detective and then went around and got into the driver's seat. The car pulled away.

My father called from the kitchen, "Watermelon's ready!"

I backed into the house and closed and locked the door. Dep snuggled down into my arms. I carried her into the brightly lit kitchen and set her on the floor beside her food and water dishes.

My mother shoved a plate of juicy pink watermelon across the kitchen island's granite top toward me. "Don't look so sad, Emily. Brent will be back."

I eased onto a stool and slid a bite of watermelon onto my spoon. "I know, and I'm used to his needing to work at odd hours. But I hate not being with him."

My mother gave my father one of her special smiles. "I understand."

I tasted the watermelon. "You two are good at choosing watermelons."

My mother grinned. "We have experience. You're quiet, Walt. What's up?"

My father put down his spoon. "I've been thinking about what those detectives said. Something about an accident at a lumber mill. I heard about one earlier this week, but I didn't pay attention."

My mother brandished her spoon as if it were a flagpole holding a flag of triumph. "Let's look it up after we finish."

We took time to appreciate the watermelon and then cleared our dishes and started the dishwasher.

In the guest room, we squeezed past the unfolded sofa bed to the desk in front of the window. My father suggested, "Emily, you're probably quickest at working a computer. You sit down, and we'll stand behind you."

I turned on the computer. "You don't need to stand." I went across the hall to my bedroom and picked up the cute little chair I kept there. Back in the guest room, I plunked the chair next to the desk chair for my mother and suggested that my father could probably see if he sat on the edge of the bed behind us.

I found an article about a recent lumber mill accident. We read it together.

My mother asked me, "Do you think this is the accident the detectives were talking about?"

"It could be. The timing—over a week ago—seems about right, but the details don't agree with what Austin told me. He said that he had been a shift supervisor and had reported unsafe conditions to the company's owner. The foreman had contradicted Austin. However, Austin told me that the conditions continued to be unsafe, and there was an accident, so he quit." I pointed at the screen. "But according to this article, a shift supervisor's negligence caused the accident, and the shift supervisor was fired. Either Austin lied about why he no longer worked there, or his boss or the company's owner fabricated a story for the reporter."

My father asked, "Which do you think it was, Emily?"

I sighed. "Hard to tell. I thought that Austin was telling me the truth, but we tend to believe the first version we hear of a story. Also, Vic let slip that Austin has O-positive blood, and Quentin told us that the blood on his handkerchief was not the rarest type, and not Kirk's. Maybe the blood on the handkerchief was O-positive."

My mother said, "Like ours."

I heard a grin in my father's voice. "And we didn't confess to it."

My mother had a sassy answer. "They didn't ask."

I toyed with the keyboard. "Mine, too. I think Brent knows that. He and Vic might actually be concentrating on Austin. We can't trust anything Austin says, and I certainly won't be alone with him."

My mother teased, "I should hope not!"

It was getting late, and I was about to shut down the computer and go to bed, but a thought struck me. I asked my parents, "Did you see Kirk's business card? He left some of them on chairs before the Musical Monday show."

My mother looked at my father. "I didn't see one. Maybe

leaving his card at the judges' table was going too far, even for Kirk. Did you see any, Walt?"

"No."

I got up. "I think I left one in my backpack."

I found it, took it into the guest room, and then held it where my parents could read it.

My mother quoted, " 'He who pays the piper calls the tune.' Hmmm."

I sank into the desk chair again and turned it toward my parents, which was tricky in the small space, but I didn't think that any of our knees ended up permanently damaged. I told my folks, "Summer, Quentin, and I thought the words on Kirk's cards were lacking in originality. But did he have another reason for that motto? He must have wanted to spread the idea around. He left his cards on windshields and in and around the businesses where he played."

My mother guessed, "Maybe he was open to requests. I only ever heard him play three tunes."

My father agreed. "Me, too."

I admitted, "The only tune I recognized was 'My Bonnie Lies over the Ocean,' and that was because the audience sang along."

My father tapped the card with his thumbnail. "I also heard him play 'The Skye Boat Song.' What was the other one, Annie?"

"I can't quite place it." She hummed a few notes that I didn't recognize, and then she leaned toward the screen. "Some people believe that 'My Bonnie Lies over the Ocean' was about Bonnie Prince Charlie escaping to the Isle of Skye, and 'The Skye Boat Song' definitely had that connection. Could the third song that Kirk played be one of the many songs about Flora MacDonald? She was legendary for helping Bonnie Prince Charlie."

Behind me, my father stood up. "Can you find a list of bagpipe songs featuring Flora MacDonald, Emily?"

"Sure."

There were several. My father leaned over my shoulder and ran his finger down the screen. "Emily, can you play a recording of a bagpipe playing 'Flora MacDonald's Lament'?"

I turned up the sound and let the mournful harmonies wail into my guest room.

In the reflection from my screen, I saw my mother give my father a high five. "That's it!"

My father asked, "What do you think, Emily?"

I studied the image of the kilted man playing a bagpipe. "I don't know. I like bagpipe music, but it all sounds the same." I drummed my fingers on the desk. "Why did Kirk play those three tunes over and over again?"

My mother often saw the humorous side of things. "Maybe those were the only tunes he knew, and the motto has nothing to do with accepting money for playing requests."

My father guessed, "Maybe he was going to play those three tunes until someone paid the piper to play a larger assortment."

We all laughed. I shut down the computer, picked up Kirk's card and Dep, and went to bed.

Several hours later, in the pre-dawn, my tired mind nudged my father's guess into a slightly different theory.

Maybe Kirk had not been hinting that someone should pay him to enlarge his repertoire.

Maybe, instead, he had hoped to scare someone into paying him to stop playing the three tunes he'd been repeating all over town.

My phone announced, in much too sprightly a fashion, that it was time to get up. I muttered, "Extortion! Emily, your theories are far-fetched, and you're not awake, and you won't think clearly until you drink that first cup of coffee at Deputy Donut."

Unlike me, Dep was instantly awake and ready to start the morning.

Walking to work during another warm, sunny morning, I told myself that my extortion theory was ridiculous. Vic would sneer at it, and he'd be right. Kirk couldn't have been the first person to use an old saying as a motto on a business card.

Chapter 23

It was Saturday, Skit Saturday, and all four of us were working at Deputy Donut. Helping with the first batches of donuts for our morning customers and sipping the bold and invigorating goodness of the day's special coffee, a dark roast from Sumatra, I pictured the distant future when Brent and I were both retired, wearing comfy slippers and contentedly sipping coffee in front of a roaring fire.

Jocelyn teased me, "Emily, I can tell by the faraway look on your face that you're thinking about Brent."

Olivia spread orange frosting on fudge donuts. "And her wedding day. You must be excited."

I picked up a tray of pistachio cream–filled donuts. "I am."

Jocelyn thumped the rolling pin onto a ball of dough. "I can hardly wait."

At the fryers, Tom grinned as if he were the father of the bride, which, in a way, he was. Memories of Alec would always be a strong bond between us.

We had considered closing Deputy Donut on my wedding day since Tom, Olivia, and Jocelyn would all be attending, but the company catering our rehearsal dinner and reception had extra staff available, so we had hired them for the day of the wedding. *Only nine more days . . .* I slid the tray into the display case and turned to face the other three. "It's beginning to seem real."

Jocelyn's eyes twinkled. "What are you going to wear when you walk down the aisle, Emily?" She asked me that question nearly every day.

As always, I made a zipping motion across my mouth. "You mean down the forest path? Not telling."

Olivia joked, "A long white dress with a train so she can collect dead leaves and slimy snails on the way down the hill."

I picked up the tray that Olivia had finished frosting. "You got it."

Jocelyn suggested, "Jeans and a T-shirt."

Tom shook a basket of sizzling donuts above the oil. "She'll be dressier than that. She'll wear her Deputy Donut uniform and hat. Probably the long pants like we wear in the winter instead of shorts. Long pants are more formal."

Jocelyn put on a fake serious face. "But with sneakers."

I agreed. "Sneakers forever."

Olivia tilted her head. "But what will Brent wear?"

I opened the display case. "That's easy. I'll be in black and white, so he'll wear a tux."

Jocelyn turned to Olivia. "Did you hear that? She's admitted she's wearing black and white."

I slid the tray into the case. "Tom's the one who guessed I was wearing a Deputy Donut uniform."

In dark and forbidding tones, Jocelyn threatened, "I'm going across the driveway to Thrills and Frills. I'll force Madame Monique to tell me if you asked for a veil to hang from your Deputy Donut cap."

Laughing at the image, I told them, "Now that you've guessed what my entire outfit will be, I'd better warn you to make donuts shaped and decorated like flowers and put them together for my bouquet."

Jocelyn snapped her fingers. "With tons of frosting, so that whoever catches it will have to be careful."

Pretending horror, Olivia backed away. "I'm not going to try to catch it."

Jocelyn muttered loudly enough for all of us to hear, "Someone might accidentally bat icing flowers into your hair."

Tom chimed in, "No problem. There's a lake right there. You can dive in."

I made an exaggerated frown. "No frosting allowed in that crystal-clear lake."

Customers began arriving, and the four of us acted more decorously, but even though the Knitpickers and retired men didn't come in on weekends, they had helped set a happy and comradely tone that spilled over when they weren't there.

About halfway through the morning, Ed, the server from the Fireplug, came in. He looked surprised at the noisy bantering of our customers with one another and with us. He put on a game-looking grin, found a table, and sat down. As far as I knew, he'd never been inside Deputy Donut before Wednesday morning, when he'd complained that Kirk's theft of his charge cards had prevented him from buying an engagement ring in time for his proposal, and now he was back, the second time in one week. I asked what he'd like.

"Just that normal coffee you brought me last time."

"Medium-roast Colombian. It's really good."

"That's what I thought."

I poured it and set the fragrant, steaming mug in front of him.

He thanked me. "You know, you're good at giving advice, and not just about coffee. You said I should give my girl some time and bring her the ring, and she'd come around."

I couldn't help a big smile. "Did it work?"

He spooned sugar into his coffee. "Not yet, but I'm not giving up. I'm going to choose a ring and try again. The police found my wallet and charge cards in that bagpiper's van, but not my phone or the money from my wallet."

Not wanting to admit that the police had already told me that, I simply nodded.

Ed went on, "Anyway, you're not to think that the thieving bagpiper ruined my life—far from it. For one thing, the police pointed out that Kirk might not have been the person who put those things in his van. I was just kind of depressed when I was in here last time and ready to blame anyone, you know?"

I said, "I know." I couldn't help wondering what had mellowed him. Maybe it had been time, as he seemed to want me to believe. Or maybe he didn't want anyone suspecting that he had killed Kirk. Trying not to look like I suspected I could be talking to a murderer, I added, "I wonder what made Kirk think it was okay to steal from people."

Ed poured cream into his coffee. "I don't know. It wasn't like he didn't have a job. He was the high school janitor. He didn't have to go around stealing or trying to make money from screeching on those bagpipes."

"It seemed to me that he kept playing the same songs over and over again."

Ed stopped pouring the cream a half second before his mug would have overflowed. "I wouldn't know. They all sound like train wrecks to me."

"It wasn't very original, like what he wrote on his business card."

"What was that?"

Hoping that no one else in the shop, especially Tom, Jocelyn, and Olivia, would realize that I was perhaps being too inquisitive around a possible murder suspect, I asked as innocently as I could manage, "Didn't you see what was on it?"

Ed flushed. "I never saw his card."

I knew I should drop the subject, but I couldn't help prodding, "He left one on a table in the Fireplug. I think you put it into your pocket with the tip he left."

"Did I? I don't remember." Ed's flush subsided. "Oh, wait. I can guess what happened. If anyone puts advertising in the pub without asking, we discard it. So, I must have stuck it into my pocket to throw out later, but I think I forgot." He toyed with his spoon. "It must've ended up as dryer lint. In fact, I'm sure it did. I found paper crumbs. What was on it?"

"Just an old saying. 'He who pays the piper calls the tune.' Not very original."

"It doesn't make sense, either, but he must've thought it was clever." Looking down, he stirred his coffee. Not much sloshed onto the table. "There's just no understanding some people."

I agreed and asked if I could get him anything else.

"No, I'll just drink this and head on to work. It's going to be a long day. Hey, aren't you supposed to be helping at tonight's big party, too? I'm tending the bar."

"Yes. Jocelyn and I will serve donuts and other treats."

"See you there, then."

I checked on other customers, and the next time I looked toward Ed's table, he had gone.

Chapter 24

✺

Shortly after lunch, Cindy arrived, blew a kiss to Tom, and told us, "The neighbor girls have had so much fun performing that they've worked up another act. I dropped them off at their first stop, and now I can sit on your patio to watch today's skits."

I suggested, "You could sit inside in the air-conditioning again."

"It's not as humid today, and besides, I'd like to record them on my phone for their parents." She bit her lip. "I hope their skit goes well. They came up with it really quickly."

I went outside with her. It was early enough that many of our tables, all of them shaded from the early afternoon sun, were still available. She chose a spot where she'd have an unobstructed view of the sidewalk and the acts.

I asked her, "Would you like iced coffee or tea today? Another *affogato*?"

"I'm hungry for one of your chocolate donuts with vanilla frosting."

"Today, we're topping some of those with fresh raspberries, if you'd like."

"I'd like. An iced mocha should go well with that." She held up two fingers. "Actually, make it two of those donuts."

I brought her the coffee and donuts. The only other people on the patio were talking and laughing. I quietly asked Cindy, "Do you know if there's to be a funeral for Kirk? I haven't seen an obituary."

She pulled her plate closer. "There won't be one here. I think his ashes will be sent to his sister in Chicago."

"Is that where he lived before he moved here?"

"I think so."

Deborah had said that Penny moved to Fallingbrook from Chicago. Did Penny and Kirk have a shared history that Penny had avoided telling me about? Cindy wouldn't know the answer to that, but she might know the answer to my next question. "Could Kirk have met Lisa-Ruth Schomoset in Chicago?"

Cindy looked startled. "I don't know where Lisa-Ruth lived before. She's been here about five years, and he only moved here at the beginning of the school year. What makes you think Lisa-Ruth and Kirk could have known each other before?"

I straightened the placemat across the table from Cindy. "I wondered if Kirk had a longstanding grudge against Lisa-Ruth, something that caused him to make it look like she had stolen money."

"Not that I know of, but I wasn't present when they were first introduced, so I can't be sure. She's awkward around adults, but her students think she's fantastic. She's helped many of them get into music programs in college. She really knows her field, and they love learning from her. You don't suspect Lisa-Ruth of murdering him, do you, Emily?"

"I was just wondering if she might have wanted revenge for that stunt with the money. In any case, I'm guessing that she didn't take a mug from the table here on Tuesday. I think Kirk might have grabbed it from her table after we all turned our backs."

"That would have required some quick work in the middle

of playing a bagpipe, but I don't think Lisa-Ruth took it, so who else could have?" She didn't seem to require an answer. She went on, "She emailed the kids' parents and some of us teachers a link of the video she'd taken with her phone. You and I thought she could have put the mug into her bag, but it was probably her phone." Naturally, Cindy reminded me, "But leave the investigating to the police, Emily. Talk to Brent. Will you be seeing him soon?"

"I hope so. Maybe he'll make it to tonight's show." I glanced down Wisconsin Street. "I think the first group of touring actors is on its way. I'd better take some more orders."

Cindy reached for her spoon. "I hope you can make it outside in time to see Tom's and my neighbor kids."

"I hope so, too, but we have to make lots of donuts for tonight's gala."

By the time I'd taken orders for customers at another table and brought them their treats, a pair of teen boys were staging a swordfight on the sidewalk while a distressed damsel in a flowing gown flapped her hands in an apparent attempt to stop them. The swords looked almost real but sounded and flexed like they were made of rubber. After some realistic—if you discounted the swords' floppiness—fight choreography, the damsel stepped in, knocked both swords to the sidewalk, grabbed one of the boys by the hand, and dragged him away like a prized possession. The other boy grinned at the audience and made an exaggerated shrug that seamlessly turned into a courtly bow. He picked up both swords. Brandishing one in each hand, he followed the other two toward the Fireplug. We all clapped.

Olivia, Jocelyn, and I took over the donut making and decorating and sent Tom out to watch the skits with Cindy.

Their four neighbor girls had signed up late for Skit Saturday, and they were the last performers on that afternoon's schedule. Figuring that we could take a break from making donuts and donut holes for that night's gala, Jocelyn, Olivia, and I slipped out onto the patio.

Oinking and snorting, the three smallest girls lugged their cardboard carton cauldron to the sidewalk in front of Deputy Donut. They were wearing pink shirts and shorts, pink pinned-on curly construction-paper tails, pink construction-paper ears fastened to headbands, and rubber piggy snouts. Since portraying the three weird sisters from Macbeth, they'd painted higher, brighter flames curling around the cauldron painted on their carton.

They set the carton on the sidewalk and reached inside.

The tallest girl, dressed head-to-toe in shaggy fake fur and sporting a bushy gray tail, pointed wolflike ears, and drawn-on whiskers and nose, stalked with menacing growls toward the three little piggies.

The smallest girl pulled a ribbon-tied bundle of drinking straws out of the carton. With a big smile, she stood facing us and holding the bundle above her head.

The next-smallest girl held two sticks in a rooflike angle over her head.

The biggest of the three little piggies pulled a brick out of the carton and held it over her head.

Snarling and slashing at the air with her mittened hands, the "wolf" pranced to the girl with the straws. The wolf huffed and puffed, and the straws, still tied in their bundle, fell from the littlest piggy's hands. She ran to the next girl and helped hold up the two-stick roof.

With great drama, the wolf blew the sticks down. The two girls ran to the third girl and helped hold up the brick.

The wolf huffed and puffed to no effect while the three little piggies giggled and oinked.

The wolf made climbing motions and then seemed to accidentally claw the cardboard cauldron onto its side and topple into it.

In obvious glee, the three little piggies danced around the fake fire and the cauldron containing the fallen wolf.

The wolf crawled out of the carton, and all four of the girls bowed to the audience. The three smallest girls set the carton upright, thrust the bundle of straws, the sticks, and the brick into it, and dragged it toward the Fireplug. The wolf slunk after them.

On the patio, we cheered and applauded until the four girls would no longer be able to hear us.

Cindy gathered her things. "I'll go meet the girls at Frisky Pomegranate and take them home."

"Why do I get the feeling that you're helping the oldest girl look after the others all summer?"

"I keep a benevolent and mostly non-interfering eye on them, and they know they can call on me if they need anything while their parents are at work, but other than driving them places from time to time and letting them play with pottery and other art projects, I don't do much."

I hugged her. "You're a wonder."

"Not really. They're all creative and a joy to be around, so the time I spend with them does more for me than it does for them."

Tom and I looked at each other, and then nodded. I offered, "Would you like to bring them all to Deputy Donut sometime? We'll give them a cooking lesson or donuts to decorate."

Tom added, "We wouldn't let them near the deep fryers."

Cindy shouldered her bag. "That would be fun. I'll run the idea past their parents. I know they'll like it. And the girls will, too."

She strode up the street toward the Fireplug, where the oldest girl, the actual babysitter, appeared to be capering, in full huff-and-puff mode, around the little piggies.

After all of our customers left, Tom, Jocelyn, Olivia, and I cleared the patio tables. Inside, we moved the OPEN sign in our front door to COME BACK TOMORROW and locked the front door. We gathered everything that Jocelyn and I would need to take to the gala later that night after the Skit Saturday show, and then we got the shop ready for the Jolly Cops.

When we finished, Tom wished Jocelyn and me good luck with the gala and reminded us, "Olivia and I will open the shop in the morning, and you two can come in later, after you get a good night's sleep."

Jocelyn gave him a big smile. "Thanks, but it'll be fun. And the party is supposed to end at nine thirty. We should be back here by ten, and it won't take us long to clean up and put everything away."

We thanked one another, and I started walking home with Dep.

A block from my house, a black SUV pulled up beside us.

Chapter 25

❧

It was Brent's own car, which might have meant that he wasn't on duty, but he got out, and I could see that he was dressed for work, in a gray suit, white shirt, and navy tie. He came around the front of the car. "I hoped I'd find you." He strode to me, wrapped me in a bear hug, and murmured into my hair. "I've missed you."

My broad smile matching his, I looked up at him. "I've missed you, too."

Dep wound her leash around our ankles. "Mew."

Laughing, I bent and untangled us. "Dep, honey, today's not the day we tie the knot." I picked her up and gazed into Brent's amused eyes. "Can you come to dinner?"

"Sorry, no. I'm expected back at the office, but I needed to talk to you."

I inadvertently tightened my hands around Dep. "My . . . parents?" My voice came out barely above a whisper.

Brent quickly shook his head. "Nothing to do with them." He gave my upper arm a comforting squeeze. "Sorry for worrying you. As far as I know, they're fine, and they're not high on Vic's list of suspects. Don't worry about that. I just wanted to tell you who is and who isn't on Vic's list. I should say our list." Tiny dinosaurs were woven into his tie.

I loved this man. In nine days, I was going to marry him. I

couldn't keep secrets from him or lie to him. I managed a pained, "I'm sorry."

He merely smiled down at me. "For what?"

"I went and talked to the woman who lives across the road from Penny O'Lander."

"You did?"

My fast heartbeats must have bothered Dep. She wriggled. I clutched her tighter and explained, "I told Deborah to call the police, and she seemed eager to have Penny, and maybe Tiffany, too, arrested. She said she would call you."

"She did, but she didn't tell us about you."

I gave him a wan smile. I'd guessed correctly that Deborah might leave me out of what she believed was her independent crime-solving. I apologized again. "I probably shouldn't have gone out there, but I thought I might be able to give Deborah a nudge that would help Penny."

"I wish you'd let me handle it. There are only those three houses on that stretch of road, and when Frisky Pomegranate's open, Deborah is the only person around."

"I didn't realize that when I went out there, but I was pretty sure from the way that Penny described Deborah that Deborah was eccentric, but not dangerous, at least not to me."

"Did you think you would be better at tricking Deborah into telling the truth than I would be?" His smile took the sting from his words.

"Encouraging, not tricking. And I know you could have let Deborah set a trap for herself and fall into it. But Vic? Also, I wasn't even sure that I would succeed in meeting Deborah or getting her to do anything. I thought I might be going for a short drive in the country, but it all worked out. She told me she knows exactly when Penny comes and goes because she keeps a spreadsheet."

Brent's mouth twitched. "She showed it to me. It's extensive. Vic didn't think that both of us needed to go to the initial interview with Deborah. I went by myself, and Vic was right. One detective was enough, though I think she might have preferred a larger audience."

"If I were Penny, I'd move away. Oh, right. She is. Tiffany should, too. Deborah is kind of creepy and overzealous."

"I agree. After I talked to Deborah, I looked into Penny's husband's death. It was ruled as natural causes. Penny was away from him for eleven hours that day, and he died about eight hours after she left. They ate lunch together, and he did the dishes—his fingerprints were on the dishes in the drainer. He was older than Penny, and retired. He usually took afternoon naps. That day, he didn't wake up."

"I'm glad to hear that a woman who serves food to the public is not a murderer."

"Always good to know. Another person we've cleared is Summer's young friend, Quentin Admiral. The murderer used Quentin's handkerchief to sop up his own blood from a scratch Kirk made while defending himself with a Frisky Pomegranate knife."

"So, you need to find someone with a scratch, someone whose fingerprints might be on the knife from Frisky Pomegranate, unless he used Quentin's handkerchief to wipe prints off the knife."

Brent's smile broadened. "You got it. And it's very likely someone with O-positive blood. Not Quentin and not Penny."

"But it could be . . . who? My parents? Me? You?"

"We're not suspected. At least, not by me."

"Uh-oh, Brent. There's a problem with the handkerchief theory."

"What?"

I had a feeling he'd already thought of it. "Would a murderer leave a handkerchief stained with his own blood at a scene?"

"It's been known to happen. Maybe the killer expected the rain to wash away all of the blood. He might have even moved Kirk's arm accidentally, covering most of the handkerchief."

I repeated "the killer." Shuddering, I changed the subject slightly. "You said you wanted to tell me who is still on your list."

"It's possible that the murderer is not yet on our radar. But I need you to stay away from two people you mentioned—Ed Ellbonder, the server at the Fireplug, and Austin Berwin, the man who was driving around in the vicinity after Kirk ran through your parking lot toward his van, where someone apparently caught up with him and killed him."

"Does either of them have a wound that could have been made by a Frisky Pomegranate knife?"

"We are not yet doing body searches."

"I've never seen Austin in a short-sleeved shirt, but Ed was wearing one on Monday evening. Ever since then, when I've seen him, he's worn a long-sleeved shirt."

Brent took out his notebook, wrote in it, and then told me, "One thing about Austin. He was telling the truth about his job. The company owner has since realized that Austin's whistleblowing was right. The foreman was the one who created the unsafe conditions, and that man has since been fired."

"Where was that foreman early Wednesday morning?"

"At a party in Gooseleg." Brent thrust the notebook into a pocket. "So, although we don't know who actually killed Kirk, and it might not have been either Austin or Ed, I need you to keep your distance from them, and don't ask them questions about Wednesday morning."

"Ed and I are both working at the party tonight." Dep's purring vibrated against me.

"You won't be alone with him, will you?"

"There should be a crowd, and Jocelyn will be with me. Is there any possibility that you'll be there?"

He leaned down and kissed my forehead. "I wish I could. And now that I've said what I needed to say, I should let you go. It sounds like you have a busy evening ahead."

"You might, too. I hope you can clear this up soon so we can relax and have fun just thinking about our wedding."

He winked. "I think about it often. And don't worry, I've already packed for our trip, and I won't miss any of the events we've planned. Again, let me know if you need me to do anything. After all, Vic is in charge of this investigation."

"You already did a lot. Everything's under control."

He gave me another bear hug. Dep, too, since she was still in my arms. He turned toward his SUV.

I reached out and clutched at his jacket sleeve. "Wait."

He faced me, a question in his eyes.

I asked, "Do you know what kind of car Deborah drives?"

"Why?"

"I'll be disappointed if it's a new one."

He laughed. "I understand why. Did you see inside her house?"

"No, but her outfit provided clues about her favorite time period. What's the inside of her house like?"

"It's a perfectly preserved museum of furniture and décor from around 1955."

I couldn't help laughing. "I'm not surprised."

"What car do you picture her driving?"

"Something like a 1958 Mercury with lots of gold and shiny things."

He accused, "You've seen her in it."

I shook my head. "Not that I can remember."

"She doesn't drive it much, but you're right. After I talked to her, I looked up her car license details. She owns a two-toned bronze and tan 1958 Mercury Turnpike Cruiser. They had lots of chrome and that concave panel along the rear fins."

I confessed, "I wanted to peek into her garage."

He threw back his head and laughed. "So did I. Maybe someday she'll show us the car."

"You'd have to arrest Penny for at least two murders and give Deborah credit for solving the cases before she might be willing to do that, and I don't need to see her car that badly."

He kissed me again, rubbed Dep's head, and turned toward his SUV.

Hugging Dep, I watched him drive away.

Chapter 26

✿

Knowing that we could enjoy lots of snacks at the party later that evening, my parents had made us a light dinner—a salad of fresh tomatoes, cucumbers, and feta with an olive oil and herb dressing. We finished quickly and headed toward the front door.

Dep made it clear that she wanted to go with us. I picked her up. "Sorry, Dep, but I don't think you'd like either the show or the Fallingbrook Arts Festival's wrap-up gala."

Dep bopped her head against my chin. I held her while my parents edged through a narrow gap between the door and the jamb, then I set the wiggly cat down and prevented her from following me. Running down the porch steps, I heard an indignant yowl. I felt sorry for my cute little kitty, but she was so expressive that I had to smile.

At Wisconsin Street, when we were about to turn north, Summer strode toward us from the south. I thought she hesitated, almost as if she didn't want us to see her. Maybe she thought I still believed that Quentin could have been guilty of murder. Sometimes I was no better at hiding my emotions than Dep was.

My parents stopped walking, which made it clear that we were waiting for Summer, and she started across Maple Street toward us.

My mother called, "Summer! How wonderful to run into you. Let's try to find seats together at the show."

I smiled and nodded encouragement.

Summer caught up to us. "I'm hoping to meet Quentin there."

My mother linked her arm with my father's. "The more, the merrier. I like that talented young man." She and my father started toward the square again, forcing Summer and me to walk together.

I looked up at her. She stared straight ahead.

Hoping I hadn't destroyed our friendship by not quite trusting her protégé, I told her, "I'm sorry for acting suspicious of Quentin. I never really believed he was guilty, but I was keeping an open mind. Brent told me he's cleared Quentin."

She looked down at me, and her smile seemed to be her usual friendly one. "I understand, and I'm sure you weren't the only one who noticed Quentin's anger at coming in second. But I know him. His anger doesn't last long, and he wouldn't kill someone over a little thing like that. He wouldn't kill anyone, period. Also, his parents' cabin is even smaller than ours. They knew Quentin didn't go out that night, and they told the police that, too." Her musical laugh boomed out. "Your handsome detective will always be my hero. Have the police arrested someone?"

"Not that I know of."

She made a pretense of checking over her shoulder, and then she whispered dramatically, "So, the murderer is still among us . . ."

"Or a thousand miles away."

"Let's hope so!"

We found seats near the front of the audience. Moments before the first skit began, Quentin folded himself into the chair that Summer had saved for him. The performances didn't involve music, but he and my parents seemed to enjoy them anyway, especially the three cute piggies and the almost as cute wolf.

I had to leave before the Skit Saturday show was over. Apologizing, I slipped out of my seat. I hurried south along paths through the almost deserted square. Nearly everyone in town was near the bandstand.

At Deputy Donut, Jocelyn had already chained her bike to the stand beside the back steps. I pulled our 1950 Ford delivery car out of its garage and parked it near our loading dock. Jocelyn and I packed the car with everything we expected to need at the gala.

Jocelyn loved driving that car, so I climbed into the passenger seat, fastened the seat belt that had been added long after the car was manufactured, and let Jocelyn drive the short blocks to the fire station. Its overhead doors were rolled up, and the fire trucks had been removed from the vast indoor space. They were farther east, along the street.

Inside the hall, people were arranging food on tables near the walls. Scott and a couple of his firefighters helped take our things to the table reserved for us. It was in a back corner, perpendicular to the table set up as a bar. Ed turned around from setting beer cups on shelves behind the makeshift bar and waved to us. He was again wearing a white, long-sleeved shirt without a Fireplug logo.

After everything we'd brought for the gala was on our table and on the shelves behind it, I asked Jocelyn if she'd prefer to return our delivery car to Deputy Donut or start setting up. Jocelyn should be safe out there. Ed would probably stay in the firehall, and even if Austin showed up between here and Deputy Donut, Jocelyn wouldn't be alone with him. The show in the north end of the square had attracted a large audience, but the streets and sidewalks wouldn't be totally empty at this time of evening. Besides, it was still fully light.

Jocelyn pulled the Ford's keys out of her pocket. "I'd love to drive it again. I won't be long." She strode toward the car.

I taped a Deputy Donut banner to the part of the white tablecloth hanging over the front of the table, and then I settled my Deputy Donut hat onto my curls and tied on an apron. I arranged our urn of fresh Colombian coffee, cups, packets of sweeteners, and creamers on the end of the table closest to Ed's bar and set paper plates and napkins on the other end.

Finally, I was ready for the fun part. Wearing new food-handlers' gloves, I set out three large wooden platters that were actually slices of tree trunks with the bark still on the edges. Next, I filled small bowls with peanut brittle, home-made fudge, caramels, and nuts, and placed them on the boards with spaces between them. We'd brought double fudge donuts, raised donuts with vanilla frosting, old-fashioned donuts with butterscotch frosting, raised donuts frosted in pink strawberry frosting and liberally dusted with multicolored sprinkles, and mini-donuts and donut holes in nearly every flavor we'd made that day. I filled the spots between the bowls with fresh donuts, and then scattered orange segments, strawberries, and blueberries over the donuts. Last, I sprinkled candied orange peels and violets over everything else. The boards were covered with goodies.

I walked to the front of the table and gazed at my creations.

Ed came from his bar and pointed at the platters. "Those are too pretty to eat."

"Help yourself. We brought lots. We can fill in the spaces."

Smiling, he backed away. "I'm not going to be the first to ruin it. I'll leave that to our guests." He retreated behind his bar.

Wearing her Deputy Donut hat, Jocelyn rushed to me. "The Skit Saturday show is over, and people are heading this way." She looked down at our table. "Wow, Emily, I'm glad I took the car back and left you to do the artistic stuff. Those are perfect!" She handed me the car keys. "I put the donut car into its garage."

I thanked her, and we went behind the table. Jocelyn put on a Deputy Donut apron. The firefighters had kindly set up folding chairs for us, but we didn't have time to sit down. The three little pigs and the big bad wolf galloped to our table. The littlest pig shouted, "We won third prize!" The other three girls shushed her, but all of them were smiling. Their parents helped the girls choose mini-donuts, nuts, fruit, and one piece of candy each and then steered them toward the front of the hall. One of the mothers told the girls, "It's almost bedtime. Eat up so we can go home."

Although we were in the back of the hall, people crowded around our table.

Jocelyn murmured to me, "I hope we brought enough."

"I'm sure we did. Would you like to wander around and find whatever you want to eat?"

"Okay. Shall I bring you a plate of food, or would you rather take a turn around the hall yourself?"

"I'll wait for you to come back, and then I'll go."

"I'll try to leave you something." She pointed at her hat. "We'll be walking advertisements."

While she was socializing and trying the offerings from other participants, Quentin and Summer came to the Deputy Donut table. Quentin bit into a gooey double fudge donut. "Maybe I shouldn't have let myself be tempted by this, Emily. When we're at the lake, my folks and I seldom leave except when we need groceries. Summer's been telling us about the great shops in town, but, except for this festival, I usually just chill out at the lake. I obviously have to visit Deputy Donut."

I suggested, "And bring your parents."

"I will if I can get them out of their kayaks or their chairs on the deck. They take stacks of books out there."

I handed him a napkin. "I've been to Summer's parents'

place on Deepwish Lake. I can understand not wanting to leave. The woods and the lake are gorgeous and can be calming." On one occasion, they'd been far from calming, but I thrust those memories away and suggested, "If you come into town when Deputy Donut is open, come in for donuts to take back to your folks."

"Okay." He glanced at my left hand and grinned. "Now how many days is it until your wedding?"

"Nine. It's a week from Monday, at Chicory Lake, where Brent lives, about a half hour north of here."

Quentin gripped his paper plate in both hands like an earnest boy. "I've been thinking, and I don't want to pressure you, so if you don't like my idea, just tell me. I don't know what music you've planned, but I'd like to compose and play a fanfare for you. It could be as you come down the aisle or when you walk back up. Or during your reception, or anything. I'm not inviting myself to the celebration. It's just something I'd like to do."

I was touched. Hand over heart, I answered, "I'd love that."

He asked, "Would your fiancé, though?"

"I'm sure he would."

"Tell me about the music you've already planned."

I listed the music that Brent and I, consulting with the string quartet who would play it, had chosen. I added, "The 'aisle' I'll be walking down and back up is actually a wooded pathway between Brent's home on the hill and the shore. The ceremony will be in a tent on the shore, and the reception in a tent on the lawn higher up."

Quentin's quick smile lit his face. "Perfect! What do you think, Summer?" Raising one eyebrow, he made motions with his arms as if paddling a canoe or a kayak.

Summer's eyes sparkled. "I agree." She turned to me. "He's really good. Not only at playing but at composing, too."

I smiled back. "I don't doubt it. I'll talk to Brent. He might have more ideas."

Summer turned her head toward the south, as if she could see Deepwish Lake. "I know what. See if you can drag him away from work some evening, come to my parents' place, bring your kayaks, and you can both talk to Quentin there."

"We'd love that! Maybe, if Brent can make it, we can aim for a few days from now, to give Quentin enough time."

Quentin had been quietly humming. "I've got some ideas. I'll head back to the lake to start putting them together. See you later." He strode away.

Summer watched him weave through the crowd toward the open door. "He's like that. He gets something into his head, like a string of notes, and he has to rush off and work on the rest of the melody. I'm going to leave, too, but I'm not going to the lake, not at this time of night. Our driveway is still tricky in the dark." She started toward the front of the building.

Jocelyn returned and helped other people select donuts from our boards.

My parents joined us, and I decided to tour the hall with them. I took off my apron, but left my Deputy Donut hat on.

Tasting delicious snacks, my parents and I wandered through the gala together. Between the three of us, we knew almost everyone, and we spent time discussing the success of the festival and the many different treats we were eating.

At the open doorways, my mother gave me a peck on the cheek. "We'll go now. The temperature is perfect for a stroll to your place, Emily." Except for a slight glow toward the west, the sky was now dark, and stars were beginning to show.

I glanced back at the big clock high on the fire station's back wall. "The party's due to end in about a half hour. I'll see you at home after the guests leave and Jocelyn and I take everything back to Deputy Donut. But don't feel you have to wait up for me."

My father patted a hand over a pretend yawn. "We might not. It's been a long week for old folks."

My mother teased, "Speak for yourself."

Holding hands, they started west along Oak Street.

I was about to go inside when I noticed a man standing in the shadows between trees in the square across the street. He seemed to be watching my parents, but then he turned and must have noticed me staring at him.

Austin Berwin.

He started toward me.

Chapter 27

✼

Halfway across Oak Street, Austin pointed toward the fire station. "What's going on?"

I glanced over my shoulder. The firehall was welcoming, with its huge overhead doors open, its interior brightly lit, and more than fifty people inside laughing, talking, and carrying drinks or plates of food. Best of all, those people were near me, almost as close as Austin was. I faced him again. "It's the final gala for the Fallingbrook Arts Festival."

"Is it open to everyone?"

"Sure. It's winding down, though, and there's probably not much food left. But come in."

"I didn't participate in the festival, so maybe I shouldn't."

"Sorry for not making the food sound appetizing. Everything's good. A half hour ago, our Deputy Donut table still had lots of donuts and other treats. We don't want leftovers."

He stared toward the interior of the firehall as if searching for someone in particular. Finally, he shook his head. "I guess I won't. I love your donuts and coffee, but I'll come to Deputy Donut for them." His smile seeming far from sincere, he added, "Sometime when I'm really hungry."

He angled across Oak Street and headed toward Wisconsin Street.

The direction that my parents had gone.

Austin had to have guessed, after my questions about where he'd been driving early Wednesday morning, that I could suspect him of murder.

While he'd been lurking among trees in the square, had he seen me with my parents? Had he guessed they were people I might care strongly about?

And had he noticed them turning south down Wisconsin Street?

Standing on the sidewalk in front of the firehall's parking apron, I watched him. At Wisconsin Street, he hesitated and peered south. My heart thudded. I considered following him to make certain he was not chasing my parents. *Stay away from him.* I pulled my phone out of my pocket.

Austin turned his head toward me. I stepped back toward the firehall, but not in time. He waved.

In an attempt to hide my phone, I held it close to my hip while I waved back with my free hand.

To my relief, Austin headed north.

My relief ebbed. He had come from the square, which was north of the fire station, and now he was again heading north.

I tried to convince myself that the lights and sounds from the gala had caused him to detour south to see what was going on, and he was merely returning to wherever he'd been going in the first place.

But what if he merely walked north to the next street, turned west, and then walked—or drove—south through the parking lots where I wouldn't be able to see him?

He might end up close to my parents. Already, trees in the square hid him from me.

I texted my father that a man might be following him and my mother, and that the man could be on foot or driving a burgundy Honda Civic. I urged them to avoid him, hurry to my place, and lock themselves inside.

I called Brent and told him where I was, approximately where my parents were, and that Austin Berwin could be stalking them.

Brent asked, "Are you sure he's not following you?"

"I'm at the firehall with plenty of other people around. The party's scheduled to end in less than a half hour. Jocelyn and I will stay together until we finish putting everything away in Deputy Donut, and then we'll walk together to the corner where we usually part company. My parents should be safely locked inside my place by then."

"I'll send a patrol car out to have a look around. Misty and Hooligan are on duty tonight."

"Thanks, Brent. It's possibly nothing, but . . ."

"It's better to call than not. And I'm here at the police station, almost right next door to where you are now. Would you like me to come over?"

I smiled. "Of course I would like that, but it's not necessary. Austin will be long gone by the time Jocelyn and I leave the firehall."

"He should be." Brent's tone of voice was a reminder that Austin could still come to the party. Which wouldn't be surprising, since I had invited him. He had turned me down, but what if he changed his mind?

I told Brent, "I'll call you if I need you."

"Or call emergency."

"Okay. Good night, Brent."

I could barely hear Brent's reply over the chatter of a group leaving the gala. One of the women's high heels rang out on the concrete.

I sent another text to my father to let him know that Misty and Hooligan might cruise past to keep an eye on my parents.

My father replied that no one seemed to be following them. They'd soon be locked inside with Dep and a pot of herbal tea.

I pocketed my phone and wended my way to the back corner of the hall.

Jocelyn had moved from behind our table to beside it, next to the Fireplug's temporary bar. Arms folded, Ed was leaning against a wall, smiling and talking to her.

Maybe I should have told Jocelyn that Brent had warned me to stay away from Ed.

I told myself to calm down. Jocelyn was not alone with Ed, and although people had begun leaving, there were still at least forty people in the firehall, including Scott and his fit and muscular firefighters. Besides, only moments ago, I'd been trying to protect my parents from Austin. It wasn't likely that both Ed and Austin were dangerous, and it was possible that neither of them was.

Jocelyn was probably perfectly safe.

Probably.

Instead of stopping to talk to more people, I joined her and Ed between our table and the bar.

The Deputy Donut table had been more popular than we expected, and we were running out of treats. Jocelyn asked me, "Should I go back for more?"

I didn't want her roaming around outside alone where Austin Berwin might be, but I only said with more nonchalance than I felt, "The party's nearly over. Let's hope we run out completely. We'll have less to carry back."

Jocelyn looked toward the open doorways. "I could get the car. We can take things back in it."

"I think we can carry everything."

She gave me an assessing look, but said only, "I should attach a huge basket to my bike for times like this."

I laughed. "Hardly necessary. We'll get the donut car if we need it." I glanced at Ed. "Did Harold get a delivery bike for the Fireplug yet? I haven't seen you riding around town on one."

My question must have embarrassed Ed. He blushed and

mumbled, "It was something more fun than a bike, and I was going to get to operate it."

Jocelyn, who biked all over town, cocked her head up at him. "What could be more fun than a bike?"

Ed shuffled his feet. "I do my bike-riding at the gym."

Jocelyn persisted. "What was Harold going to get? A motorcycle? A toy tractor?"

Ed's face reddened more. "I'm not supposed to tell. Anyway, I don't know when we're getting it or if we are. I mean, it's not like we can't use his van to deliver things."

I asked, "Is that how you brought your kegs and beer cups here tonight?"

Ed pointed at a substantial hand truck in the corner between our two tables. "I used that dolly and brought things through the parking lot from our back door to the back door here."

Maybe Ed was embarrassed, afraid that Harold thought he was incapable of operating the delivery vehicle. I was picturing an electric scooter or a tiny van. I thought that Ed might retreat behind his own table again, but he stayed nearby and watched Jocelyn and me consolidate the contents of the three donut platters onto two. We put the third platter on the shelf with our emptied bakery boxes and food containers.

Mr. Wordsworth, the high school English teacher who had helped judge that evening's Skit Saturday show and the Theatrical Thursday show, stared down at the two remaining donut platters as if trying to decide what to choose, and then he lifted his face and gazed at the fuzzy donuts on the fronts of Jocelyn's and my Deputy Donut hats. "Are you two responsible for this table?" Did he always speak like a stern schoolteacher?

I smiled. "Yes. Help yourself."

Instead of trying any of the goodies on our two remaining platters, he pointed a forefinger at them. "Presentation is everything. I'd have to give you only a C-plus on this. Those wooden planks do not look sanitary. Why did you use them instead of stainless steel that you can sanitize in steamy, soapy water?"

I answered. "These don't look it, but they're sealed and completely washable. Donut charcuterie boards are the latest rage in serving donuts."

Mr. Wordsworth's face turned purple, and his eyes bulged as if he were about to choke. "Charcuterie? For your information, charcuterie is the French word for cold cuts or a store selling them. I don't see any meat on these boards, not that I would find the combination appetizing."

Jocelyn contemplated the platters in dismay so dramatic she could have won a ribbon in the Skit Saturday show. "Oh, dear, our maple-bacon donuts must have been too popular. We seem to have run out of them."

She knew as well as I did that we hadn't brought any maple-bacon donuts to the party.

Gulping down a laugh, I stood as tall as I could, which made me as tall as Jocelyn, a little shorter than Mr. Wordsworth, and still a lot shorter than Ed. I suggested, "Maybe we should call them 'donuterie boards.' "

Mr. Wordsworth's eyes opened wider and bulged even more. "Nudery?"

I faked an apologetic expression. "I guess we'd have to pronounce it 'donuttery'."

Jocelyn muttered out the side of her mouth, "Get thee to a nuttery."

Mr. Wordsworth did not, apparently, hear her, which was just as well. He stabbed an index finger downward. "One of your platters has bare spots."

I opened my mouth and closed it again. Beside me, Jocelyn quivered. On my other side, Ed widened his stance and folded his arms across his chest, and I wished that his sleeve wasn't hiding his forearm. I'd like to have seen Mr. Wordsworth's face when Ed's spider tattoo appeared to jump.

Mr. Wordsworth raised the accusatory finger into the air.

"I know what you're going to say. The evening is almost over, and you're running out of inventory. Your boss could have informed you that it is your job to always have plenty on hand to make sure that this never happens." He picked up a double fudge donut from the platter that hadn't had, until then, a bare spot, and he continued his harangue. "Professionals know that diners prefer to see a bountiful table. Food that has been picked over is far from appealing. I was fortunate enough to take a Caribbean cruise eleven and a half years ago, and the buffet was always overflowing. There was never anything missing, even on the last evening of the cruise." With his free hand, he rearranged donuts and bowls of treats on one of the platters. "There. I've put a more artistic touch to your platter."

I didn't know what to say. Jocelyn was also uncharacteristically quiet.

Mr. Wordsworth bit into the donut. "This is actually good, considering that it can't be fresh."

Jocelyn's quivering had become more like shaking. Ed unfolded his arms and took a step toward the much-smaller man. Preparing myself to grab Ed if he lunged at Mr. Wordsworth, I managed a strangled and insincere thanks for what the English teacher probably believed was a compliment.

He might not have noticed. He went on with hints he undoubtedly thought were helpful. "I teach drama, and the plays and musicals I produce at Fallingbrook High have received excellent reviews." Ignoring Ed, he pinned Jocelyn and me in the glare of those prominent, light blue eyes. "Have you two attended any of them?"

I wanted to squirm like I might have when I was a student, which, fortunately for me, was before this teacher started working at Fallingbrook High. I put on another fake smile. "Not since I was a student."

Jocelyn inserted, "Me, neither."

The finger that had pointed at our donut charcuterie

boards and had lifted into the air in warning now aimed itself at Jocelyn and me and shook in a scolding. "You'll have to start coming to them. The students need community support." I wanted to explain that Jocelyn was about to return to college, but Mr. Wordsworth continued talking. "We're known for our special effects, and this year, we'll be using a drone. I won't tell you what all I plan to do with it, but I promise you, it'll get your attention." He gulped down another bite of donut and stared into the distance. "We were going to have one of the school staff play his bagpipe at the production, but he suffered an unfortunate accident. You probably don't know this, but the tubes on bagpipes without fingering holes each play a different, single background note. Those pipes are called drones. So, we were going to have two different sorts of drones in the production." He gave us a smile. "Don't worry. I'll make it work. One of my students will have to learn to play the bagpipe. For the amount of time he'll be on stage, he won't need to be as proficient as our former staff member was."

Appearing totally serious, Jocelyn asked, "And will you have a colony of bees in the production, also?"

I stepped back for fear I might erupt into giggles.

Mr. Wordsworth's dramatically confused expression seemed to be more of a criticism of Jocelyn than of his own inability to understand her. "Bees? Why would we? Oh, I get you. Worker bees. Drones. Very funny, miss." He took another bite of his donut, and then held it in front of his face and studied it. "Drone," he said slowly. "That staff member who . . . er . . . suffered the unfortunate mishap could have been called a 'drone nut.' And you could make some dull and tasteless donuts and call them 'dronuts.' Huh? Huh? What do you think of that, young ladies?"

Jocelyn echoed his earlier words so seriously that I was probably the only one who knew she was mocking him. "Very funny, sir."

Drone.

Drones could be used to deliver things. Like hamburgers and fries.

Like a broken mug to the driveway of one of the owners of the shop where the mug had originated . . .

I couldn't say a thing. A thousand suspicions crowded into my mind, and I regretted having moved back where I could see both Jocelyn's and Ed's faces.

They could see mine.

And I wished that they couldn't.

Chapter 28

If Ed guessed what I was thinking, I could be in danger.

If Jocelyn guessed what I was thinking, and let it show on her face, she might also be in danger.

Trying to hide my face from both of them, I looked down at the donut-filled wooden boards on our table. Although sparser than when we'd first arranged them, they still looked appetizing.

I could barely register what I was seeing.

Drone, I thought again. When I'd asked Ed about the Fireplug's possible new delivery method, Ed had blushed and mumbled. I'd wondered if he was embarrassed because Harold had decided Ed would not be able to operate the new vehicle, whatever it was.

But what if the delivery method was a drone, and Ed had already operated it? His blush could have been because he didn't want me to know that he'd ever seen it, let alone flown it.

Meanwhile, Mr. Wordsworth was droning on and on about the shows he had produced in previous schools.

Ever since I'd looked down to prevent Jocelyn and Ed from guessing my thoughts, Jocelyn had been giving Mr. Wordsworth encouraging, one-word replies.

Drone.

Around the time that Kirk had been killed, my parents and I had heard a buzzing noise. It had slowly diminished. My parents had seen flashing lights, and I hadn't. They'd been sleeping in the front of the house. My bedroom was in the back.

With its lights flashing and its motor buzzing, a drone could have flown above the street, hovered low over my driveway, delivered its payload, and then lifted off and flown away.

Why would a murderer have used a drone to remove the weapon from a murder scene?

If he hadn't wanted to be seen carrying the mug, he could have left it where it was or hidden it underneath his jacket.

How big would a drone have to be to carry an earthenware mug? Surely, Ed hadn't been hauling a drone around while chasing his intended victim. After the murder, he could have taken the drone to the scene, but showing up there right after killing Kirk would have been risky. It was more likely that he would have removed the mug from the scene immediately and taken the mug to the drone.

If Ed lived in one of the houses behind where Kirk had parked his van, Ed could have hopped the fence, carried the mug inside where he would not have been in the view of security cameras, and attached the mug to the drone. Then he could have taken it out to his front yard and sent the drone and the mug away.

Why had he flown them to my driveway, and not to a stand of trees or bushes where the mug would be less likely to have been discovered? He must have hoped to cast suspicion on someone besides himself, and he'd chosen me because I was one of Deputy Donut's owners.

But why remove the mug at all? Our logo on the mug would have automatically turned us into suspects.

And . . . a drone? If Ed had chosen me to look guilty, he could have delivered the mug on foot or with a vehicle.

I hoped the others weren't noticing how long I'd been intently staring at the platter of donuts, fruit, and candies.

Security cameras on buildings along the route from Kirk's camper van to my house would be pointed at sidewalks and streets, not toward rooftops and the sky. Maybe Ed had wanted the drone to evade detection by flying above the range of the cameras. Most likely, Ed had decided it was safest to be indoors during an electrical storm, and had sent the drone out into it instead.

And after the drone had dropped off the mug, where had the drone gone? Maybe Ed had directed the drone to return to him.

The instruction booklet I'd seen in the ladies' room of the Fireplug might have been for a drone, but maybe there had also been an English version. It would have been reasonable for Ed to have taken the English instructions home if he was the one who needed to learn to fly the drone.

I couldn't help looking up. Ed was watching me. His eyes narrowed in apparent speculation.

I slid my gaze past him to Mr. Wordsworth. He must have realized that he again had my attention. He interrupted his monologue with a question directed toward Jocelyn and me. "What do you think?"

Jocelyn answered, "Wonderful."

I said, "Yes." I thought, *How had the drone held the mug? With pincers that left black marks on the mug's handle?*

Between bites of a second or third double fudge donut, Mr. Wordsworth explained, "Another reason presentation is so important is you don't want to risk losing your audience, or in your case, your customers."

Losing, I thought. *What if Ed lost the drone after it made its delivery? He was probably inexperienced at controlling the drone, especially during a thunderstorm.*

Mr. Wordsworth launched into the description of another musical his students had done.

What if someone planning an illegal drone flight read the instructions in a hurry and didn't remember everything he was supposed to do?

I pictured the instruction booklet I'd seen in the trash in the ladies' room at the Fireplug. I should have realized at the time that the drawings had been too complicated for attaching a hand dryer to a wall and plugging it in.

Those foreign-language instructions could have been for assembling and flying a drone. Ed had probably kept the English version, and he might have thought that even if someone noticed the brochure he'd tossed into the trash, they wouldn't be able to read it. Besides, what visitor to a ladies' room would root through the wastebasket?

It hadn't occurred to me to do that, but now I wished I had. The diagrams might have provided clues that could have led Brent to Ed, and Ed would not be in the firehall with us, and I wouldn't have to worry about what he might have seen in my face. Or what he might do about it later.

With mechanical smiles, I encouraged more people to help themselves to the rapidly disappearing goodies on our two platters. I managed to thank everyone for their compliments.

Through it all, Mr. Wordsworth continued his lectures directed at Jocelyn and me. He ignored Ed and everyone else. Unfortunately, no one was asking Ed for beer. He stayed beside our table, probably still watching me.

Something prodded at the back of my mind, and I stared blankly toward our donut charcuterie boards.

I had an uncanny feeling that I knew that the drone had gone astray after it delivered the mug to my driveway. Was I creating a false memory of hearing it somewhere else later that morning?

On the way to work? Before I'd found Kirk's body? Or after?

Not before. After. At Deputy Donut?

Or someone else had heard it.

Dep.

When I'd taken her into the office that morning, she trotted up to the ceiling, and then she hissed. Wide-eyed, she'd come running back down.

Jocelyn and I hadn't heard anything, and Jocelyn had chided Dep for possibly being startled by the sounds of birds splashing in puddles or pecking at our flat roof. But could Dep have heard a drone up there? Maybe it had still been buzzing, or one of its propellor blades had been trying to turn, but all it could do was knock repeatedly against the roof.

Dep had reacted to birds on the roof before, but she'd always seemed intrigued, not threatened or frightened like she had on Wednesday morning. As far as I knew, whatever had disturbed her hadn't bothered her after that—because she tuned it out, or because it stopped? How long would a drone's battery remain charged, especially if the drone was soaked and its motor was struggling to turn its propellors?

I wanted to call Brent and tell him my theory, but I couldn't do it in a firehall still crowded with people. Especially Ed.

I told myself that Mr. Wordsworth's monotonous lecture was lulling my mind into wandering and concocting ideas that I would recognize as ridiculous five minutes after I left the noise and activity of the gala behind. I wouldn't want to cause Brent—or Vic—to make a fruitless climb to the roof of Deputy Donut.

But for now, the far-fetched notions kept pouring into my brain.

We kept a ladder in the garage where Jocelyn had parked our donut car. After we finished putting everything away at Deputy Donut, I would insist on driving Jocelyn home in the donut car, and then I could go back, haul out the ladder, and climb high enough to peek at the roof and convince myself that nothing was up there and that my guesses about a drone were complete nonsense.

Mr. Wordsworth stared questioningly at me with his bulging eyes.

Jocelyn answered, "Yes."

I nodded. "Absolutely."

Ed stared at me, and I felt heat rising up the back of my neck. What had I just agreed to? I hoped it wasn't making costumes for the school play. Or even donating donuts to sell at intermission.

Jocelyn was studiously ignoring me. Knowing her as well as I did, I feared that she was trying to figure out what I was thinking.

Mr. Wordsworth went on with his monologue. The crowds thinned, and our donut charcuterie boards were nearly empty. Across the hall, Scott winked at me. Without changing my expression, I glanced from him to the clock on the back wall. It was 9:29. I gazed at Scott again and opened my eyes wide in what I hoped was a pleading fashion.

Scott grinned. The clock changed to 9:30. Scott strode across the hall to our corner and said loudly, "Vendors can start packing up now."

Ed merely nodded. Arms folded, he continued watching Mr. Wordsworth, still giving his spiel.

I was going to have to stay with Jocelyn until she was safely home. Maybe we could quickly pack up and leave while Ed was gathering kegs and cups and transporting them with his hand truck through the parking lot between the fire-hall and the Fireplug.

I spun around, grabbed an emptied bakery box, and placed the leftover donuts, candy, nuts, and fruit into it. I closed the box and shoved it toward Mr. Wordsworth. "Here. Thanks for telling us . . ." I broke off, not knowing how to end the sentence.

Jocelyn picked up the slack. "So much." A devilish dimple creased her cheek.

Mr. Wordsworth fumbled with the box until it was tucked

securely in his arms. For once, he seemed to have lost the ability to speak.

I suggested, "Take that home to your wife, since she must have missed the party."

He backed away. "I don't have a . . . well, I guess I should be going. They say that teachers have summers off. Not true! We work year-round."

Jocelyn put on a concerned and thoughtful look. "We know." Then she pointedly turned her back on him and began rearranging things on the shelves behind the table, things that didn't need rearranging.

I joined her.

And so, to my dismay, did Ed. He asked nicely, "Can I help you two with anything?"

Chapter 29

❦

I tried to turn a friendly smile up at Ed's face, but I was thinking, *Is this man a killer?* "We've got this," I said. "And you're here all alone, aren't you? You have more to do."

"No big deal." He stared toward the front of the firehall. "You two can stop pretending to be busy. That man left the building."

As if she didn't quite believe Ed, Jocelyn peered toward the street outside. "Well! Wasn't he interesting!"

Ed scratched at his right wrist and jostled his shirtsleeve. I stared, expecting to see a bandage or a scratch, or at the very least, a scab, but I didn't get a chance. Blushing, he pulled the sleeve down over his wrist. "I don't know if he was interesting or not. I zoned out."

I tried to come up with an opinion that would make it appear that I had not been distracted by my suspicions of Ed. "I'm sure he was, or would have been to some people."

I must not have fooled Ed. He grinned down at us. "You two weren't paying attention, either. None of us were. Who would? But I think you might have agreed to sell tickets for school plays in Deputy Donut."

Jocelyn covered her mouth with her hand. I heard a muffled, "Oops." She uncovered her mouth. "Sorry, Emily, if I agreed to something you'll have to carry out after I'm back at school."

I waved a hand in a way that I hoped looked carefree. "Think nothing of it. I guess, I mean guessed, that we can help sell tickets at Deputy Donut even when you're not there to help." I looked up at Ed. "Did he ask you to sell tickets at the Fireplug?"

"He didn't ask me anything. Or acknowledge that I was there. He wanted to impress you two."

Jocelyn replied in a succinct way that echoed my thoughts exactly. "Yuck."

Ed laughed and went back to his table. Taking the empty and partially empty kegs back to the Fireplug would require several trips. He would use the firehall's back door. Jocelyn and I would leave the way we came, through the front. We would have to pass the front of the Fireplug on our way to Deputy Donut, but Ed wouldn't be able to see us from the parking lot in back.

Jocelyn offered, "Want me to go fetch the donut car, Emily?"

I didn't want either of us wandering around in the dark when a murderer might still be in town. I picked up the coffee urn. "This is nearly empty. We can put the things we have to wash into the big plastic bag we brought for them, and the smaller bag with the banner and the tape can go inside that bag. One of us can carry the big bag, and one of us can carry the urn, and we can walk, right? Especially if we wear our hats and aprons instead of forcing them into the bag. We'll need only one trip. And we'll both get a walk that we probably want. Or need."

I was afraid that Jocelyn was going to insist on running for even more exercise and fetching our delivery car by herself, but she agreed that we didn't need it.

I let out a quiet, relieved sigh. I should be able to engineer staying with her until she was safely home.

I took the bag. Jocelyn could have carried the weight of the urn one-handed, but it was bulky. She held it by the handles on the sides. We called goodbye to Ed, greeted other people we knew on the way out, and left. The big overhead doors were still rolled all the way up.

It was fully dark outside, and still warm. Scents of pine wafted from the town square. Jocelyn and I were both short, but neither of us liked to dawdle.

She exclaimed, only loudly enough for me to hear, "That English teacher! Not only mansplaining everything, but he had to manterfere and rearrange our platters as if neither of us had any artistic talent. Which we do."

I muttered, "I'm glad he wasn't at Fallingbrook High when I was."

"I'm glad he came after I graduated, too. I might have failed English just to show him."

At the corner of Wisconsin, I looked north and south, and also back toward the fire station.

Ed wasn't in sight.

I reminded myself that Ed might not have been the villain I'd built up in my mind. We still needed to be wary of Austin. I didn't see him, either.

We turned onto Wisconsin. We were on the Fireplug's side of the street. I suggested, "Let's cross." I tried to sound casual. No cars were coming. I stepped into the street.

"Okay." Jocelyn easily kept up with me. "Jaywalking's not like you."

"I break all sorts of laws when Brent isn't looking."

"No, you don't."

I wasn't about to argue. I also wasn't about to slow down, even though our aprons, which were longer than our shorts, flapped around our knees, threatening to make us stumble. On the other side of the street, Harold was with patrons on the Fireplug's patio. Lights, lowered for atmosphere, were on inside. I didn't see Ed.

I reminded myself that when Ed returned to the Fireplug, he would need to serve customers. He wouldn't have time to chase after us.

Although I'd been out in the fresh and reviving air for several minutes, my theory about the drone still seemed possible.

We passed the front of Deputy Donut and then walked up the driveway and let ourselves in through the office. In the storeroom, we washed the charcuterie boards, the dishes, and the coffee urn and put them away.

We left through the office. I locked the back door and ran down the two steps from the porch, turned back, and told Jocelyn as nonchalantly as I could, "I don't think that either of us should be out alone at night until Kirk's murderer is caught. I'll drive you and your bike home in the donut car, and then I'll move my parents' car out of the driveway, take my car out of the garage, and stow the donut car safely in the garage overnight."

Jocelyn joined me next to her bike, chained to the stand next to the porch steps. "That's a lot of moving cars around, especially when you need to get up early."

"So do you. Besides, Tom and Olivia will open in the morning if you and I need to sleep late."

She patted her bike. "I'll walk my bike with you to your place, and then ride really fast. My parents' house is only a few blocks from yours."

I said sternly, but with a laugh in my voice, "Jocelyn. I'm your boss."

Jocelyn put her fists on her hips. "Yes, and that's why I don't want you to go clambering around on roofs by yourself." In the dimly lit parking lot, I recognized the mischief in her grin.

Chapter 30

I stared at Jocelyn for a full ten seconds before I managed to speak. "What do you mean, 'clambering on roofs'?"

"Isn't that what you were about to do?"

I opened my mouth. Nothing came out.

Jocelyn teased, "I knew what you were thinking because I was thinking it, too. That English teacher was droning on about drones, and I suddenly remembered Dep on the morning of the murder. She acted like she heard something on the roof. So, how about if I climb up there just to check? If a drone or anything else that could be evidence is up there, we can call Brent."

To steady myself, I grabbed the railing. "Was I that obvious? Ed was watching me, too."

Her eyes opened wider. "Do you think Ed might be a killer? He wasn't here when Dep acted scared of the ceiling, so I doubt that he could put it all together."

I asked, "What if Ed lost a drone that night? He would be wondering where it was. I got distracted when the English teacher was talking about drones, and Ed noticed. Ed might think I actually know where his drone is, but I don't. I'm only guessing."

"Ed's drone? Or is the drone the thing that Harold bought for deliveries and was going to let Ed operate?"

"Right, it would probably be Harold's drone, if it exists at all. I think it might. My parents and I heard strange buzzing noises around three Wednesday morning, which could have been shortly after Kirk died, and my parents saw flashing lights. The noise and the lights could have come from a drone. On Wednesday evening, my father found a broken Deputy Donut mug in my driveway. I'm guessing that we heard a drone delivering that mug."

"A mug? Why?"

"I shouldn't say." I changed the subject. "Did you and your folks hear or see anything that night?"

Jocelyn was still standing beside her bike. She hadn't unlocked it. "I didn't, and my parents have been staying at the Fallingbrook Falls Campground all summer. They haven't been in town during the past week. But . . . Ed? I didn't talk to him in Deputy Donut when he came in, and I never met him before tonight, but he seemed, I don't know, nice. And the blushes made him appear sort of innocent."

"He could have been blushing because he was lying." I told her about the instruction leaflet I'd seen in the ladies' room at the Fireplug. "I don't know for certain, but the illustrations could have been for a drone. And other things happened, too, that when I put them together, make me wonder about him."

"What sorts of things?"

"A handkerchief found at the site of Kirk's murder had blood on it, but the blood type didn't match Kirk's or the handkerchief's owner. So, it might belong to the murderer, who could have been injured while he was attacking Kirk. Ed started wearing long sleeves instead of short ones after the murder. Maybe he was trying to hide defensive wounds. This evening, one of Ed's sleeves worked itself up a little. He yanked it down, so again I wondered if he was trying to hide a cut or a bandage. Also, he had quite a grudge against Kirk. On Monday evening in the Fireplug, when Kirk was staring at a map, Ed yelled at Kirk to either buy something or get out. That rude remark really annoyed Harold."

Jocelyn laughed. "I can see why."

"Ed apologized to us and then explained that he'd been trying to protect us from Kirk."

Jocelyn opened her eyes wide. "Because of a bagpipe?"

I had to laugh at the way she emphasized *bagpipe*. I explained, "Ed complained that Kirk had stolen his wallet and phone. Because of not having his charge cards, Ed hadn't been able to offer his girlfriend a ring at the proposal party he planned, so he gave her a picture he'd cut out of a magazine instead, and she turned him down in front of friends and relatives."

Jocelyn slapped her forehead. "Ed's judgment does sound questionable. What made him carry out a ridiculous plan like that?"

"I don't know. He was really angry at Kirk before the murder, but afterward, he made a special effort to come to Deputy Donut and inform me that it wasn't such a big deal, and he hoped to change the woman's mind."

"That's a lot of suspicious behavior."

"But it doesn't work as evidence. It's gut feelings and things that happened that could be perfectly innocent." I stopped talking so I could listen. I heard voices from near the Fireplug, but no footsteps. No other people seemed to be close to us, but I spoke quietly anyway. "I can't help wondering if the murder had something to do with the motto on Kirk's business cards. Kirk left those cards all over town, but I'm not sure how Ed figures into that."

"I saw the cards, but I didn't pay attention to what they said."

"It was 'He who pays the piper calls the tune.' I know it sounds far-fetched, but that motto could have been an attempt at extortion. Maybe Kirk was trying to tell someone that if they paid him enough, he would stop playing the same three tunes over and over again. Like, maybe those tunes meant something to him and to the person he was trying to extort."

"Do you know what the three tunes were?"

"The first one was 'My Bonnie Lies over the Ocean.' Even I knew what that was. My parents recognized 'The Skye Boat Song,' and they figured out that the third one was 'Flora MacDonald's Lament.' "

Despite the darkness, Jocelyn's eyes shined with surmise and excitement. "There's a connection between those three tunes. Flora MacDonald supposedly helped Bonnie Prince Charlie escape by boat to the Isle of Skye."

I fluffed up the curls that my Deputy Donut cap had flattened. "What could it have to do with Kirk MacLean and someone in Fallingbrook centuries later?"

"Let's see what we can find on the office computer."

"Okay." I didn't want to delay going home, but maybe Jocelyn would lose her enthusiasm for exploring our roof. Or we'd learn something that would make climbing ladders at ten at night unnecessary. I unlocked the back door again and deactivated the alarms. I deliberately left the office lights off. The glow coming in through the window between the office and the kitchen was enough to prevent us from bumping into furniture and to help us find the computer's ON button. For once, I regretted having installed large windows and a glass door on the sides of our office overlooking the driveway and the parking lot. We would have to hope that Ed—or Austin— would not come close enough to see our faces, lit by the computer monitor.

I searched for combinations of words from the titles of the three tunes that Kirk had played.

And then it nearly jumped out at me, and Jocelyn let out a yelp and pointed at a headline: "Husband Sentenced in Murder of Bonnie Flora MacDonald Skye."

The article was about ten years old. Bonnie Flora

MacDonald Skye's husband, Fergus, had murdered her in the bookstore where she worked in Chicago and had attempted to cover up the crime by setting fire to the bookstore. Fergus Skye was given a life sentence.

"Chicago," I said aloud. "Two people who I originally thought might have been involved in Kirk's murder have connections to Chicago, but both of them have been cleared."

"Who?"

I was thinking of Quentin and Penny. "I shouldn't say. I don't know if Ed has ever lived in Chicago, but on Monday night, Ed saw Kirk studying a map on the wall of the Fireplug showing the area destroyed by the Great Chicago Fire of 1871. Thursday evening, when I was in the Fireplug with Samantha, Hooligan, and my parents, that map was gone. Harold explained that he'd removed it because some of his staff had found it depressing."

"Some of his staff. Did he mean Ed?"

"I think so." I didn't know if Austin Berwin or Lisa-Ruth Schomoset had connections to Chicago. Quentin would have been in his early teens when the murder occurred. I guessed that he had probably been concentrating on music and other studies at that age and wouldn't have been roving around Chicago murdering people. His parents were professors. That didn't necessarily mean they were innocent. Besides, their motive could have been much the same as Quentin's—revenge for Kirk's having distracted Quentin during the Musical Monday performance. They'd given one another alibis.

So had my parents and I, and I expected everyone to believe us. Maybe I should trust that Quentin and his parents were telling the truth, too.

I suggested, "Maybe it's a coincidence that the murdered woman's name matches the tunes Kirk was playing. Her husband was convicted. Case closed."

In the greenish light from the computer screen, Jocelyn turned to study my face. "Yes, but should it have been?"

I frowned. "Maybe they got the wrong guy, or Kirk believed that Fergus Skye had worked with an accomplice, and that accomplice either lived in Fallingbrook or was visiting during the Fallingbrook Arts Festival."

Jocelyn concluded quietly, "And Kirk expected someone to pay him to keep quiet about what he knew or suspected."

"I wonder if he had a specific person in mind. The way he left his cards everywhere and played those tunes all over Fallingbrook, he could have merely been guessing or hoping that the actual murderer or the husband's accomplice was in or near Fallingbrook."

Jocelyn looked at the article on the screen again. "The sentencing was almost ten years ago. How old do you think Ed is?"

"Early thirties?"

Jocelyn admitted, "I suppose he could be that old. Do you know if he saw one of Kirk's business cards?"

"No. I watched him put one in his pocket, but he claimed he never read it, and it ended up as dryer lint."

"That was strangely convenient."

I agreed. "Even if he didn't read the card he picked up, he had plenty of other chances to read one."

"Let's go get the ladder. If nothing's on the roof, maybe we can rule out Ed."

"We can't rule him out if he returned the drone to Harold. I don't like the way he paid attention to me when drones were mentioned. And it's not up to us to rule anyone in or out. That's Brent's job."

She retorted sensibly, "But we want to know what Dep heard on the roof."

Chapter 31

✼

We shut off the computer, reactivated the alarms, went outside, and locked the back door. Again standing in the parking lot behind Deputy Donut, I glanced up toward the building's dark parapet looming against the slightly lighter sky. The moon, only half full, cast some light, but we were in the shadow of the back corner of Thrills and Frills. I suggested, "Maybe we should wait until daylight."

Jocelyn turned toward me. "During work hours? Or after work. It would be easier to do it now. We wouldn't have to explain to anyone."

"Ed might become curious and wander down here."

"He'll have returned to work at the Fireplug by now, and they'll be open a few more hours."

I agreed that she was probably right. "But if he didn't let Harold know that he had finished at the firehall, he could check on us before he returned to work." I bit my lip. "And maybe he's innocent. There's someone else that Brent told me to stay away from, Austin Berwin. Austin was walking around this area about an hour ago. We'd be safest if we put your bike in the trunk of the donut car and I drove you home and then parked at my place."

Jocelyn waved a dismissive hand. "We'll be fine. If we

don't do this now, we'll probably lie awake all night wondering if we should have. Or if we should get up at three in the morning to do it."

That made the decision for me. I definitely did not want Jocelyn out here by herself at the hour when this murderer might be most likely to haunt the streets. I put my hands on my hips. "I've been tricked."

I refrained from looking up at the camera mounted on the porch roof. At this point, we'd done nothing particularly strange. True, we had left the office and then returned to it, but that wasn't unusual. And now we were merely chatting next to Jocelyn's chained bike. I pulled my phone out of my pocket. "If we don't want to have to explain to anyone who might look at the videos later, we should temporarily disable our rear camera." Hoping Tom wouldn't object too strenuously if he ever noticed what I did, I fiddled with my phone and turned the camera off. "Remind me to start it again after we put the ladder away."

Jocelyn started toward the garage. "Okay."

Each of us taking one end of the heavy extension ladder, we lifted it off the hooks fastened to one of the garage's interior walls. We shuffled out past the donut car and left the garage door open. We didn't talk while we carried the ladder across the parking lot, but our progress was far from silent. The clanking of aluminum seemed louder in the otherwise quiet night. We stood the ladder next to Deputy Donut's back porch so that one side of the ladder would touch the stair rail and the porch roof. All of the Deputy Donut staff had taken courses that would help us prepare for nearly anything, and one of the courses had stressed safety around ladders. After Jocelyn and I were both satisfied that we'd extended the ladder high enough, that the base of it was far enough away from the building for a proper climbing angle, and that the rubber shoes at its base were snugged against the pavement, I shined my phone light on the rung locks above us. They had snapped into place. Jocelyn unlocked her bike, used her chain to attach one side of the ladder to the porch railing, and then tried moving the ladder from side to side. It didn't budge. The main danger, aside from scary heights, would come from pushing the base of the ladder close to the building or the top of the ladder away from the parapet surrounding the roof.

I knew what was coming next.

Jocelyn decreed, "I have more experience at heights. You hold the ladder, and I'll climb up. If there's nothing to see, I'll come down, and we can put the ladder away."

"There's no arguing with you, is there?"

"None."

So, I steadied the ladder, and Jocelyn scrambled up it. The ladder remained firmly in place. Above Jocelyn, stars pricked holes in the sky's dark fabric.

The only sounds were laughter from the Fireplug's patio up the street, Jocelyn's sneakers on the rungs, the creaking of the ladder, and leaves rustling in trees behind the parking lot.

Hanging onto a rung with one hand, Jocelyn shined her phone's light toward the roof.

I waited one second, two, ten . . .

I expected her to back down the ladder, but she climbed up until her feet were at the same level as the top of the short wall surrounding the roof. Holding the ladder with both hands, she stepped sideward onto the top of the parapet. I held my breath. If she tumbled backward, she would fall only about ten feet to the porch roof, but that roof slanted down toward the parking lot, and she could roll all the way down to the pavement beyond the porch steps. Maybe she'd be able to catch herself before that happened . . .

Or I'd be able to run back and to my left and catch her. Sure. That would have been impossible.

But she was Jocelyn and didn't fall. Grasping one side of the ladder with both hands, she turned toward the ladder and jumped down onto the roof. She was safe. I exhaled.

She walked away from the ladder and the parapet and disappeared from my sight.

And then I heard a hoarse whisper. "Emily! We guessed right. It's up here."

Chapter 32

I called in a whisper every bit as shaky as hers. "Don't touch it. Come down."

Jocelyn didn't answer. Worse, she didn't reappear near the top of the ladder.

Again, I waited.

"Jocelyn?"

No answer. My whisper had been barely audible.

She didn't show up.

I couldn't wait. Reasoning that the angle of the ladder was perfect for climbing, and that because of the chain, no one needed to steady the ladder, I started up. I didn't climb as quickly as Jocelyn had.

I also didn't hear any sounds from her.

Remembering the instructions in the course we'd taken, I carefully made certain that, between my hands and my feet, I always maintained three points of contact with the ladder.

Finally, I could peek over the top of the foot-high wall surrounding the roof.

To the right of a wide brick chimney about a dozen feet from me, Jocelyn was crouching beside a small heap of wreckage.

Jocelyn had made going from the ladder to the roof look

easy. Picturing how she'd done it, I climbed until I would be able to sidestep onto the parapet.

It was easier said than done. I gripped the sides of the ladder so hard that my hands hurt, but they didn't want to let go. The ladder rattled. Jocelyn looked up. "Emily!" She leaped to her feet and ran to me. "You shouldn't have risked coming up here. I was taking pictures to show you so you wouldn't have to."

"I made it up here just fine."

She ordered, "So, go back. I'll finish taking pictures and be right down."

"Now that I've gotten this far, can you help me onto the roof?"

Muttering about needing to call the fire department to get us down, she let me grasp her hands while I stepped onto the parapet. She was strong, and I trusted her not to let me fall backward. I wasn't sure about jumping off the foot-high wall. Jocelyn helped me, and finally, with my teeth clenched, I was standing on the pea-sized gravel covering our flat roof. I refused to think about having to transfer myself from the parapet to the ladder when it was time to go back down.

I pulled my phone out of my pocket, shined its light down in front of me, and walked cautiously beside Jocelyn to a tangle of broken plastic and twisted propellors beside our wide brick chimney. I concluded aloud, "If this drone flew here during the hour or so after Kirk was murdered, the storm could have prevented the drone's camera from showing much besides rain. It really poured after my parents and I heard the buzzing and my parents saw flashing lights. Watching the video the drone sent to his phone, Ed might not have spotted the chimney in time to prevent the drone from crashing into it. Or even if he'd spotted the chimney, he probably didn't have much experience flying drones. He might have crashed it even on a sunny day."

"Apparently, he was able to carefully place that mug in

your driveway. He might have a good idea of which direction the drone went after that."

I finished the thought. "And where it landed."

"Then why didn't he come find it? Like at three some other morning?"

"Maybe, if he had killed Kirk, he decided that trying to retrieve his drone would be riskier than hoping it wouldn't be found for months or even years, and he probably suspected that the drone no longer worked and probably never would. The crash might have shattered its camera and positioning system. If so, he probably doesn't know exactly where the drone is."

Jocelyn glanced around at nearby shops. "How could he? Most of the other buildings on this block are shorter than ours. Because of the wall around our roof, small objects on our rooftop can't possibly be seen from other roofs. Not even from the Fireplug's roof. You'd need another drone." She stared toward the Fireplug. "What's that strange-looking hut with the slanting top on the Fireplug's roof?"

"It looks like an enclosed stairway."

"Maybe someone was considering adding a second story."

I gestured toward our ladder. "We should have put Deputy Donut in that building, and saved ourselves from climbing that ladder."

"Killjoy."

I became serious again. "Whoever lost the drone might have suspected that it landed on one of the buildings around here. The afternoon of the day I found Kirk's body, some of the gawkers were peering toward the tops of buildings."

"Was Ed one of them?"

"He might have been. He came into Deputy Donut that afternoon, but if he was staring up at roofs, I didn't see him do it."

Jocelyn reminded me, "We're still not sure if the drone is connected to Kirk's murder."

"No, but . . ." I practically had to stand on my head, but I finally saw the pincers that were meant to grip whatever the drone was supposed to deliver. I pointed them out to Jocelyn. "I guess those can be opened and closed remotely by the drone's pilot. The morning that Kirk died, those claws probably held the handle of the broken Deputy Donut mug until they released it in my driveway." The claws were coated in a black, rubbery-looking substance. "And they left black marks on the mug's handle. Brent and the DCI agent wondered what made those marks."

The light of my phone lit Jocelyn's face from below and cast an eerie glow over it. She tapped her cheek with a forefinger. "If Ed had been flying Harold's drone and didn't bring it back, wouldn't Harold wonder where it was, and ask him?"

"Could Harold have given him time to learn how to fly it? Also, they'd have needed a license to use it commercially. Maybe Harold left the learning process and the exams to Ed."

"If I were Ed, I'd replace the drone and hope that Harold never realized I'd crashed the first one."

"Maybe he did. I'll call Brent about this one." I looked down at my phone.

Suddenly, a bright light blazed from the north, illuminating Jocelyn and me. Instinctively turning my face away, I shoved my phone into my shorts pocket.

Jocelyn's and my elongated shadows streamed behind us over the flat roof and beyond the parapet. The shadows of our heads loomed near the top of Thrills and Frills.

I reached for Jocelyn. She yanked at my arm. Both of us gasped in shrill whispers, "Get down!"

Chapter 33

✣

I flung myself down onto the rough surface. Lying on our stomachs, Jocelyn and I were—just barely—in the shadow of the north section of the parapet. I turned my head toward her. "Where's that light coming from?"

She guessed, "Another roof? It's to the north, and across Wisconsin Street. Maybe someone climbed up that staircase on the roof of the Fireplug."

"I suspect you're right. I've been picturing Ed controlling the drone from one of the yards backing onto the parking lot where Kirk was killed, but Ed told me he's the one who opens the Fireplug in the late mornings. He must have keys. Maybe he went up to the roof of the Fireplug to send the drone and the mug to my driveway. From there, our chimney must have been in the drone's flight path. Maybe Ed didn't know where the drone went, but tonight, seeing my reaction to the word *drone*, he could have wondered if it had landed on our roof. After we left, he had plenty of time to return to the Fireplug and make an excuse to take a light up onto the roof and watch in case we showed up here."

"His light must be one of those super powerful ones." Insects danced in a horizontal stream of light a foot or two above us.

For a second, the top rungs of our ladder shined like silver beacons. Shadows writhed, and the powerful light went out.

Jocelyn complained, "Now I can barely see anything."

"Me, neither. Let's slither closer to the ladder and be ready to climb down it as soon as our eyes readjust to the darkness." We'd have to creep over there without scraping our knees and hands on the small, loose gravel more than we already had. My knees stung and burned. I hoped that, because of Jocelyn's gymnastic training, she was better at landing and hadn't hurt herself. Not that she would mention minor injuries during a crisis. I certainly was not going to confess to my own carelessness. I asked in an urgent undertone, "Do you have your Deputy Donut key?"

"Yes."

"You go down first, then. Lock yourself in."

She didn't move. "And what are you going to do?"

"Call Brent."

Naturally, she resisted. "Let me help you onto that ladder. You climb down carefully, and I'll be right behind you. Then we can call Brent."

"You can get down to safety more quickly."

"We don't know that anyone's coming here. Maybe someone was testing a new light. Or they do that every night, for fun."

I could now make out the ladder's outline above the parapet. "Go, Jocelyn."

"No, Emily. Not without you."

The ladder was probably less than a dozen feet from us, but it seemed much farther away. "Let's crawl over there, then. I'm sorry for climbing up. If I hadn't, we'd both be safely on the ground by now."

"We won't think of it as an emergency. We'll keep our final goal in mind—to lock ourselves inside Deputy Donut and call Brent. In the meantime, we'll focus on the moment and take it one step at a time. First, as you said, we will stay as low as we can and snake our way to the ladder without being seen if whoever has that light turns it on again. And we will stay calm. I can see again. Can you?"

"Yes."

Crouching, placing her fingertips and the toes of her sneakers on the gravel, and keeping her head down, she crept toward our ladder.

Although not as adept at contortions, I followed her lead. Every second that the bright light did not suddenly pinion us, I worried that Ed had stopped watching us only because he was on his way to . . . I didn't want to think about what.

I reminded myself, *one step at a time.*

Jocelyn reached the parapet first and sat down on the roof with her back against it. She patted the gravel. "Sit here, and we'll discuss our next step."

She was the expert. I sat beside her on the tiny but pointy stones. The bright light had not reappeared. No one was watching us. We would be fine. This was not an emergency. I would stay calm . . .

How was I supposed to do that? By concentrating on breathing, or by trying not to think about breathing?

One step at a time.

Jocelyn whispered, "Stay there and watch how I do this." She reached up to the ladder, held it with one hand, and eased herself to sit on the parapet with her back to dark emptiness. I told myself that the porch roof might even be less than ten feet below her.

Focus.

Next, she put both hands as high as she could on the side of the ladder next to her. She pulled her torso up, arranged her feet underneath her on the parapet, and stood, breathing easily and obviously testing her balance. From there, she made it look easy to place her right hand on the far side of the ladder and her right foot onto the nearest rung. Then she had both feet on the same rung, and she was gripping both sides of the ladder. All she had to do was carefully back down.

I opened my mouth to tell her that, having gotten that far, she should continue down the ladder, but she quickly reversed the process and sat again on the parapet with one hand holding the ladder. "Easy," she said. "But since we have no ropes or safety harness, we'll do it a little differently with you. I'll brace myself and hang onto your waistband until you're on the ladder and feel steady. Then you can start down."

"One step at a time." My inner shaking did not come through my voice. *Stay calm. Focus.*

Jocelyn grinned. She was as confident as she looked. She slid off the parapet and again sat on the roof beside me. "Your turn. Remember, I chained one side of the ladder to the porch railing. The ladder is not going to slide sideward. You'll be fine."

I grabbed the ladder with my right hand and sat on the parapet with my back to empty space above the porch roof. Holding onto the ladder, I felt secure. I slid my right hand upward and then grasped the ladder with my left hand.

Apologizing for invading my personal space, Jocelyn stood and slid her fingers behind my waistband. "I've got you. Now use the strength of your arms to pull yourself up and put your feet underneath your bum. And then straighten."

Following her instructions was difficult, but my arms were strong from carrying trays of food and drinks, and I managed to stand up. Focusing, I made certain of my balance. I moved my right hand to the right side of the ladder and my right foot onto the rung. Again checking my balance, I set my left foot on the same rung.

Jocelyn crowed in a whisper, "You did it! Now back carefully down the ladder."

I took a deep breath. I'd been concentrating so hard on moving safely from the parapet onto the ladder that I'd ignored sounds from the street, but now they reached my consciousness.

Someone was walking briskly down Wisconsin Street.

Jocelyn must have heard them, too. "Wait," she whispered. "Maybe they'll keep going."

They didn't. I heard the footsteps turn the corner onto the driveway beside Deputy Donut.

The footsteps came faster. Someone was pelting toward the back of our building.

Chapter 34

There I was, spreadeagled on that ladder while someone ran up the alley toward us.

I didn't hesitate to think or force myself to focus. As if I'd done it hundreds of times, I swung myself from the ladder back to the parapet. Jocelyn grabbed my hands and helped me off it. We both slumped down onto the roof.

I whispered, "Maybe he's not coming here."

Whoever was running stopped. Where was he?

Jocelyn and I looked at each other. The whites of her eyes glimmered. Both of us pointed toward the chimney. We nodded at each other. Crouching, we ran toward the chimney. I barely glanced at the mangled drone as I passed it.

Could the person near the base of the ladder hear the crunching of our shoes on the loose top layer of gravel?

We ducked behind the chimney, out of sight of anyone who might climb the ladder and peek over the parapet. We squatted, but because the parapet was only about a foot tall and not close to us, our heads might have been in view of anyone on the Fireplug's roof. At the moment, no light shined from there.

I thought I heard the footsteps of someone running up to our back porch and shaking the office door. We'd locked it. It must have held. There was a thump, as if someone leaped over both porch steps and landed on the parking lot, and then the ladder rattled. "Jocelyn! Emily?" I couldn't tell for sure who was calling our names in that bloodcurdling stage whisper, but it was easy to believe it was Ed.

We didn't answer.

"Come down! It's . . . life and death. You're in danger."

We knew that. We were in danger from him.

The chimney was wide, but not much wider than the two of us hunched over. We made ourselves as small as we could.

Was he armed? With what?

He had stopped calling to us. Maybe he thought we had escaped down the ladder. We would have had time if we hadn't needed to wait for our eyes to readjust to the darkness and if I'd been as accomplished on ladders as Jocelyn was. But he could have suspected we'd fled through the parking lots. He wouldn't know which way to go, and while he was searching the back alleys and streets, we could creep down and lock ourselves into Deputy Donut.

The ladder creaked. Again.

And again.

Someone was definitely climbing, as stealthily as the aluminum ladder would let him. He was heavier than either Jocelyn or me. Jocelyn pulled her phone out of her pocket, tapped it, and showed me that she had restarted Deputy Donut's rear camera.

I gave her a thumbs-up and fished in my pockets for my phone. I didn't find it. I rose up onto my knees on that sharp gravel and tried again.

My phone was missing.

Had I dropped it when I was on the ladder, focusing on safety? Wouldn't I have heard it crash onto the pavement? I fought down panic.

Creak, creak.

He was still coming up. His head would rise above the parapet any second.

I hated not being able to see where he was and what he was doing. Beside me, Jocelyn's breathing sounded almost normal, but I knew her. Her muscles would be tightly coiled. She would be ready to spring up and attack.

I eased to my left to peer around the chimney. Jocelyn tugged at my arm, and I retreated into the chimney's ridiculously meager cover.

I'd seen enough.

The top of a head had been rising above the edge of the parapet. In the darkness, the hair could have been brown, auburn, or black. It was pulled back behind a broad forehead.

Now I was certain. Our pursuer was Ed.

And I'd seen something else every bit as frightening, if not more.

Its screen mirroring the starlit sky, my phone lay on the roof between me and the ladder. The phone must have slipped out of my pocket while we were duckwalking across the roof. If I'd heard my phone land, I must have unconsciously attributed the sound to our sneakers on the gravel.

My phone was only five feet from me, but it might as well have been miles away. I would not be able to retrieve it without moving into Ed's view.

The ladder creaked again.

Jocelyn stared at me. Barely above a breath, I whispered, "Ed." I mimed holding a pretend phone and working the keypad with my thumbs. Even though she wouldn't be able to see the phone from her position, I pointed toward where it was.

With a quick nod, Jocelyn gave me her phone. Its screen lit her serious face and seemed dangerously bright in the darkness behind the chimney.

Mouthing a thanks, I shielded her phone's screen with my hand.

I had a new problem.

Brent's number. On my phone, I didn't have to tap in the entire thing.

I knew his number, didn't I? I squeezed my eyes shut.

I remembered the area code but blanked on the rest. *Stay calm. It will come to you.*

I could call emergency, but how would I make myself understood without alerting the man on the ladder? If I could contact Brent, I could whisper. He would understand and send help.

The ladder creaked. Was Ed going back down?

Jocelyn must have noticed my hesitation. She gently removed the phone from my trembling hands, scrolled through screens, and handed it back to me.

I should have remembered that everyone who worked at Deputy Donut kept one another's emergency contacts on our phones. My finger hovered over the screen, ready to tap the connection to Brent.

From the ladder, Ed swore underneath his breath.

By the light of Jocelyn's phone, she and I stared at each other again. She still didn't look as panicky as I felt.

The ladder clanked, and something thudded down onto the roof, as if Ed had landed on both feet at once.

He was breathing heavily, walking as softly as a big man could on gravel.

Toward us.

Chapter 35

❧

As far as I knew, Ed had not yet figured out that Jocelyn and I were behind the chimney. I closed my hand over Jocelyn's phone and held my breath. I didn't dare make the call. Even if I said nothing, Ed might hear Brent answer or be able to see a glow from the phone. For the same reason, phoning emergency was out of the question.

Ed muttered, "So, that's where it went." A rattle and a scrape made me think he kicked the drone. His light swept east, along the gravel south of the chimney, close to me.

The beam stopped moving.

Ed said in an eerily quiet voice, "A phone?" The beam of light jerked, and Ed whispered hoarsely, "Emily? Jocelyn? Where are you?" His footsteps landed softly.

It was inevitable. He was coming around the chimney. He would see us.

We couldn't go around the south side of the chimney. One man could, by himself, fling his arms out to the sides and block off the space between the south parapet and the chimney, and nothing besides that one-foot-high wall would protect us from falling all the way to the driveway below. Especially if we were pushed.

We could run to the north side of the roof, but he would

hear us, and although we would be about thirty feet from him, he could easily chase us.

It occurred to me, belatedly, that the parapet had probably been built for appearance, not to protect the few people who might venture up to the roof. The building was a hundred years old or more and had been renovated many times, but had the parapet, even in the beginning, been reinforced? Maybe it was only bricks held together by aging mortar with vinyl siding attached to the outside. The slightest nudge might send bricks, mortar, siding, and the nudger plummeting to the ground. Because of our building's high ceilings, the roof was about one and a half stories up.

Jocelyn and I silently consulted each other, and then rose to our feet. I could tell she was mentally flexing her muscles, ready to strike, and I felt almost as tense. She looked serene. I probably did not.

Ed came around the chimney, halted, and stared at us. "What's going on?" As if our silence unnerved him, he stood still. The only thing in his hands was my phone.

I countered with a question. "What are you doing here?"

He held out the phone like a peace offering. "Does this belong to one of you?"

I didn't dare look away from Ed to call Brent. I answered tersely. "It's mine. Set it on the roof and back away from it, hands up." I sounded like an amateur actor in a cliché-ridden old movie.

Ed raised both of his hands. One was empty, and the other held my phone. "Whoa, easy there, Emily." He bent and laid my phone gently on the roof, and then he stood, raised both hands again, revealing his bare palms, and backed two steps toward the south parapet. "All I did was warn you two to get out of here. It's not safe."

Knowing I needed to concentrate on Ed and on making sure that no one, including Ed, went close to the edge, I continued to ignore Jocelyn's phone, still clutched to my chest. "What do you mean, Ed?" I tried not to sound aggressive.

He pointed toward the base of the chimney. "There's a broken drone up here. I don't know how, but it might have something to do with that bagpiper's murder."

I asked, "How do you know it was a murder?"

Ed spoke between lips tightened by, I thought, anger. "Everyone knows that. The police taped off a parking lot for days, and they've been going around asking innocent people stupid questions."

Innocent people, I thought. Ed obviously thought he could convince Jocelyn and me that he was one of them. But a few minutes before, he must have been up on the roof of the Fireplug, spying in our direction, and when he saw the pinpricks of light from our phones, he'd turned on a much more powerful light and recognized us. Then he'd run to Deputy Donut.

Maybe he was hoping we'd start down the ladder, and he could push us off it onto the pavement.

I asked him, "What made you come over here just now and climb onto the roof?"

"I already said. To tell you that you were in danger. You *are* in danger, both of you. You need to get down to safety. Now."

I pointed at the tangle of metal and plastic. "Did you think we were in danger from a broken drone?" I winced. I hadn't meant to sound sarcastic.

"No! I was on the Fireplug's patio, and I saw this enormous beam of light shining from the roof of the Fireplug over to here. I remembered the look on your face, Emily, this evening when that bore of a teacher was talking about drones. It was like you suddenly thought of something important but didn't want anyone else to know what it was. Jocelyn, too. Both of you looked secretive. I didn't think about it again until I saw that light shining this way, and then it went out. On the chance that you two were up here on the roof searching for a lost drone, and you didn't know that someone who might have killed a man might be coming after you, I ran here to warn you. I saw that ladder propped up on the building and guessed you were up here, so I climbed up. Why were you hiding from me?" He sounded hurt.

He was a good actor. Maybe he should have participated in Theatrical Thursday and Skit Saturday.

Again, I didn't answer his question. Instead, I asked quietly, "Ed, who do you think might be coming after Jocelyn and me?"

"My boss, of course. Harold's the one who has a flashlight with about a million candlepower. He likes gadgets. He took the staff up to the roof of the Fireplug once and showed us how far straight up that light could shine. It was like this column of white going miles into the sky, and you could see bugs and dust and things flying through it, really cool. But tonight I figured he'd seen something in this direction, and I remembered how you two looked at the party when drones were mentioned, and I got worried that you might have found Harold's drone, and he might have been using it for something criminal. I'm worried for you two, not for me."

That was generous, but I wasn't ready to let Ed get away with making up stories. I reminded him, "At the party, you said that Harold hadn't bought the fun new delivery thing."

Ed glanced nervously northward. No light was shining from that direction. "That's what he said. A long time ago, he told me he was ordering one, and he would let me fly it, and then he said it hadn't come and he didn't know if it would. But I'm pretty sure he ordered one and it did come, because I saw packaging and an instruction booklet that had to have been from a drone when I emptied trash at the Fireplug. The instruction booklet wasn't in English, so I couldn't read it, but the drawings were for a drone, I'm almost certain. That was after the bagpiper died."

Ed gazed toward the Fireplug. The enormous light still had

not come back on. Ed looked back at us. "Also, around then, Harold seemed to be searching for something, like on the ground and in parking lots, and he was even staring up toward the tops of buildings. So, I wondered. If Harold bought a drone, maybe he wasn't good at running it. He could have lost it. And then I thought that maybe you two had seen or heard the drone somewhere, and then, right there in the party, you both seemed to put a bunch of guesses about drones together. So, I thought you two might look for Harold's drone to try to connect it to the murder. I'm not saying that broken thing over there was connected to the murder, but why else was Harold saying he hadn't ordered a drone? As far as I could tell, it had already come, and he'd unpacked it and had probably assembled it."

Everything Ed was saying could have been about Harold.

More likely, Ed was talking about himself and what he had done—thrown out the instructions and lost the drone.

I asked a question that was sure to make both Ed and Jocelyn believe that my jangling nerves were making me babble. "Do you know why Harold removed the map of the 1871 Chicago Fire? The bagpiper was looking at it before he died, and the next time I was in the Fireplug, it was gone." Harold had told me he'd removed it because his staff had found it depressing.

Again, Ed turned the answer back to his boss. "Harold said it was depressing. I guess it reminded him of his previous pub, which was in one of the Chicago neighborhoods that was rebuilt after a fire way back in 1871 destroyed it. When Harold first bought the Fireplug, he said that his Chicago pub was totaled when the bookstore next door was torched. A man had killed his wife in that bookstore. Harold was proud of being the star witness who helped put that man in prison. Harold used his insurance money to buy the Fireplug."

If Ed was telling the truth, I had a good guess at why Harold might have murdered Kirk. Maybe Harold had been involved in the murder of Bonnie Flora MacDonald Skye and had realized that Kirk knew about it or guessed the truth. If Harold had wanted Kirk to keep quiet, Harold would have to pay the piper to call off the tunes.

If Ed was telling the truth . . . Again, Ed could have been talking about what he himself had done.

Ed said slowly, as if thinking it through, "Y'know, Harold could've been the one who killed that woman and torched his own pub. Like, for, you know, the insurance money. And maybe that bagpiper figured something out, so he had to be eliminated, too."

Our ladder rattled. Our discussion had masked the sounds of someone approaching.

And furtively climbing the ladder.

Jocelyn and I froze in position.

The whites of his eyes huge in the darkness, Ed picked up my phone and charged toward us.

Chapter 36

I braced myself, ready to shove Ed away if he tried to push Jocelyn or me over the edge, and I half expected Jocelyn to turn a cartwheel and kick him in the chin.

She didn't move, but I knew she was also preparing to defend us.

Ed put his fingers on his lips and squeezed behind the chimney with us. We all stood straight and still, our arms down at our sides. Ed didn't touch either of us.

Tensely, I listened.

The person who, judging by the sounds, was cautiously moving from the ladder to the top of the parapet, didn't speak. The soles of his shoes barely crunched on the roof's gravel surface. He was coming toward us.

The footsteps stopped, and I heard little besides the beat of my heart and a burst of song from up the street at the Fireplug. And then he spoke into the silence. "So, that's where it is." They were almost the exact words Ed had muttered when he saw the drone. Only this time, it was Harold's voice. He said more loudly, in his usual jolly pub-owner tones, "I know you're behind the chimney. You can come out now."

With his eyes closed, Ed took deep breaths but otherwise didn't move.

I gave Jocelyn her phone, edged past Ed, and walked around

the south side of the chimney. Standing west of the chimney, Harold watched me. Even in the relative darkness, I saw his small but superior smile, as if he pitied me for my foolishness. Jocelyn and Ed followed me out of the laughable shelter of the chimney.

Harold glared at Ed. "I heard some of the fantasies you were weaving, Ed. I had nothing to do with the burning of my pub in Chicago, and nothing to do with the murder of Bonnie Skye. Her husband torched the bookstore where she worked and where he'd left her body. My pub was next door. The fire destroyed it. I was an eyewitness and was able to testify that I saw Bonnie and her husband go into the building, and only him coming out. He's in prison where he belongs. I didn't know her, or them, but Kirk MacLean did. He refused to believe that Skye could kill his wife, and he started scouring the country for evidence against anybody and everybody. He even followed me to Fallingbrook and got a job here. I'm not sure what MacLean had in mind if he unearthed someone that he could scare into thinking that he, Kirk MacLean, had some sort of evidence against them. People like him would use any excuse to make money, including threatening someone with exposure. But MacLean was never going to find anyone besides Bonnie's husband. The right person is behind bars, no matter what MacLean wanted to believe. Maybe MacLean could play the pipes, but he couldn't do much of anything else, and he certainly could not solve crimes. They'll probably discover that MacLean's death was an accident." Harold bent over the drone.

I warned, "Don't touch that drone. It could be evidence."

Harold's laugh sounded warm, but still tinged with the underlying pity I'd seen on his face moments before. "It's okay. I've forgiven Ed for stealing it and destroying it. I'm sure you meant to return it, Ed, and it's not your fault that you're useless and crashed my drone. I'm not going to report the theft. Your punishment will be losing your job."

Harold untucked his white dress shirt, picked up the drone, wrapped it in the front of his shirt, and cradled it against his chest almost like it was a baby. He even rubbed his shirttails against the drone's arms and legs as if to warm it. Or to wipe fingerprints off it . . .

Carrying the drone, he started toward the ladder.

Ed hadn't said a word. A shaft of light from the half-moon, now sinking in the west beyond the parking lot, shined on his right arm, making the spider tattoo seem to jump. As if that beam of light were a burning needle, Ed took off, racing toward Harold. He ran past his boss, though, into the shadows, and leaped up onto the parapet.

Afraid he was going to fall, I yelled, "Don't!"

Ed grasped the ladder and swung his feet onto it.

Harold shouted, "Ed! Stop!"

The ladder clanked. Hanging onto both sides of it, Ed started down.

My phone peeked out from the top of his shirt pocket.

I flew after him. "Give me back my phone!"

Light flashed behind me, and something hard slammed into the backs of my knees.

My shins grazed the top of the parapet. I was about to plunge over the foot-high wall onto the porch roof.

I shot my left hand out and grabbed the side of the ladder. It had all happened so quickly that I'd barely noticed Jocelyn's scream. Shocked almost as much by her panic as by my almost catastrophic loss of balance, I fell against the ladder and wrapped my arm around it.

The ladder rattled. Although knowing I risked making myself dizzy, I peered downward.

Below me, Ed jumped off the ladder's bottom rungs. He didn't waste a second looking up to see if anyone might be following him. He dashed around the back corner of Deputy Donut and out of my sight.

Harold ran toward me. "Emily, what are you doing up

here? Sorry! I didn't mean to hit you with that thing. I was trying to stop Ed, and that thing is harder to throw than it looks."

That thing? He'd flung the drone at Ed and had hit me instead?

He must have. The drone was lying between my sneakers and Harold's. One of its propellors turned lazily. Another had broken off and was lying near the base of the parapet.

Breathing heavily, especially for her, Jocelyn pulled me away from the ladder, the parapet, and the drone. "Are you okay, Emily?"

"Sure." The backs of my knees stung, and in my dazed state, all I could think of was that I was glad I'd chosen a wedding dress that would cover my knees. Their fronts would be scraped and scabbed, and their backs might be yellow and purple by the next Monday, still nine days away.

Focus.

I rasped out, "Let's go farther from this parapet. I'm not sure how much stress it can withstand."

Harold seemed to be listening to Ed, who was still running north. "The way Ed threw himself at that wall and over it, I think it can withstand a lot. What are you two doing up here? If he chased you up here, I'm sorry. I should never have hired him. He was a good employee most of the time, but he lacks judgment. I should never have let him be the one to learn to fly that drone. And to make matters worse, it disappeared the night that Kirk MacLean died. I don't know what Ed was doing out that night besides crashing my drone, but I can't help wondering why he was flying it in the storm, especially that night." He paused and asked, "*Did* he chase you two up here?"

Harold had hurled that drone with surprising force.

It had fallen short of Ed on the ladder. It had nearly pitched me headfirst off the roof.

To give Harold credit, aiming a broken drone with propellors spinning drunkenly had to be difficult.

But had Harold truly been aiming at Ed? Or at me?

Jocelyn squeezed my wrist and pulled me farther from Harold.

Ed and Harold had each blamed the other for crashing the drone, and both had implied that the other one might have been involved in Kirk's death. Who had been lying?

Or had both of them participated in killing Kirk and causing the murder weapon to fly away in the claws of a drone?

Chapter 37

✺

I didn't trust Ed, and I was not going to trust Harold, either. But I could tell Harold part of the truth. "Ed didn't chase us. We were working next to him at the party in the firehall." Attempting to sound sincere, I dolloped on a frosting of untruth. "Jocelyn and I were talking about this safety course we'd taken and how we were planning to practice our ladder skills, and he . . ."

Fortunately, Jocelyn figured out what I was trying to do. She took over the story. "He said he'd like to do that, too." I hoped that Harold didn't understand how unusual it was for her breath to catch, as if from fear, in her throat. She added more confidently, "He said, correctly, that a third person would make the exercise safer." She nodded toward the top of the ladder, still showing over the parapet. "And he's obviously experienced with ladders."

Jocelyn stopped to inhale, and I finished for her. "So, he came here, too."

Harold pulled a phone from his pocket. "Maybe he knew all along where he'd crashed my drone, and he didn't want you two finding it without him coming along to make up lies about it. Maybe he is, as you say, experienced with ladders, but maybe not. He could have just been desperate to flee. It's no wonder. While he was lying to you about me, he was obviously confessing to murdering MacLean. I'll get the police to track him down." Harold tapped his phone screen and then reported in a deep and serious voice, "My employee, Ed Ellbonder, who's about six-four and two hundred pounds and has tattoos and long dark hair that he usually wears in a ponytail, stole from me and from my friend, Emily Westhill, and he confessed to murdering that bagpiper. I heard him running north in the parking lots behind the west side of Wisconsin Street. He should be close to Oak Street by now." Harold disconnected and assured us, "They'll catch him." He gestured toward the ladder. "Shall I help you ladies practice going back down?"

Jocelyn shook her head. "I've lost my nerve."

"Me, too," I said.

Harold smoothed his untucked shirt as if his palms could iron out the wrinkles he'd made by wrapping his shirttails around the drone. "I didn't hear everything Ed was saying about me, but what I heard was lies."

How much had Harold actually heard?

And then I thought of something I should have considered before.

Ed had told us on Monday evening that his phone had been stolen. Had he been telling the truth? According to the police, his and Quentin's wallets were in Kirk's van, but Ed's phone wasn't. If Ed's phone had truly been stolen on Monday, he hadn't been watching the drone's progress early Wednesday morning on his own phone.

He could have used another device, though, so whether his phone was stolen or not didn't prove anything. But it was a possible clue that Harold was the one making up stories.

And then I thought of other possible evidence against Harold. He had mentioned cutting through parking lots on his way to and from work. He probably lived somewhere near me. Our working hours were so different that I'd never seen him when Dep and I were walking to and from Deputy

Donut, but he could have driven past my house when I was gardening in the front yard or the donut car was in the driveway, and he could have known where I lived.

Maybe Harold lived in one of the houses that backed onto the parking lot near where Kirk had parked his van. I'd pictured Ed hopping a fence and fleeing from the scene into one of those houses. It could have been Harold.

Jocelyn touched her phone's screen.

Harold asked, "What are you doing? I already called the police. They'll catch Ed."

Jocelyn didn't look up from her phone. "I'm calling the fire department to get us down." She managed to sound bored, although I was sure she was as anxious about Harold as I was. And that flash I'd seen before the drone rammed me? Had Jocelyn taken a picture of Harold throwing it?

He strode to her and ripped her phone out of her hand. "I said I'd help you." His fury told me that he probably did suspect that Jocelyn had photographed him. He threw her phone. It skimmed across the parapet near the ladder and slid off toward the porch roof and the hard parking lot.

Jocelyn stared at him. "Why did you do that?" She didn't have to pretend amazement. Plus, she was probably thinking the same thing I was—Harold wouldn't have destroyed her phone if he expected either of us to live to tell anyone how it had ended up on the ground. If Harold was contemplating throwing both of us off the roof, he must have thought we had believed what Ed had told us.

Harold calmed down slightly, but I could hear the anger simmering underneath his voice. "We don't need the fire department or anyone else. You two need to get yourselves down for your own sakes, or you'll never brave climbing a ladder again. You are both going down that ladder. You first, and then Emily. I'll help you."

He would undoubtedly help us down, probably by pushing us off the parapet the moment we tried to step onto the ladder. He'd say we fell accidentally, breaking Jocelyn's phone, and probably our skulls, too.

I edged farther from him.

He turned toward me. "Where are you going?"

That was a good question. The ladder wasn't safe for us while he was anywhere near it, and neither was the roof. I had never before thought of Deputy Donut as small. At the moment, its roof seemed barely bigger than a trampoline, an image I quickly tried to drive from my mind.

The drone was the only thing up there resembling a weapon. I dashed to it, picked it up, faced Harold, and let go of every pretense of believing or trusting him. "Don't come closer."

He merely laughed and started toward Jocelyn. She ran. He chased her. She dodged around the north side of the chimney. With the awkward drone in my arms slowing me down, I ran after both of them. We were two against one, and Jocelyn and I were both strong, but Harold was big and undoubtedly stronger.

Possibly hoping to meet Jocelyn on the other side of the chimney, Harold headed toward the south side of the chimney, the side that was closest to the edge.

Jocelyn must have anticipated that move. She came back around the north side of the chimney and waited, her back to me and her face toward the chimney, but several paces from it.

Harold raced out from behind the north side of the chimney.

He wouldn't have recognized Jocelyn's stance, but I did.

Almost exactly as I'd pictured her defending us from Ed, she turned a flip, rammed Harold's chin with her feet, and knocked him onto his back.

Except for their feet on the gravel, Jocelyn and Harold had been quiet, but I'd been screaming, the ineffectual croak of nightmares. I closed my mouth and ran to Jocelyn and the man lying on the roof.

Jocelyn whipped off her belt, flipped Harold onto his side

and then onto his stomach. As if she'd had police training, she straddled him, pulled his wrists together behind his back, and wound her belt around them. She extracted his phone from his back pocket, tossed it onto the roof, and sat where the phone had been.

Harold called us all sorts of names, told us exactly what he thought should happen to us, and struggled, kicking his feet.

I held his incapacitated drone above his head and warned, "You don't want me to drop this, Harold."

Harold's shirtsleeves had ridden up, exposing a thick white bandage above his left wrist.

Suddenly I remembered that while Ed had been with us on the roof, his sleeves had been rolled up, both of his sleeves. Without noticing the significance, I'd seen his spider tattoo.

It had been too dark to be sure that he had no cuts, scratches, bruises, or bandages on his arms, but I hadn't spotted any.

If Kirk had tried to stab someone with his ceremonial dagger or the knife from Frisky Pomegranate, it had probably been Harold. Which didn't prove that Ed was innocent. Half afraid of seeing Ed sneaking up the ladder, I glanced nervously at it. No one was there.

Jocelyn reached her arms up toward me. I lowered the drone into her hands, took off my own belt, and wrapped it around Harold's ankles. Jocelyn informed him, "I have your drone now, and if you move, it could fall out of my hands onto your head. It might hurt."

Harold growled, "What do you two think you're doing? I came up to rescue you from Ed, and this is the thanks I get."

I picked up his phone from the roof, sat on his calves with my back to Jocelyn, and hunted for a button to awaken his phone. Harold flailed.

Sirens sounded from the direction of the police station. I had planned to call emergency but had not yet done it.

In the darkness, I heard Harold smack his lips. "That'll be

the police, finally going after Ed." Judging from what I'd heard of his side of the conversation, with no pauses and no one apparently asking him questions or telling him to stay on the line, I doubted that he had actually called them. He urged, "You two can get off me, now."

We didn't, and despite Harold's squirming, I caused his phone to come on.

An engine roared. It sounded like a fire truck. It came closer.

Scarlet and white lights swung around, coloring nearby buildings.

On Wisconsin Street below us, brakes hissed. The siren quieted, leaving my ears ringing. Lights flashed around and around, the truck engine continued running, and a radio stuttered out staticky sounds.

No one near the fire truck could have possibly heard any of us on the roof, but we all shouted for help. Harold's voice was loudest.

Chapter 38

❧

I didn't need Harold's password to call emergency on his phone.

Over his noisy protests, I told the dispatcher that we needed the police. "We're on the roof, so it would be helpful if the fire department came and brought a ladder truck."

The dispatcher told me to stay on the line.

On the street below us, the engine continued roaring, and I heard more vehicles arrive. The strobing lights were disorienting, first bright, then dark, red, white, shifting the shadows around us and causing the chimney to appear to waver. Machinery clanked and whirred. People shouted. I wondered if anyone was paying attention to that staticky, and to me incomprehensible, radio.

A man who sounded like a slightly muffled Scott hollered, "Brent! Wait!"

In disbelief, I told the dispatcher, "I think they're already here."

"Really?" She drew the word out like she didn't believe me, which wasn't surprising. She'd barely had time to contact them. "Stay on the line until you're sure."

Aluminum railings inched toward the parapet on the front of the building. The railings rose higher, and I realized they were the side rails of the fire department's aerial ladder. The top of the ladder hovered over the parapet, not quite touching it.

In full gear, complete with a light shining from the front of his helmet, Scott scrambled off the ladder and then turned and helped Brent onto the roof. Brent was wearing one of his neatly tailored dark business suits.

I told the dispatcher, "The police and fire department have arrived."

"Apparently, we received a call ten minutes ago." She sounded mystified.

I thanked her, and we disconnected.

I wanted to run to Brent, but I stayed where I was, sitting on Harold's calves.

The front of Scott's helmet cast a shadow over his face, and the light beaming from it made it hard to see his expression, but judging by Brent's, we were an astonishing sight. Jocelyn and I were sitting on Harold as if we were riding a horse—and it was bucking—with her facing the head and me facing the tail. Jocelyn was undoubtedly still holding that battered drone above Harold's head. I calmly set his phone down on the roof beside me and pushed down with both hands on Harold's ankles. Even though my belt tied his ankles together, his feet were still too active for me to feel completely safe.

Brent ran to us. "What's going on?" Behind him, a firefighter helped Vic Throppen, also in a suit, off the fire truck's ladder and onto the roof. Vic snapped pictures of Harold, Jocelyn, me, and everything surrounding us.

Harold bellowed, "These two harpies attacked me."

Vic stated coldly, "They're getting off you. Right now. And you there, set that thing down. Carefully." Still sitting on Harold's legs, I looked over my shoulder at Vic. He was talking to Jocelyn. "Better yet, wait." He unbuttoned his suit jacket, pulled out a large tan paper square, and unfolded it. He had climbed to our roof carrying an empty but sizeable evidence bag. He ordered Jocelyn, "Slide it into this without touching more of it than you have to." He held the bag open, and Jocelyn wrestled the drone into it. Harold was now lying still.

Vic reminded Jocelyn and me, "You two ladies, get off him."

Brent had to know that neither Jocelyn nor I would attack someone unless we had to. He reached down both of his hands. Jocelyn and I each took one and stood. Brent let us go and pointed at the chimney. "Go over there and wait until we can get you down from here." Although I suspected that he wanted to laugh at the way we'd looked when he first spotted us sitting on Harold, Brent had controlled his voice. He sounded brisk and official.

Vic threw all three of us a suspicious glance. "And no talking to each other. Hear?"

Jocelyn and I nodded and turned toward the chimney.

Brent called after us, "Emily, your knees are bleeding."

I looked down. I'd skinned them more than I'd realized. It was almost like being ten years old again. I held the palms of my hands toward him although, due to the distance and the dim lighting, he probably wouldn't be able to see the scrapes and scratches. "I fell."

"They're bleeding in back, too." Brisk and official had turned into alarmed and official.

Vic was kneeling, unfastening the belt around Harold's ankles. He signaled to Scott, and Scott started working on the belt around Harold's wrists.

I pointed at Harold. "He threw that broken drone at me. It nearly knocked me off the roof."

Harold sat on the roof, pulled his knees up, and rubbed his ankles. He winced as if in pain. "I wasn't aiming at her. I came up here because I was afraid that my employee, Ed Ellbonder, was menacing the two harp—er, women. I accused Ed, and he ran toward that ladder over there. He'd stolen Emily's phone. I didn't know she was going to chase him trying to get it back. I tried to stop him by throwing the drone at him, but it's hard to aim a shape like that. It missed Ed, but it hit Emily. If she's willing to tell the truth, she'll admit that I apologized to her."

I backed against the rough bricks of the chimney beside Jocelyn and nodded. "He apologized."

Jocelyn added, "But—"

Vic interrupted harshly. "I told you two not to talk."

Brent didn't say anything, but he was watching me and frowning in obvious concern. I glanced meaningfully toward the ladder that Jocelyn and I had set up at the back of the building. A light from the aerial ladder illuminated the top of our ladder.

Brent had been behind our building enough to know that the ladder had recently appeared there, and he must have understood my silent warning about the escape route Harold might take. He said to no one in particular, "Police officers are stationed at the base of the ladder at the back of the building." He threw me another look and spoke into his radio. "Send paramedics to the front of Deputy Donut. Firefighters will help them up to the roof. People up here might be injured."

Trying to show without speaking that I didn't need medical help, I flapped my hands, but Brent didn't retract his request.

More firefighters had climbed their ladder. About ten of them surrounded Harold and stared down at him. I hoped that being in the center of the glow from their helmet lights intimidated Harold. To me, the firefighters appeared merely curious. And like they were looking forward to regaling their friends and families with tales of the peculiar rooftop call they'd made that night. Their enormous boots shuffled on the gravel.

Brent and Vic helped Harold to his feet.

Vic demanded, "What went on here tonight?"

Harold's posture was confident, upright, and apparently relaxed. "I'll tell you the honest truth."

Beside me, Jocelyn pretended to stifle a cough. She was probably thinking the same thing I was—that liars were probably fond of terms like "honest truth." Vic was studying Harold, not us. I jabbed Jocelyn's arm with an elbow. I was careful not to look at her. I might have laughed aloud.

Harold pointed toward us. "I came up here to rescue those two women from Ed. I called him out on the lies he was telling them, but instead of waiting for you folks to come, he ran away."

Vic asked, "What lies?"

Harold's answer was quick. "He was projecting, telling them I'd done the things he had done."

Vic straightened his suit jacket. "Can you be more specific?"

"He said I flew my drone and lost it. But he's the one who did that. I'd given him permission to learn to fly it, pass the exam, and everything, but he must not have bothered with the exam. He took that drone out late at night. Maybe he thought no one would notice because of the storm. He probably thought no one was outside. I expected him to be still assembling my drone and learning how to fly it. Then, tonight, he abandoned his post on the patio of the Fireplug— I'm the owner, you know—and snuck over here. It turned out that he'd somehow noticed these two women with flashlights up here on the roof. That must have been when he figured out where the drone he'd lost had gone. He chased them up here—"

Vic interrupted. "Were they already here, or did he chase them up here?"

"Sorry," Harold said. "They must have already been up here. He followed them." He pointed at our ladder. "Up the ladder and everything. When I got here, he was saying not only that I'd flown the drone, but that I did it on the night that the bagpiper died. He had some story about the bag-piper trying to extort me over the death of some woman in Chicago."

Brent had been watching Harold. He glanced toward me. I gave my head a slight nod, and Brent returned his attention to Vic and Harold.

Vic asked Harold, "What do you suppose your employee did with the drone that night?"

Harold was taller than Vic. He stood up straighter. "I have a theory. Ed killed that bagpiper. Maybe it was an accident, but afterward, he attached the mug he'd killed him with to my drone."

Vic turned quickly and glared at me.

Harold didn't seem to notice. He puffed out his chest. "And then Ed sent the drone to deliver the mug far from the scene, but when he tried to get the drone back, he crashed it. He must have figured he could just leave my drone here and replace it so I'd never know what he'd done. It could have been years before anyone came up here." Harold shook his head like someone pondering a difficult subject. "I have to admire him for flying that drone as well as he did with little or no experience."

Vic had returned to paying attention to Harold, but Brent was watching me. He raised an eyebrow and cocked his head slightly.

I turned my palms up to indicate that I didn't know who had told Harold that a mug was involved in Kirk's murder.

Maybe no one had needed to tell Harold. I suspected that he'd known, long before anyone else did, about that mug, where it had gone, and how it had gotten there.

Chapter 39

✵

As I understood it, the only people besides the murderer who were certain that a Deputy Donut mug had been involved in Kirk's murder were the police, my parents, and me. That evening, I'd given Jocelyn some pretty strong hints about the mug, but I'd been with her ever since, and she hadn't repeated the information. I was sure that my parents wouldn't have told anyone.

As if assessing possible escape routes, Harold glanced for a second toward the ladder that Jocelyn and I had set up. Maybe he wondered if Brent had been bluffing about police officers stationed near the foot of the ladder.

There was a short, tense silence, and then Brent suggested to Vic, "Maybe we should go back to the station and finish taking this man's statement in comfort." And probably away from curious firefighters. And Jocelyn and me.

"Detective Fyne, you go with him," Vic ordered. "I'll stay here and question the two women. Separately."

Harold bent toward his phone, still lying on the roof where I'd set it.

I called urgently, "Brent!"

Putting out a hand to stop Harold from reaching his phone, Brent looked at me. So did Vic.

I shouted, "Take his phone! Ed's was stolen, probably before . . ."

I didn't have to finish the sentence. Brent nodded and slipped Harold's phone into his jacket pocket.

Harold objected. "That's mine."

Brent stayed calm and neutral. "You'll get it back."

He wasn't the only one who understood what I'd meant by "before." Harold tangled himself in more lies. "If my phone has videos on it of the night of the bagpiper's death, that will prove that Ed stole my drone and also borrowed my phone to watch where it went."

Patiently, Brent stated, "We'll check everything out."

Again, Harold shot a quick look toward the ladder leaning against the back of our building. Brent stayed within inches of him.

A siren sounded on the street below us. Scott waved Brent and Harold away from the top of the aerial ladder and directed a couple of firefighters to go down and help the paramedics climb to the roof.

A minute later, firefighters helped Samantha and her partner, wearing their emergency medical technician uniforms and lugging cases of equipment, onto the roof.

Brent pointed toward the chimney. "Emily and Jocelyn have scraped knees, and the backs of Emily's legs are cut."

I started to say I was fine, but Harold spoke instead. "Those two women injured me when they tackled me."

Staring toward the bandage on Harold's left forearm, Vic asked, "Did they already give you first aid?" Vic's barely disguised sarcasm showed that he was not believing everything Harold said. I hid my triumphant smirk from Harold but aimed it at Jocelyn. She grinned and made another fake cough.

Harold yanked his shirtsleeve down to cover the bandage. "That's old. The one with the straight hair kicked me in the chin and knocked me down. I hit my head."

Samantha looked up into his face. "Did you black out?"

"Probably not for long, but I'll tell you what. I'll go to the police station and file a complaint of assault against the two women, and then a policeman can accompany me to the hospital, and an actual doctor can assess my injuries so that charges can be laid."

Vic snapped, "Fine. And we'll do the same with Ms. Westhill. You admitted that you threw the drone that hit her."

Harold lowered his chin and rounded his shoulders in patently fake humility. "I didn't do that on purpose. Those two attacked me for no good reason."

Samantha threw him a withering glare. "He probably should be checked for concussion. He's not making sense." Instead of examining him, however, she and her partner strode toward Jocelyn and me.

Harold bunched his hands into fists. "Don't listen to that ambulance driver. She and Emily have been at my pub together. They're friends. They'd say anything."

Muttering underneath her breath about being called an "ambulance driver," Samantha shined a powerful flashlight at Jocelyn's and my knees.

Scott spoke to Vic. "Sir, if you don't mind, I'd like to remove the civilians from the roof as soon as possible in case another call comes in. We don't want to strand anyone."

Vic rapped out, "Fine." Or was he repeating Brent's last name? He added, "I'll be glad to be on solid ground again."

Brent smiled at me. "Maybe Emily and Jocelyn can take you into Deputy Donut and give you some decent coffee."

Vic didn't answer.

Samantha quietly told Scott that she needed to assess Jocelyn's and my injuries before letting us climb down any ladders. She had me turn around. "The cuts in back don't look too bad, Emily, but we'll clean you both up, and then we'll see, okay?"

Surely Vic wouldn't mind if I talked to Samantha and her partner, but I limited my answer to, "Sure."

With her partner aiming a flashlight, Samantha started cleaning our knees and palms and tweezing out grit.

Brent spoke into his radio. "Come around to the front and meet me at the ladder truck, please." He turned to Scott. "Okay, we're ready to go down."

Harold pushed past firefighters between him and their ladder, but one of the firefighters stopped him and clambered onto the ladder first.

Harold complained, "You don't need to go ahead of me as if I were a toddler."

Scott had been watching Samantha's first aid. His face fiercer than I'd ever seen it, he snapped, "Rules."

Harold started backing down the ladder. He looked up at Brent. "If those girls"—he had downgraded us from harpies and women—"can be questioned in their donut shop, allow me to treat you to a burger and a beer at my pub."

Brent's smile was perfunctory. "I'll have to pass."

Samantha tackled the backs of my knees with a burning liquid. "Sorry if it stings."

"It's no worse than the cuts were."

Brent called to Samantha, "Is Emily cleared to climb down the fire truck's ladder?"

Samantha picked up her medical kit. "If she feels like it. She doesn't need stitches."

I said loudly enough for Brent to hear, "I'd rather climb down myself than be lowered in some sort of weird contraption."

Brent gave me a thumbs-up, let a firefighter precede him, and started down the ladder. Firefighters climbed down between him and Samantha and between Samantha and her partner. Scott, a couple of his firefighters, and Vic stood at the edge and watched them go.

I decided that Brent's command to stand near the chimney had applied only when Harold was on the roof being questioned, so I went to the side of the roof overlooking Wisconsin Street, too.

A patrol car was stopped at an angle, more or less facing north, in the southbound lane of Wisconsin Street. Two police officers got out of the cruiser, a tall blond woman and a shorter, agile man. Misty and Hooligan.

Harold reached the sidewalk and was quickly surrounded by firefighters and Brent. After conferring with Brent for a second, Hooligan escorted Harold into the rear of Misty and Hooligan's patrol car. Misty climbed into the driver's seat, Hooligan took his usual place in the passenger seat, and Brent headed for an unmarked cruiser. He wasn't leaving Vic without transportation, though. Another unmarked car was near the fire truck.

What Vic didn't have any longer was backup from other police officers. I sensed that he was fuming. He might have thought that if Jocelyn and I arrived on Wisconsin Street before he did, we might run away. Or he might have been afraid that one of us would use the ladder we had erected. That was not going to happen if I could help it.

He must have decided that we were less likely to escape him if he left us on the roof with firefighters than if he let us arrive on the sidewalk before he did. Firefighters helped him down the aerial ladder, and then Jocelyn.

Scott guided my footing on the fire truck's ladder. Because of its high siderails and gradual angle, backing down wasn't scary. Well, compared to going from our parapet to our ladder, it wasn't.

Chapter 40

❧

Jocelyn and Vic were waiting for me beside the fire truck. I asked Vic, "Would you like to come into our shop to take our statements? As Brent said, we'll make coffee." I hoped Vic wouldn't insist on taking us to the police station. I didn't want to be anywhere near Harold.

"That'll be fine."

I opened our front door and flicked on lights.

Vic asked me, "Can your assistant make the coffee while I talk to you?"

Jocelyn answered for me, "Sure. You have a choice. I can grind some of today's special beans. They're from Sumatra. Or we have a smooth Colombian. Or we can open tomorrow's special. It's from Bolivia, which doesn't produce a lot of coffee, so it's unusual. You might think that we added chocolate to it, but we didn't."

Vic's smile made him look less predatory. "Let me try the Bolivian."

"And some of today's donuts?"

"I'd like a couple. You choose."

I led him to the table farthest from the kitchen and lifted two chairs down from where we'd set them upside down on the table.

We sat.

Vic took out his notebook. "Who did you tell about that mug?"

"Only Jocelyn, and I only hinted to her about it tonight, right before we climbed to the roof. The only people she encountered after that and before you folks joined us were Ed and Harold. She didn't say anything about the mug to either of them."

"Your parents knew about it, right?"

"Yes, from my theories and your fingerprinting."

"Who did they tell?"

"Probably no one. They've been focusing on the Fallingbrook Arts Festival and on helping Brent and me get ready for our wedding. My first husband was also a detective. My parents know about keeping quiet about investigations."

Vic scribbled in his notebook. "Did you tell Ed Ellbonder?"

"No, and he didn't mention it during his accusations of Harold."

"How do you suppose Harold knew about it?"

I gave Vic a level stare. "There's one obvious way."

To my surprise, Vic nodded. "We need to rule out other ways he could have found out about it before we jump to that conclusion."

"Those black marks on the mug's handle could have been made by the coating on the drone's claws."

"I thought the same thing. The forensics lab can test for that."

"I find it interesting that Harold conveniently came up with the theory that the drone had been used to deliver the mug somewhere. Ed said nothing like that." I told him that Harold probably lived in my neighborhood and knew which house was mine. I concluded with, "He could live in one of the houses next to the lot where Kirk parked his van."

"He's not one of the homeowners, but we'll check. Maybe

he's a renter or lives across the street or somewhere else nearby. He wasn't on our radar until tonight." Vic wrote in his
notebook and then looked up at me. "Anything else?"

"When he was talking to us, he admitted he owned a pub
next door to a bookstore that burned down with the body of
a woman inside it. His supposed eyewitness testimony put
the woman's husband in jail for her murder. I think that
woman was Bonnie Flora MacDonald Skye, and her incar-
cerated husband is Fergus Skye. I found an article about his
conviction on the internet." I repeated my theory about the
three tunes that Kirk MacLean had played and the possible
warning in the motto on his business cards. Finally, I told
Vic, "Harold guessed aloud to Jocelyn and me that Kirk was
trying to frighten Ed into paying Kirk not to tell the police
that Ed had participated in that murder in Chicago over ten
years ago. What if it was Harold, not Ed, who Kirk was trying to extort? Did Ed have any connection to the Skye couple? Has Ed ever been in Chicago?"

"We'll look into all of it."

Jocelyn brought Vic his mug of coffee and a plate holding
a double fudge donut and a baked carrot cake donut with
cream cheese frosting. She handed me a mug of calming
chamomile tea and an old-fashioned donut spiced with lots
of nutmeg—chamomile to help me sleep, no doubt, and nutmeg to fill that sleep with dreams. Or, after our experience on
the roof, nightmares . . . *Dreams*, I firmly told myself, *of
Brent*. Even before my first sip of tea, I felt warmer.

Jocelyn retreated to the kitchen, and I said to Vic, "You
saw the bandage on Harold's left forearm. Was Kirk right-
handed?"

"He was."

"Everything Harold said about Ed could have been pro-
jection, telling us what he actually did, but saying that Ed
did it."

"And vice-versa."

"Almost as soon as Harold arrived on the roof, I told him not to touch the drone because it might be evidence. He picked it up and rubbed his shirttails over it. He could have been wiping off fingerprints."

"His own and—did anyone else touch it?"

"Not then. I picked it up after he threw it, and when you came up onto the roof, Jocelyn was holding it. We attacked him because he chased Jocelyn around the chimney. It sounds silly, but he wasn't playing games. I'm sure he meant for both of us to end up sprawled on the pavement one and a half stories down."

"That's a serious accusation."

"He kept telling us, rather forcefully, to start down the ladder, and he'd help us down. I didn't trust the sort of 'help' he might have given us. I didn't see him actually hurl the drone, which he claimed to have aimed at Ed, but he missed Ed by a lot, and if I hadn't grabbed that ladder, I probably would have been knocked off balance and over the parapet. Jocelyn might have a better idea of where he was trying to throw it."

"When Harold threw that drone, why were you close to Ed, and to the edge?"

I gave Vic a rueful smile. "Ed had my phone. I chased after him because I wanted it back. I shouldn't have been so impulsive."

"Can you describe your phone?"

I told him the make and model. "It's in a pink case printed with gray cats and pink and brown donuts."

He reached into the inner chest pocket of his jacket, pulled out a phone, and set it in front of me. "Like this?"

I was careful not to touch it. "Exactly like that."

"Is yours password-protected?"

"Yes."

"Can you try turning this one on?"

"Is it okay if I touch it? I mean, if it's mine, it has Ed's fingerprints on it."

"And mine. It's okay. About the first thing that Ed told us was that this was your phone."

"You caught him, then, after Harold called you?"

"I don't have a record of any calls from Harold. And we didn't 'catch' Ed. He came to us with that phone. He'd used it to phone emergency shortly after he reached the ground. He said that you and Jocelyn were on the roof here"—he pointed toward the ceiling—"with someone he thought might have murdered Kirk MacLean. He wanted us to send someone to rescue you. He was in a panic. He's waiting in the police station now to give his statement."

"That's how all of you got here about two seconds after I called emergency using Harold's phone. Without," I admitted, "asking him if I could." I tapped my password onto the screen of the phone Vic had handed me. The phone came on. "This is my phone." I checked the call record. "I didn't make the most recent call. Someone else called emergency." I showed Vic.

He nodded. "Okay, but there's one thing I don't understand. Ed said you and Jocelyn were already on the roof when he arrived and climbed up there. Why were you and Jocelyn on the roof in the dark?"

I took a deep breath and explained hearing the word *drone* at the party that evening and then wondering if a drone could have caused the buzzing I'd heard early the morning that Kirk died, the flashing lights my parents had noticed, and, a little later, my cat's acting like something was on the roof. "Because of the timing, I also started wondering if the drone had been involved in Kirk's death or in moving the mug. Jocelyn was with me at the party. When drones were being mentioned, she also remembered my cat's reaction to something on the roof the morning Kirk died. After the party,

Jocelyn and I looked up combinations of words from the titles of the three tunes that Kirk had played, and we found the article I told you about. We didn't know what to make of it." I gave Vic all the reasons why Jocelyn and I wondered if Ed might have flown the drone and crashed it on the roof. "Jocelyn and I decided to check. We found the crashed drone, but before we could call Brent or climb down, Ed showed up."

"Had you told Ed about your plans?"

"No."

"Why do you suppose he followed you?"

I told Vic about Ed noticing a light shining from the roof of the Fireplug toward our roof. "Ed said Harold owned one of those super-powerful lights."

"That's something we can look for with a search warrant." Vic sounded pleased. He wrote in his notebook and then asked, "Did you take pictures of any of this evening's events?"

"Only the drone. Then we heard someone—it turned out to be Ed—start up the ladder, and we kind of duckwalked to hide behind the chimney. My phone must have fallen out of my shorts pocket. Ed picked it up. I guess he hasn't replaced his stolen phone."

"Apparently not. He said he didn't mean to take yours with him, but he was in a hurry to get away from Harold and get help for you two."

"And you believe him?"

"We're beginning to."

"I am, too. I think Harold is Kirk's murderer, and unless he and Ed worked together, Ed is innocent. Do I get to keep my phone? You don't need it for evidence?"

"Not unless you want to charge Ed with stealing it."

"I don't."

"Can you show me the photos you took of the drone this evening?"

The photos showed very little, only the mangled drone, the twisted propellors, and the black-coated pincers. "Jocelyn took some, too, but Harold threw her phone off the roof. It's probably broken."

"We might be able to retrieve photos from it, anyway. But did I hear you correctly? Did you say that Harold threw Jocelyn's phone off the roof?"

"Yes. She said she was calling the fire department to bring a ladder and get us off the roof, but Harold must not have wanted her to call for any sort of help. After he destroyed her phone, I remembered that Ed's phone had been stolen before Kirk was murdered, so it was unlikely that Ed had been watching the video the drone was transmitting. Not using his own phone. Besides, whether or not Harold had killed Kirk, Ed hadn't threatened Jocelyn and me, but Harold had hit me with the drone and thrown Jocelyn's phone off the roof. Then she ran from him. He chased her, so we knew he was a danger to us. Jocelyn knocked him down with her feet."

Vic raised his eyebrows and glanced toward Jocelyn, humming in the kitchen.

I smiled. "Yes, that tiny woman. She no longer competes as a gymnast, but she coaches, and she's still in shape. I held the drone over Harold's head while she fastened her belt around his wrists and sat on him, and then she held the drone over his head while I belted his ankles and sat on his legs. Holding him down wasn't easy. And for the record, his head might have landed on the roof, and he could have been stunned for a second—who wouldn't be? But if he actually blacked out, it was only for a second or two. His complaints weren't polite, but they were articulate."

Vic whistled under his breath and continued writing. He finished and looked up. "Can you get Jocelyn, now? Maybe you can find something to do in the kitchen."

"Refill your coffee?"

"I'm okay."

"Then I'll go into the office. I'll stay inside until you folks allow us in the parking lot. Jocelyn's smashed phone is out there, and maybe other evidence."

"We should have people back there soon."

I signaled to Jocelyn. She took my place at the table.

Closing myself inside the office, I overheard Jocelyn's angry, "He purposely aimed that thing at Emily! He could have knocked her off the roof. She could have been badly injured or worse."

The office was mostly dark, except for glows coming through the windows on all four sides. The parking lot was brighter than usual. Someone had set up a powerful portable light near the end of the driveway, and Misty and Hooligan were shining their own lights on the pavement.

I didn't see the remains of Jocelyn's phone. I opened the back door, stuck my head out, and called to Misty and Hooligan. "Did you find Jocelyn's phone?"

Misty shook her head.

I changed my question to, "Did you find pieces of a phone?"

Hooligan answered, "We haven't found evidence of anything."

I had an idea. "I saw the phone slide off the parapet. Lots was going on, and I don't remember hearing anything breaking." I pointed above my head. "Maybe it landed up there."

Hooligan brushed his hands together. "And there's a ladder right here."

I couldn't help warning, "Be careful!"

Misty smiled. "We have all kinds of strange training and experience. Who used the ladder to climb onto the roof?"

"Jocelyn and I, then Ed came up, then Harold."

Hooligan made a pretend sad face. "And we weren't invited to the party."

"You'd have been more than welcome."

Misty checked the ladder's footing. Apparently, it was still secure.

Hooligan started up the ladder.

Misty held the ladder with both hands. "You should have called us instead of climbing ladders in the dark."

I defended myself. "I wasn't sure it was a police matter."

Misty glared at me. "So?"

"I know. I should have called. By the time I knew for sure, I'd lost my phone." All of my police officer friends, including my late husband, had informed me that they would rather be called for something that turned out to be nothing than to not be called when they could have prevented something terrible from happening.

Hooligan stopped climbing. I could see only his pantlegs from the shins down and his boots. He went up one more rung. "Aha! It must have fallen onto the porch roof and slid into the gutter." He rose to his toes.

Misty warned, "Careful!"

He grunted. "Got it! It's protected by a tough case. I don't see any damage." He climbed down the ladder and joined Misty on the pavement. The top of a paper evidence bag stuck out of a pocket on his armored vest.

Misty let go of the ladder. "Emily, is Detective Throppen still inside?"

"Yes, talking to Jocelyn."

Misty looked at Hooligan. "Let's take this to him."

I let them inside and switched on the office lights.

Vic turned toward us and watched Misty and Hooligan, with Jocelyn's phone in his outstretched hand, walk toward them.

I followed.

Chapter 41

❧

Misty apologized to Vic for interrupting his conversation with Jocelyn.

Hooligan showed the phone to the pair at the table. "We found this outside."

Jocelyn gasped softly. "It's not smashed."

Vic asked her, "Is it the one you said Harold threw off the roof?"

"Yes. And he did throw it. Emily saw it, too."

Misty explained, "It landed on the porch roof. Hooligan climbed up and got it."

Vic accepted the phone and handed it to Jocelyn. "Can you see if it works?"

She turned it on and gave him a thin smile. "It seems okay."

Vic asked her, "Did you take pictures while you were on the roof?"

"Yes. I'll show you." She tapped and scrolled. "I have lots of angles of the drone, and then, yes! Harold picked up the drone and was holding it like a baby, and he seemed to be cleaning it with his shirttails. I wondered if he was wiping fingerprints off it, so I started a video. And look!"

Vic got up and stood next to her. Misty, Hooligan, and I crowded around.

Jocelyn started the video from the beginning. Harold was holding the drone, looking down at it, and wiping it with his shirt. A blur ran past, heading toward the ladder. Jocelyn explained, "That's Ed." Harold yelled at him to stop, and another blur followed Ed past Jocelyn's camera. "That's Emily, running after Ed." Ed flung himself onto the parapet and the ladder. My voice, tinny over Jocelyn's speaker, demanded my phone. While I was still a couple of feet from the ladder, Harold heaved the drone toward me. It hit the back of my knees, bending them and throwing me into the parapet.

Beside me, Misty and Hooligan gasped, and Misty grabbed my wrist as if to assure herself I was unhurt.

In the video, I teetered for less than a second. It had seemed much longer. I grabbed the ladder, and then the roof swung crazily. Except it wasn't the roof that was swaying. Jocelyn told us, "I started running before I turned off the video." The video ended. "I reached Emily shortly before Harold did."

I added shakily, "And she pulled me away from the edge before he could do what the drone failed to do."

Vic asked Jocelyn to replay the video. We watched it again.

Misty said, "Harold missed Ed by several feet. Maybe his aim was terrible, but that sure looks like he knew he was too late to hit Ed with the drone, and he aimed at Emily on purpose."

Jocelyn's voice came out as sharp and hard as broken glass. "He did."

Vic told her, "We'll get investigators to go up there and study angles and distances. Along with the video, they'll be able to tell exactly how bad—or good—Harold's aim was."

Hooligan asked, "Emily, why did he throw it at you? I'm not denying that that's what it looks like, but why?"

My words were as dry as my mouth. "Harold had heard Ed telling Jocelyn and me that he thought Harold had killed a woman in Chicago, and that Harold probably killed Kirk because Kirk might have known or guessed the truth. Harold needed to prevent Jocelyn and me from telling anyone else. I think he would have liked to have knocked Ed off that ladder, but he was concentrating on wiping his fingerprints off that drone and wasn't fast enough. After he threw that drone and I didn't fall over the parapet, Harold tried to convince Jocelyn and me to face our fears and climb down the ladder, but we refused."

Jocelyn spread her hands out on the tabletop with its cheerful painting of a donut coated in peach-colored icing and decorated with chocolate heart-shaped sprinkles. "I was afraid he might push us off the parapet while we were transferring from it to the ladder." She held her phone on her open palm. "I know why he tried to destroy my phone. He suspected I might have photos or a video showing him hurling that broken drone at Emily. And I did!" She and I gave each other a high five.

Vic brought me back to earth. "Emily, can we have a look at the videos from your security cameras?"

"The front, yes, but the back—"

Jocelyn didn't let me finish. "The back one was off for a while, but I restarted it when Ed was climbing the ladder."

I ignored the obvious way that Misty was staring at me.

We all went into the office, and I turned on the computer. First, we looked at the videos from the street. Carrying the urn and the big bag and wearing our Deputy Donut aprons and hats, Jocelyn and I walked quickly from north to south past the front of the store. I was obviously talking. A half hour later, Ed dashed south along the sidewalk in front of Deputy Donut. He stared toward our front windows but didn't slacken his pace. A few minutes after that, Harold strolled south. He stared up toward our roof.

I said, "When Jocelyn and I were on the roof, I heard Ed running toward our building, but I didn't hear Harold approach until the ladder creaked."

Jocelyn said, "Same here."

"Judging by the way he's walking," Misty suggested, "he's trying to set his feet down quietly."

Vic praised her. "Good observation."

"Oh, I'm observant, all right." Knowing she was aiming that dig at Jocelyn and me and our non-explanation of why the rear video camera had been "off for a while," I felt like shrinking and hiding under the desk.

We sped the video up, but no one else appeared in it until the first fire truck arrived.

The video from the camera attached to our back porch roof showed Jocelyn and me carrying the urn and bag inside and then returning to the porch without our aprons and hats. Then there was nothing until someone wearing dark pants and shoes started up the ladder. His top half wasn't in the camera's range.

Vic asked, "Who's that?"

Jocelyn was quick to answer. "Harold, probably. I got the camera going again after Ed was almost up to the roof, so he didn't show up."

A few minutes later, Ed jumped off the bottom rungs of the ladder. He took my phone out of his shirt pocket and tore north through the parking lot.

Hooligan apologized to Vic, "I'm afraid I might have smeared fingerprints when I climbed the ladder to look for Jocelyn's phone. I went about halfway up."

"Not a problem," Vic answered. "Law enforcement saw Harold up there, and Ed went down that ladder before you went up, which probably destroyed a few of Harold's prints. Where is that ladder usually kept?"

I answered, "In the garage at the back of the parking lot."

Vic asked me, "If we have Misty and Hooligan put it away, being careful not to touch much of the top of it, can we access it tomorrow to take prints from it? I'd rather not leave it out and have more calls tonight about people roaming around on your roof."

"That would be great," I said. "Thanks." I told Misty and Hooligan, "We left the garage door open."

They both frowned at me.

I explained, "We didn't expect to be away from it more than a few moments."

Jocelyn added, "And we had our hands full of ladder." She gave Misty and Hooligan the key to her bike lock so they could unchain the ladder.

Vic held up a hand. "Misty and Hooligan, don't go until after I check in with Brent." He took out his own phone. "Hey, Brent." He was silent for a few seconds, listening to Brent on the phone and studying my face. "Footage on Harold's phone shows the drone flying from the roof of the Fireplug to Emily's driveway and setting the mug down there? Excellent!" He listened quietly again. "And flying back in heavy rain, and then the video suddenly ends? Perfect. Keep the person of interest there. We need to follow up on a few things, but I suspect he's our killer. I'm going to email you some pictures and a video." He glanced again at me. "And Emily's going to email you segments from the security cameras here at Deputy Donut." I nodded and started isolating the relevant clips from the videos. Vic added to Brent, "Don't let the video I'm sending you from up on the roof give you a heart attack. It was taken before you and I went up there tonight, and Emily is still with me, and she's fine." He listened for a few seconds. I couldn't hear what Brent was saying, but Vic, studying Misty, said, "I'll ask her." He lowered the phone and asked, "Misty, where were you from around midnight on Tuesday until around four in the morning on Wednesday?" He aimed the phone toward Misty.

She said loudly, "Working, part of the time in the office, and part of the time out on patrol with Hooligan. We were inside the office during the entire storm."

Vic took the phone back and asked, "Did you hear that, Brent?" After a second's pause, Vic grinned at us and said, "I'll be right there. Keep the suspect with you."

In a few short moments, Harold had gone from being a person of interest to a suspect. Because . . . ?

Misty sputtered. "Did that scum of a pub-owner claim that he'd been with *me* that night?"

Vic tapped Jocelyn's phone, sending Brent the video and photos. "Apparently, but your department will have records of where you actually were."

"As if! I would never . . . I'm a happily married woman, still a newlywed!"

Hooligan and I grinned at each other. I added, "And unlike Harold, her husband is respectable."

Misty muttered, "Faint praise."

Vic grinned at her. "Fallingbrook is lucky to have first responders like you two, Scott, and Brent. And those EMTs who looked after Jocelyn and Emily up on the roof this evening, too. Did I understand correctly that Samantha is your wife, Hooligan?"

Hooligan's smile was proud and loving. "Yes. And Misty and Emily introduced her to me."

I corrected him. "Misty did. I arrived moments later. You and Samantha were already smitten."

Hooligan's smile widened.

Vic handed Jocelyn her phone. "I've also sent your photos and that incriminating video to myself. I'd like your pictures, too, Emily, or can you send them to Brent? I should get over there. It appears that we have an arrest to make."

"Sure." I was too exhausted and drained to be jubilant or even relieved about the impending arrest. Maybe I would believe the danger was over for all of us if and when Harold was actually behind bars. I sent the files to Brent.

Vic thanked me, thanked all of us, strode to the front door, and left. Jocelyn locked the door. Misty and Hooligan went out through the office. Jocelyn and I carried the dirty dishes to the storeroom and put them into the dishwasher, and then we turned out lights and set alarms. Our back porch wasn't taped off, so we went out that way.

Outside, police tape blocked off only the area between the porch and the corner of our building next to the driveway. Misty was dismantling the portable light. Hooligan gave Jocelyn her key. "We chained your bike to the stand."

Jocelyn grinned and pocketed the key.

He turned to me. "We put your ladder away, closed your garage door, and tested it. It's locked. We'll leave this police tape here until investigators have a better look in the morning."

I thanked him and gazed up at the parapet, still intact and dark against the starry sky. "I doubt that there's much to find. Ed and Harold both arrived on foot, and they probably didn't drop things all over the place on the way."

Hooligan closed the portable light into the cruiser's trunk. "Do you two want a ride?"

Jocelyn pointed to her again-locked bike. "I'll walk my bike beside Emily until she gets home, and then ride the rest of the way. I doubt that we'll find any more murderers out tonight."

Misty glared at our building, but she must have been thinking about the Fireplug up the street or the police station beyond it. "We'll head into work and maybe get in on the booking process. That . . . that murderer claimed I spent the night with him! Who does he think he is?" She paused and aimed a finger at me. "And Emily, don't you go thinking that I was more upset about that disgusting allegation than I was about seeing a video of you almost being pitched off the roof."

Chapter 42

❧

Still glowering, Misty got into the driver's seat of the cruiser and slammed the door. Hooligan grinned at me and then clambered into the passenger seat. They took off.

The sound of their engine dwindled, and then all we heard were insects announcing that the evening was still warm with enough humidity to soften the air. No noise came from the Fireplug. Harold's congeniality had helped the pub thrive. His murdering might end the pub—and his freedom.

If Kirk had simply gone to the authorities with his theories about the death of the woman whose name figured in bagpipe tunes, he would probably be alive today. His greedy attempt at extortion had destroyed him. I sighed.

Jocelyn glanced at me, but if she were having similar thoughts, she didn't put them into words. I made certain that our alarms were reset and the video cameras were rolling. "I'm actually surprised we got out of here before the Jolly Cops arrived."

Jocelyn unlocked her bike. "With probably an hour to spare."

With her bike rolling beside us, we walked quickly through the quiet streets. We were both tired, and maybe a little giddy, but we didn't say much. We stopped at the path leading from the sidewalk to my front porch. The welcoming outdoor light was still on.

A large black SUV swooped to the curb beside us. Leaving the engine running and the driver's door of the unmarked police vehicle open, Brent ran to the sidewalk and grabbed me in a fierce hug. "I had to assure myself that you were all right."

I laughed into his suit jacket. "You saw both of us after Jocelyn took that video, and we were fine then. Besides, we'd told you about Harold throwing that thing at me."

Brent released me but held onto my elbows. "I know." He looked at Jocelyn. "How're you doing, Jocelyn?"

"I'm fine." She pointed at the SUV. "Or I was until your monster cruiser came snarling up to the curb like it was about to attack us." I could tell she was joking.

Brent could, too. Pretending to be insulted, he teased, "I drive with only the lightest of touches. I'll show you, Jocelyn. Let's squeeze your bike into the back, and I'll take you home to make sure you arrive safely." He glanced toward my porch. "After Emily locks herself inside her house."

Jocelyn clutched at her heart. "Oooh, Emily, such a masterful man." She faced Brent. "That's woman-speak for *bossy*."

"I know." He opened the SUV's back hatch. "And it's people-speak for *rattled*."

"Okay." Jocelyn wheeled her bike to the vehicle. "I'm only complying because I don't want to waste your time arguing. You need to go back to the police station and lock that guy up." She and Brent lifted the bike into the back of the SUV.

I asked Brent, "Are you arresting him?"

He managed to close the hatch without damaging the bike. "What do you think?"

"You'd better be."

"Masterful woman! Yes, on multiple charges."

Like Jocelyn, I didn't want to delay him. I ran up onto my porch, went inside, locked the door, and looked out the living room window.

Jocelyn was in the SUV's passenger seat. Standing beside the open driver's door, Brent waved over the top of the SUV at me, and then he lowered himself into the vehicle, closed his door, and sped off.

"Mew?"

At my feet, Dep blinked sleepily up at me. I scooped her into my arms, kissed the orange-stripy spot on her forehead, and whispered, "I'm glad you missed that adventure, Dep."

She purred. I carried her upstairs. The guest room door was shut, and at least one of my parents was snoring. It was Sunday, already. Brent's and my wedding day was only eight days away.

I had so much to do that the eight days passed quickly. They also dragged.

I saw Brent briefly when he and Vic came into Deputy Donut to ask Jocelyn and me questions, but I talked to him over the phone most evenings.

And then it was Sunday again, my first day of two weeks of vacation, most of which I would spend with Brent. Everything was in place for the rehearsal, the rehearsal dinner, the wedding, and the reception. And our honeymoon. Well, almost. My father cleaned my engagement ring until the sapphire sparkled. I finished my packing, closed my suitcase, and grinned in happy anticipation.

Late in the afternoon, I dressed in a cobalt blue sundress and black patent sandals. I grabbed my small black patent purse and walked down to the living room.

My parents were already there. My father wore a new tan-and-white-checked blazer, an open-necked white shirt, and khakis. My mother's dress was understated, for her, in leafy green silk. Her eyes gleamed with pride. And maybe a few tears. "Emily, that dress matches your eyes perfectly. You look wonderful."

"So do you two."

Brent arrived, and Dep immediately tried to cover his dark blue suit with cat hairs. He finally put her down, and we all managed to go outside without allowing Dep to join us.

Brushing at his jacket, Brent escorted me to his car's passenger seat. He got in and waited for my parents' car to back out of my driveway. With them following us, we started toward Brent's home out in the woods.

He tossed a quick, loving smile at me. "It's finally happening, Em."

"Yes." Afraid of impending tears that could have made me wish I'd worn red to match my eyes, I changed the subject. "How's the investigation going?"

"Ever the romantic! It's going well. In addition to the video he kept on his phone of sending that chipped mug to your place and the video Jocelyn took of him throwing that broken drone at you, the blood on Quentin's handkerchief matches Harold's blood type. We're still waiting for the results of the DNA test. We naturally rejected Harold's ridiculous, spur-of-the-moment alibi of being with Misty the night of the murder, and it turned out that Ed had an alibi for the time of the murder, after all. He was with his girlfriend, but their relationship was so fragile that he didn't want to bring her into it, didn't want us bothering her. He knew he was innocent, and it didn't occur to him that others might think he was guilty."

"I'm glad he has an alibi. I hope the relationship with the girlfriend improves, but from what he told me, she might not value him as much as she could. He's a good guy, but I'm afraid that he might not quite meet her standards."

"Not everyone is as lucky as I am."

"Watch the road."

"Masterful woman. And there's more news. At Vic's urging, a District Attorney in Illinois is looking into the Skye murder case. This new DA replaced the one who prosecuted Fergus Skye."

"Do you think they'll charge Harold with that murder, plus the arson?"

"They might. It seems that important evidence might have been neglected during the original trial, and Fergus Skye was convicted largely on Harold's testimony, and because the DA at the time, and also probably the jury, knew how often the spouse is the culprit."

Lake-dotted forests surrounded the village of Fallingbrook, and we were soon out in semi-wilderness. A half hour from town, on the right, a long driveway led to Brent's chalet, so far from the road that we couldn't see it nestled in its clearing in the forest. This time, we drove on past his driveway. The road curved down between stands of pine toward Chicory Lake, the lake I thought of as "Brent's Lake," although he owned only part of the shoreline. Near the bottom of the hill, Brent turned right, into the parking area of a business offering boat rentals and carriage rides. The owner of the property was one of Brent's closest neighbors.

My parents parked near us, and we all stepped out into the pine-scented air. Slightly downhill from us, wavelets lapped at a small beach.

Misty, Scott, Hooligan, and Samantha arrived seconds later, and Reverend Christopher pulled in while my parents, Brent, and I were greeting the others.

All of us could have walked the quarter mile to the wedding tent on Brent's section of the shore, but Brent and I surprised everyone with rides in the restored antique carriages that we had also reserved for the next day, when the carriages' owner and his wife and their grown sons and daughters would shuttle our guests to the wedding and back. After the ceremony, the guests would drive up to Brent's driveway and park there for the reception.

The large white wedding tent had been erected close to Brent's sandy beach, the boathouse that stored our kayaks, and his dock. We clambered out of the carriages.

For a few seconds, I stood still, absorbing the beauty of the late-afternoon sun glittering on the lake and the humidity-hazed forests on the far shore, and then I turned around and returned Brent's smile.

I was my own person. No one was giving me away. Misty, Samantha, and I left the others to wait for us in the tent and hiked a short distance up the trail past the S curve, where pines hid us from the people below. Although the only music was the burbling stream to our right and a chorus of birdsong, we practiced our procession, Samantha first, then Misty. When I thought that Misty would be near the tent, I walked slowly down the trail.

In the tent, Brent took my hand, and we faced Reverend Christopher and the lake. Reverend Christopher guided us through a summary of the ceremony. He had also officiated at Samantha and Hooligan's wedding and Misty and Scott's, and most of the plan was familiar.

After the rehearsal, we all drove to a cozy dinner club. Our out-of-town friends and relatives joined us there for dinner. If everyone else felt even a tenth as happy and loved as I did, they had a wonderful evening.

I could have gone home with my parents in their car and let Brent return to his chalet sooner, but Brent wanted to drive me himself before he went home. On the way to Fallingbrook, I fell into a contented sleep.

* * *

The next afternoon, the sky was clear blue and the temperature was perfect, at least for those of us who would be wearing sleeveless dresses. Some of the men might be a little warm, but Brent and I weren't sticklers for formality. Jackets and ties could be removed, and no one would complain.

Samantha, Misty, and I changed into our dresses in one of Brent's spare bedrooms. Unlike the wedding guests riding in horse-drawn carriages in the valley, my two attendants and I would walk down and return up—with our husbands—the forest trail. We'd chosen to wear flat shoes and dresses that brushed the tops of our calves. Even if breezes lifted my hem slightly, the bruises and cuts on my knees should not be visible.

I had decided against wearing a veil—I'd done the whole white wedding thing before, when Alec had been my groom and Brent had been his best man, and Samantha and Misty had been my attendants. This was a new marriage, and even though many of the wedding participants were the same, Brent and I wanted this wedding to be different. Brent and I would always revere our memories of Alec.

My dress was bright, shimmery silver. Like Misty's and Samantha's dresses, it didn't scream *wedding* and could be worn other times. Misty's dress was the lavender-hued silver of early morning mist. Samantha's was the silvery blue of Chicory Lake when filmy clouds cast sheer drapes between the sky and the earth. The bodices of Misty's and my dresses were fitted. Samantha had opted for a looser style.

She turned to check her makeup in the mirror, and I became certain that I'd been right about why she hadn't ordered a beer the night we'd gone to the Fireplug together.

Samantha had the cutest baby bump.

Misty was also staring at Samantha. Misty's and my eyes met in the mirror. Misty winked at me.

I gasped, "Samantha! Are you and Hooligan expecting?"

She put on a saucy grin. "Expecting what?"

"I . . . um . . ." I looked to Misty for help. Misty only grinned.

Samantha smiled so much that her eyes nearly disappeared.

I demanded, "When were you going to tell us?"

"After you get back from your honeymoon. This is your and Brent's big day, not ours."

I rushed to hug her. "Are you kidding? You just made it even better."

Between more hugs and exclaiming, we almost made ourselves late.

Clutching our bouquets—roses and lavender, not the donuts that Jocelyn, Olivia, and I had joked about—the three of us strolled quietly down the trail together. The woods were at their summertime prettiest. We stopped at the top of the curve. Now, in addition to the stream rushing downhill beside us and the birds chirping in trees, we could hear the string quartet playing in the tent in the valley. Samantha started down the trail and went out of our sight. As planned, the string quartet began playing the processional as soon as they saw her.

Misty started down the hill.

I counted twenty seconds after she disappeared beyond the trees, and then I began my solo walk down the wooded pathway. I thought I was being both sedate and stately, but my smile must have been huge.

Finally, I could see the tent, the people in it, and the string quartet. As previously arranged, they stopped playing when I came into view.

Brent's smile was at least as big as mine.

From out on the lake, a cornet fanfare burst forth, the notes clear and pure. I could barely see the canoe, but I knew that Summer was paddling it with Quentin as passenger. His composition and playing were perfect, haunting, and magical, with echoes that almost made it sound like other cornets around the lake harmonized with his.

I walked in time to the majestic strains, toward friends, relatives, and Brent.

And toward our new life together.

RECIPES

Double Fudge Donuts

These donuts are baked in specially formed donut pans. The Fallingbrook Arts Festival and Emily's wedding take place in August, a time when many of us have an abundance of a certain vegetable. You won't taste it, but it will make your donuts extra fudgy.

Extra refined coconut oil for greasing the donut pan
1 tablespoon ground flaxseed
3 tablespoons water
⅝ cup all-purpose flour—no need to sift first
½ cup granulated sugar
⅓ cup cocoa powder, sifted
½ teaspoon baking powder
¼ teaspoon salt
1 ounce unsweetened baker's chocolate
¼ cup refined coconut oil, melted
½ teaspoon vanilla extract
1 cup grated unpeeled zucchini and/or yellow summer
   squash—don't drain or squeeze

Preheat the oven to 325° F. Grease the wells of a six-donut full-sized (not a mini) donut pan.

In a small bowl, stir flaxseed and water. Set aside.

In a medium bowl, whisk together the flour, sugar, cocoa powder, baking powder, and salt.

In a small microwaveable bowl, heat the baker's chocolate and refined coconut oil together in 30-second bursts of medium heat in your microwave oven, stirring between bursts until the oil and chocolate are melted and blended. Microwave ovens vary; times are approximate.

In a large bowl, whisk together the melted and blended chocolate and coconut oil, the vanilla, and the flaxseed and water mixture. Stir in the zucchini and/or yellow summer squash.

Add the dry ingredients to the zucchini mixture and stir to blend. Allow to sit for a minute to allow the zucchini to dampen the mixture, and then stir until the batter is uniformly moist.

Carefully spoon the batter into the wells in the donut pan.

Bake for 30-35 minutes until a toothpick comes out clean (but possibly fudgy).

Invert the pan to release the donuts. You may need to use a small silicone spatula to ease them out.

Frost the rounded tops of the donuts with fudge frosting (below).

Fudge Frosting

1 cup sugar
⅜ cup whole milk
1 tablespoon light corn syrup
2 tablespoons cocoa powder
1 tablespoon butter
½ teaspoon vanilla extract

Place sugar, milk, corn syrup, and cocoa powder into a heavy-bottomed saucepan.

With a wooden spoon, stir gently over moderate heat until blended, then stir only to keep frosting from burning—lower the heat if necessary.

Cook until the mixture reaches 233° F.

Remove from heat.

Place the butter on top. Do not stir.

Set aside until pan is warm to the touch.

Add vanilla.

Beat until the frosting thickens.

Immediately frost the donuts.

Hint: Leftover frosting can be spread onto aluminum foil. When cool, slide off the foil and cut into squares of delicious fudge.

Lemon-Curd Long Johns

1 dab of butter
1½ cups whole milk, warmed to 111° F
1 tablespoon instant dry (powdered) yeast
3 tablespoons granulated sugar
1 egg, room temperature
4 cups all-purpose flour
½ teaspoon salt
6 tablespoons butter, softened, almost liquid
lemon curd (purchased or made from scratch—see below for recipe)
powdered sugar
vegetable oil with a smoke point of 400° F or higher (or follow your deep fryer's instruction manual)

A mixer with a dough hook attachment is easiest for this recipe, but if you don't have a dough hook, mix as much as you can with your mixer and finish kneading by hand.

Rub the dab of butter around the inside of a large bowl and set the bowl aside.

In a large mixer bowl, combine the milk, yeast, and sugar. Let sit for 5 minutes. Small bubbles will appear as the yeast does its job.

In a separate small bowl, whisk the egg until it's a uniform texture.

Whisk the beaten egg into the yeast mixture until it's blended.

Place the flour and salt into another large bowl and stir it with a whisk or a dinner fork.

Using a dough hook, stir the yeast mixture on low.

Running the mixer on low, add ⅓ of the flour mixture. Continue mixing, stopping to scrape down the sides of the bowl until the dough is a consistent texture.

Add another ⅓ of the flour mixture and continue mixing with the dough hook.

Add the melted butter 1 tablespoon at a time and continue mixing, stopping the mixer to scrape down the sides of the bowl until the dough is blended.

Add the remaining flour mixture and continue stirring on low until the dough begins to clump together.

Increase the mixer speed slightly and knead the dough until the dough forms a ball and begins cleaning the sides of the bowl. This takes only about 3 minutes.

Place the dough into the greased bowl and cover with a wet (but not dripping) kitchen towel. Allow the dough to rise to double in size. The time will vary depending on temperature and humidity.

Cover the bowl, wet towel and all, with plastic wrap.

Refrigerate 4–6 hours or overnight. The dough will shrink—there will be no need to punch it down.

Line a cookie sheet or baking tray with a silicone pad or parchment paper or use a nonstick cookie sheet and set aside.

Form the dough into balls about 2 inches in diameter, leaving the balls in the bowl covered with plastic wrap.

One at a time, stretch the dough balls into lozenge shapes (Long Johns) about 5 inches long.

Place the Long Johns on the parchment-lined baking tray and cover with the wet towel. When all of the Long Johns have been covered, let them sit about a half hour for their second rising.

Heat the oil to 350° F.

Working in batches and not crowding the Long Johns, fry them 1½ minutes on each side.

Drain on paper towels.

When the Long Johns have cooled, slice them partway through like a hot dog bun, and spread about 1 tablespoon (or to taste) of lemon curd (see below) on the lower half of the Long John. Cover with the top half. Using a small sieve, sprinkle the tops with powdered sugar.

Lemon Curd

Use this flavorful spread anywhere you might use jam or jelly (but not with peanut butter, perhaps). Try it on Long Johns (above), toast, pancakes, or muffins. Top cakes or brownies with it. You might even simply eat it with a spoon . . .

½ cup white sugar
1 tablespoon cornstarch
½ cup whole milk
¼ cup fresh lemon juice (about 2 lemons, depending on size
   and juiciness)
3 teaspoons fine lemon zest

Zest and then juice lemons. Extra zest can be frozen for later.

In a heavy-bottomed pot, preferably enameled to prevent the lemon from reacting with metal, whisk the sugar and cornstarch together until well blended.

Whisk in the milk, lemon juice, and lemon zest.

Heat the mixture on medium heat, whisking briskly and constantly until the sauce thickens. Don't stop whisking while the mixture is being heated.

Remove the pan from the heat and pour the curd into a heatproof bowl.

Cover the bowl tightly and chill.

Visit our website at
KensingtonBooks.com
to sign up for our newsletters, read
more from your favorite authors, see
books by series, view reading group
guides, and more!

Become a Part of Our
Between the Chapters Book Club
Community and Join the Conversation